TURBULENT WATERS

A Pacific Northwest Thriller

JES HART STONE

TURBULENT WATERS

A Pacific Northwest Thriller

JES HART STONE

Sidekick Press
Bellingham, Washington
United States of America

Publisher's Note: This is a work of fiction. Names, characters, places, and incidents are a product of the author's imagination. Locales and public names are sometimes used for atmospheric purposes. Any resemblance to actual people, living or dead, or to businesses, companies, events, institutions, or locales is coincidental.

Sidekick Press
2950 Newmarket Street
Suite 101-329
Bellingham, Washington 98226
www.sidekickpress.com

Turbulent Waters/Jessica H. Stone, PhD

ISBN 978-1-958808-04-7
LCCN 2022946119

Cover Design: Andrea Gabriel

Dedicated to Jack Remick

La discipline est notre obligation envers le cadeau.

In fluid dynamics, turbulent flow is motion characterized by chaotic changes in pressure.

—G.K. Batchelor, University of Cambridge

1

Jake Burton knew next to nothing about diesel maintenance, but he knew about the marine mechanic's thirst for Canadian whiskey, and he knew how to negotiate with thirsty men.

"See that blue Ford pickup?" Jake said. "There's a brand new bottle of Crown Royal still in the box under the passenger's seat. I could toss that in to sweeten the pie."

The mechanic shielded his eyes against the morning sunlight and looked across the marina parking lot. "You mean that old beater?"

Jake nodded. "Deal?"

"I dunno. State law says every boat's gotta have a certified captain and a licensed and bonded mechanic aboard. Fines are high if the Coast Guard catches you."

"Nobody's gonna catch me—you said it yourself, the engine in that boat is running smooth, and the trip only lasts four hours. You'll be back on board for the afternoon tour."

Jake pressed the knuckle of his thumb against his upper lip to stop an itch. He pulled a fifty from his wallet—held it out.

"Here, take the morning off. Go get yourself a big breakfast."

The mechanic stared at Ulysses S. Grant. He scratched his head. "I could lose my job—"

Jake stuffed the bill into the pocket of the mechanic's oil-stained coveralls. The other man remained still. Jake pulled another bill from his wallet.

"Okay, look, here's another twenty. Honest, that's all I've got. You've officially cleaned me out." He held the empty wallet open.

The mechanic shifted from one foot to the other, pulled his left ear lobe, and sighed. He took the bill and pushed it into his pocket with the fifty.

"Yeah, okay, deal. Don't forget to ask the captain for permission before boarding, and make sure you bring my box back the minute you get off the boat. And don't lose any of my tools overboard." Without another word, he shuffled off to the blue truck, the purple box, purple bag, and golden liquid.

Jake started to dig through the contents of the borrowed toolbox, but his effort was interrupted by the deep threatening notes of Mussorgsky's "Night on Bald Mountain."

"Can't talk now, Marilyn. I'm heading into work." He held the phone a few inches from his ear.

"Jake, I know you talked to Emily last week."

"I didn't call her."

"It doesn't matter who dials, Jake. No contact is no contact."

"Look, I didn't know it was her—didn't recognize the number."

"You didn't because our daughter rifled through her troop leader's purse for that phone."

"If you'd let her have her own cell—"

"While the other girls were decoupaging baskets, our daughter was breaking the law. I hope you're pleased with yourself."

"Lighten up, Marilyn. She's just a little kid who wanted to talk to her dad."

"You encouraged her to break the restraining order. You're turning her into a criminal."

"For God's sake, Marilyn, she's seven."

"You're supposed to be the adult here, Jake. This is precisely the kind of irresponsible behavior that caused the accident. If you'd pay more attention—be more responsible—we wouldn't be having this conversation."

"Give it a rest, Marilyn."

"And—wait a minute, why are you going to work now?"

"What do you care?" he said.

"You told me you worked the night shift."

"Well, I—"

"Is this another lie, Jake?"

"No, Marilyn, it's not a lie," Jake lied. "I am on the night shift, but the day guy called in sick. What do you want?"

"I had a long talk with my father last night," she said.

"What does he want now?"

"We talked about Emily—about how she's acting out more and more every day."

"She's going through a stage," Jake said.

"Dr. Burlington was there as well."

"Great. So now you think she's a criminal and crazy."

"Dr. Burlington suggested that Emily may be rebelling because of—"

"Because of what?"

"Separation anxiety."

"I told you a hundred times—the kid needs her dad. You don't have to waste money on a shrink to figure that out. All she needs is—"

"Listen to me, Jake. My father is willing to give you another chance. There's an opening on the Board—it could lead to bigger things. Besides, it pays more than you're making pushing a broom. Father knows people who can get you appointed. He says if you take this, he'll have a conversation with the judge—maybe lift the re—"

"I don't want to go through it again. Not now. Not ever," he said.

"I can't believe you're so selfish."

"Let me see my daughter."

"My father is only trying to help."

"I don't need his help. I need my kid."

"If you'd let the past go—get off your pathetic pity pot and join the human race—"

"Marilyn, Richard was my best friend—of course, friendship is something you can't understand but no matter what you say or how much your dad tries to bribe me—"

Dead air.

Nothing but a slab of glass and aluminum against his ear. She'd hung up.

"Typical," he said.

Jake slipped the phone into the pocket of his stiff, new canvas coveralls and returned to the contents of the toolbox. Pipe wrench, socket set, screwdrivers, wire cutters, ball-peen hammer—nothing too exotic. Jake figured with these and a little bullshit, he could fake four hours of engine maintenance.

He reached to scratch his chin but stopped before damaging the imitation beard he'd spent the past two hours applying. At first, he'd planned to wear the beard and mustache he'd found online, but no matter how much he tried to make the things look real, they didn't. So, he studied YouTube videos until he learned to apply flesh-colored glue and professional-grade facial hair. The process was messy, time-consuming, and expensive. Still, after several failed attempts, he convinced himself that he could pass for a scruffy mechanic in need of a shave. But the damn things itched him worse than poison oak, and it was all he could do to refrain from scratching. Still, deception was necessary—he'd live with the itching.

He slapped on a baseball cap purloined from the marina and scanned the scene—a postcard-perfect village nestled on the banks of the Strait of Juan de Fuca. Dollops of whipped cream clouds reflected in low, olive-colored ripples, gulls wheeling free on high winds called out in shrill squeals or floated, nonchalant, on the water's surface. A small, resting flotilla of fishing boats tugged ever so gently against their moorings. The fresh, moist breeze brushed Jake's face, and everything smelled of the sea— salt and fish, vinegar tang, and musky decay.

At the bottom of the sloping parking lot, a single wooden dock led to the *Hattie Belle*—a pretty little trawler-turned-whale-watching boat. Jake guessed about forty-eight to fifty feet in length, wood construction, old, but in good repair. She gleamed with white paint—two baby-blue stripes circled her hull. From his vantage point, he could see a sliver of deck painted in the same light blue.

A gaggle of second graders clustered on the dock beside the vessel—jumping, clapping, laughing. Most of them wore jeans and sweatshirts or shorts and t's—small backpacks slung over their shoulders. Only a couple of them appeared anxious as their parents returned to parked cars. Jake sought out Emily. She'd be the only little girl wearing a dress—Marilyn insisted on dresses. Emily wouldn't be nervous. She'd be excited, curious, eager. His Emily was a trooper—willing to take risks.

Daddy! It's me, Emily!

Em—where are you?

I'm at scouts. I borrowed Mrs. Derby's phone to call you.

Honey, you know I can't—

Listen, Daddy. We're going to watch whales! Miss O is taking us to watch whales. It's a field trip. You can come.

Emily, if I could—

No, really. Mommy isn't coming. And Miss O doesn't know you, and I'll pretend I don't know you. You could dress up!

Dress up?

Like on Halloween. Or that time you pretended to be Santa Claus.

Emily, it's only a couple more months until I see the judge again. This time we'll—

Daddy, we can ride on a boat and watch whales together. Pleeeassse, Daddy.

Several children now stood at the edge of the dock and pointed to the water below. Jake spotted Emily in a moss-colored dress and a yellow button-down sweater. Though her hair was caught in a ponytail, the breeze fluffed out pale wisps, and she looked like a summer dandelion sending wishes on the wind. You can't say no to a kid like that.

He scanned the cars in the lot—the new cream-colored Mercedes wasn't in sight. Either Marilyn had come and gone, or she'd had the sitter drop Emily off. Time and time again, he'd argued that he was more qualified to take their daughter to school than some spacey high-school girl who'd only recently learned to drive. But Marilyn held firm to the temporary restraining order. Even though the whole thing was bogus—the handiwork of a high-priced lawyer—if he got caught, he'd end up in court. Again. This time, he might lose everything. Forever.

He checked his watch—0800. He stood, and with a sharp kick, Jake slammed the lid of the metal tool chest. The loud clang echoed across the water and startled dozens of seabirds. The bright morning sky filled with squawking and flight.

2

Tyler Butterfield drummed his fingers on the steering wheel, then bit at a hangnail already ragged and bloody.

"Idiots," he muttered. No doubt those dipshits forgot why they went in there. *Drumthor is probably trying to hit on some girl. Probably trying to get her to pay for their Monsters and Kit-Kats.* He stared at his finger, then wiped the new bead of blood on his jeans. "Idiots," he said again. He pushed his sunglasses up to his hairline and peered through the car's cracked windshield to the door of the Always Open Stop and Shop.

Advertising posters obscured the door and windows. Budweiser, six-pack for $7.99. Cigarettes, all cartons 10% off with military ID. Drink Coke. Hot dogs, 2 for $3.50. Flyers for community events—most long past—competed for space between the ads. Tyler squinted to read the flyers: Christ the King Easter Sunday Pageant, Southside Neighborhood Yard Sale, Annual Walk for the Doggies, and Girl Scout Cookies now available. The windows offered no visibility—no way to see what his friends were doing. Tyler glanced down at his finger again. He picked at a scrap of loose flesh. More blood.

3

The work-weary man at the register looked across the aisle to the Cool Ranch Dorito clock—almost eight. A half-hour until he could go home. He glanced at a faded photo taped to the side of the register—his plump wife sat surrounded by their tribe of small children. Behind her, in the distant background, an old, slow elephant lumbered by. The man sighed—caught a glimpse of himself in the wavy plexiglass of a display case.

He looked like someone in need of a warm meal and a set of clean clothes. He looked like a man in need of sleep. He scratched his belly through his stained and rumpled white shirt as he watched a meth-thin woman count out change from a plastic jar. *Tip money or maybe trick money.* You can tell a lot about where a person's money comes from by the time of day they show up to spend it.

The woman counted out enough to cover two cans of cat food (chicken and liver in gravy), a box of tampons, and a bottle of the cheapest white wine the store stocked. Her fingers shook as she pushed the coins across the counter.

4

Spike Drumthor leaned in—his tone low.

"When she's out the door, we move. Got it?"

They stood by the hot dog cooker where the security cameras lacked a view of the franks making slow rotations.

Kevin Woods pointed one chubby finger at the hot dogs.

"Yeah, got it. But I'm gonna get me a couple-a these first."

"For fuck's sake, fat ass. This ain't a picnic. We didn't come here so you could stuff your face. Stick to the plan." Spike glared at Kevin.

Kevin lowered his hand and stepped away from the cooker. Spike punched him on his shoulder and glanced up toward the corner—to the security camera with its blinking red light. Kevin swallowed hard and moved back to his spot close to the rotating heater.

Spike mouthed the word "loser." In a practiced move, he slicked his hair back then pushed his hand into the left pocket of his jacket. A jacket too heavy and too hot even for early morning, but Spike liked the way he looked in black leather, and besides, he needed the pockets. He touched the thin cotton of the pillowcase they planned to load with cash and the thick wool of his ski mask. The masks had been his idea from the start—Butterfield thought they were a bad idea. Butterfield was an amateur.

You're not going to be wearing them when you go in, so the guy will know what you look like. Besides, you'll be on camera when you walk in, so the masks are one more thing to get rid of and one more thing that can go wrong.

You're what's wrong, Butterfield. I know what I'm doing.

The two had argued the mask issue while they'd passed Spike's bottle of Cuervo and a joint until Kevin stuck in his two cents.

I think the masks are cool. We're robbers, right? All robbers wear masks.

Whatever. You two jerks wear masks. I don't care—I'll be in the car.

Tyler had killed the joint and flicked the tiny, finger-burning roach into the empty Cuervo bottle.

5

Neil Edward turned the key and silenced his cruiser's rumble and the radio prattle about crooked politicians and a predicted low-pressure system. He sat still and sucked in the sea breeze that rustled the stack of reports he'd flung on the dash.

He glanced at the bag of scones he'd picked up on the way—thought about eating one in the car but considered Jennette and decided to wait. From the parking lot, he could survey most of the area he'd sworn to serve and protect. Sheriff Neil Edward Longcarver rested his hands on the steering wheel and scanned his domain.

Otter's Run and the Makah Reservation were the only communities in Neah, the smallest of the two counties on the peninsula. Laid out much like a tic-tac-toe board, the town consisted of two parallel main streets intersected by a set of perpendicular side streets. Cul-de-sacs and winding lanes feathered off the larger thoroughfares to form loose neighborhoods.

The Otter's Run Sheriff's Office squatted on one of the two low hills flanking the town. On the opposite hill, a severe, ivy-covered building cast a slanted shadow. Built over a hundred years ago to hold the criminally insane, the structure now housed the Ruth Hudson Elementary School.

Neil Edward squinted and searched for the predicted dark clouds, but only seagulls squabbled and squealed overhead. His cartilage crackled as he twisted his neck and shoulders from side to side. Too stiff.

To the north of town, at the bottom of a long slope, the waters of the Strait of Juan de Fuca glistened in the morning sunlight.

Tucked into a cozy bay, the Mary Cove Marina gave shelter to a dozen or so fishing boats, a couple of barges, a smattering of yachts, and a small fleet of whale-watching vessels.

The fleet—consisting of five individually owned and operated boats—was the only reason tourists came to town. Unlike mega tour boats that packed whale watchers and general party seekers onto three or four decks, the smaller vessels could only carry fifteen or twenty passengers at best. One of their websites proclaimed, "Cocktails and loud music detract from the beauty of nature. We promise you an intimate and exhilarating experience with the creatures of the sea."

For some folks, that was enough. And, for the residents of Otter's Run—the ones who sought peace and quiet in the small bedroom community—it was perfect.

Except for a few incidents with fireworks around the Fourth of July and some petty vandalism every Halloween, Otter's Run stayed sleepy and safe. Neil Edward liked to think that his long tenure as sheriff had something to do with the last bit, but he didn't kid himself. All the action—tourism, commerce, and criminal activity—flourished in the county capital of Port Angeles, forty-five minutes east along the peninsula's coast.

Otter's Run was close enough to the big waterfront city to make an evening at a swanky restaurant doable but close enough to the rez to pay his respects at his parent's graves and catch up with old buddies over a game of cards. His little town was far enough away from both extremes for breathing room. And that suited Sheriff Neil Edward Longcarver just fine.

He stretched, felt a twinge in his shoulder. Time to retire, or hit the gym, or at least get a massage. There was a new therapist in town—a gal who practiced some kind of bodywork that he couldn't pronounce. She had a nose ring and a head of hair that looked like an old squirrel pelt, and she charged too much for a guy on a sheriff's salary, but she worked wonders on aching muscles. Plus, she smelled like vanilla frosting.

He groaned as he pushed himself from the cruiser. He couldn't afford to retire—would most likely work until he died. And the gym? No way. Neil Edward grabbed the paper bag and the reports, slammed the door with his hip, and climbed the three steps to his office. Pricey or not, after work, he'd go for a massage.

"Miss O! Miss O! I hafta go potty."

"Karlie, try to hold it a little longer, okay? There's a bathroom on the boat. Please hold it just a little bit longer."

"Miss O, can we pet the whales? My dad says you can pet whales in California."

"Ryan, we talked about this—these whales are in the wild, not in a petting tank."

"Miss O, Jenny dropped her shoe in the water."

Tamara O'Dwyer looked across the dock in time to see a skinny, red-headed girl lob her remaining shoe over the edge. It hit with a soft plop, and after one twirl on the surface, it slipped under the water and drifted out of sight. Seven children cheered—even a boy who'd been whimpering a moment before now giggled as the tiny sandal disappeared.

Only one child missed the show. Facing away from the others, she crossed her legs, held her hands to her crotch, and chanted, "A little longer. Just a little bit longer."

Tamara pushed a strand of curling black hair off her forehead. Despite the warmth of the morning sun, a cool breeze chased gooseflesh over her bare arms. *Would the t-shirt and capris be warm enough for this outing? Too late now.*

"Children, get in line. We're getting on the boat soon. Come on, everybody hold hands."

"Miss O, what about my shoes?"

The young teacher bit her lip and scanned the parking lot. Most of the parents were gone, and it was unlikely that even one could be convinced to volunteer to help with this field trip. Besides, that idea had been quashed.

Behind all the pretentious pomp and public relations, the school operated on a worn-thin shoestring. Budget cuts meant that most field trips had been canceled—not enough money to hire additional staff to chaperone.

Tamara had doggedly argued that field trips were critical to providing the children with a well-rounded education and that college-bound seniors from Port Angeles High would make perfect field trip assistants.

The idealistic novice, and the fiscally conscious headmaster, had disputed the topic until one of the senior teachers informed her younger colleague that the headmaster didn't like being challenged and that the first year of employment was probationary. Still, Tamara persisted.

The process had taken weeks, and despite assurance from the high school's principal that only top-ranking students would participate in the program, the headmaster wasn't a hundred percent on board. He reminded Tamara that her first-year review was coming soon and should anything go wrong with this plan of hers, well—

She mumbled under her breath.

"Damn it, where are those helpers?" She turned to the grinning barefoot girl.

"Well, Jenny, your shoes are down there with the fishies now. Guess you'll have to be a barefoot pirate girl for this trip."

The child skipped down the dock, stopped once, and twirled.

"Yayyyyy! I'm a pirate girl!"

"I wanna be a pirate."

"Me too!"

"Me too! I'm a pirate!"

"Children, put your shoes back on! No skipping—you'll fall in the water. Shoes on. Everybody. Now!"

Tyler shifted in his seat, reached to the console for his cigarettes, and stopped. Hailey was allergic to smoke. As far as Tyler Butterfield was concerned, Hailey was the best thing that had ever come into his life. She was the reason he fought this craving. She had become his reason for a lot of things in the past few months. She might even be what that lame-ass French teacher had called a raisin tetra—or something like that. For sure, she was the reason he was sitting, bored, in this crappy car, waiting for two jerks to grab cash from the Always Open Stop and Shop.

For the hundredth time, he tapped his phone. Hailey's senior pic on the lock screen. Hailey with her satin hair, clear skin, and a smile that never stopped. No tattoos. Didn't smoke and, except for the champagne her father had poured on her eighteenth birthday, didn't drink. Only girl who ever said no to him. All the others wanted it—they came to him—practically begged. All he had to do was give them "the look." But Hailey was waiting. She was waiting for college, waiting for a career, waiting until the right one came along. More than anything he'd ever wanted, Tyler wanted to be the right one, but keeping up with Hailey wasn't easy, and it took bucks. He tossed the phone next to the unopened smokes, looked up at the Always Open, and back down at his phone— 8:00 a.m.

8

Despite cool morning temperatures, Willow had opted to lower the convertible top for the drive from the suburbs to the marina. Tangled hair was a small price for the heady feeling of freedom in the open vehicle. Besides, it was rare for any of them to drive a family car to school and rarer still when the loaner was a parent's bright red mid-life crisis.

"OMG," Aiysha said. "He's soooooo cute."

"Lemme see." Kaitlyn's arm shot between the front seats to the back. Four slim fingers waggled and flashed lime green nail polish.

"Give it."

"Okay, you can look but don't touch. This boy is MINE." Laughing, Aiysha pressed the phone into her friend's upturned hand. She leaned against the back seat and tilted her head skyward. Closing her eyes, she hummed along with the radio. The wind tugged her curls into twisted knots.

"Man, I love driving Dad's car. I think we should skip that stupid teacher's assistant thing and drive around all day. I bet we could make it to Forks and get back before final period." Blond hair streaked with lavender lashed Willow's face as she leaned forward to pat the leather dashboard. She took a deep breath—the wind smelled of moist earth and cedar trees.

"I'm in." Kaitlyn turned in her seat and waved the phone at her friend.

"Here," she said. "He's cute, but I think we can do waaaay better. Especially in *this* car."

With an exaggerated pout, Aiysha leaned forward and grabbed her phone. She took a moment to look at the grinning ebony football player who posed shirtless while cuddling a fluffy white kitten. She sighed and swiped left.

Willow looked at the dash. She punched the accelerator—the car lurched forward.

"I'm serious, you guys. We could so do this. We have, like, an almost full tank, and I have my mom's credit card. We can fill up before we get home. No one would know."

"Let's do it!" Kaitlyn cranked the radio up a notch.

The rush of wind and blaring music forced Aiysha to raise her voice. She continued to swipe, look, reject, swipe as she yelled to her friends.

"You bitches are crazy. I need these credits to make up for missing that science test. Besides, old lady Johanson will have a shit-fit if we don't show up at that boat."

Willow twisted toward the back to tease her friend.

"The test you missed because you skipped and spent the day at the mall with that jerk. Right?"

"Hey, watch the road," Kaitlyn yelled.

Willow turned in time to see the gaping pothole in the right lane but not in time to swerve. They all jumped. Kaitlyn screamed, the phone flew from Aiysha's swiping fingers, Willow clamped tight to the steering wheel—struggled to hold steady. *Thwap, thwap, thwap.* The flat slapped the pavement as the car slowed to a stop. Willow glanced at the clock on the dash—8:00.

Bleach fumes stung his eyes. Neil Edward left the front door ajar, walked the room, and opened windows. Dropping the reports and the bag of scones on his deputy's desk, he noticed a small ribbon-tied box next to the stapler and tape dispenser. No question, the box held a garter—something fancy, maybe satin or lace.

He poked his head through the doorway to the area housing a single, unoccupied jail cell, the lavatory, and two shelves of office supplies. As the only paid employees of the Neah County Sheriff's Office, he and his deputy split the work—everything from law enforcement to janitorial duty.

He heard the toilet flush and backed through the door in time to miss getting whacked by the business end of a soaking mop.

"Morning, Jennette."

Jennette burst out of the bathroom. She waved the mop in his face and plopped a bucket on the floor in front of him. She'd tucked the hem of her 1950s style poodle skirt in the waistband giving him an agreeable view of her legs—the skinny pale white one and the curvy, hand-carved madrone wood number. Today, her wooden leg sported a lacy garter in the same bright yellow as her high-topped tennis shoes.

"Damn drunken men," she said. "Piss or spit on the floor—every one of 'em—no good and useless." She stopped and grinned at him—the silver star inlaid in her front tooth winked.

"No offense, Sheriff."

"None taken." He and Jennette shared thirty years of history—all the way back to the days when he'd worked law enforcement on the reservation, and she'd tended bar at the Blue Balls n

Beer. Pretty much nothing she did could offend him, although she still surprised him from time to time.

Twirling the mop handle like a majorette in a parade, Jennette plopped the head into the bucket. Foamy water sloshed out. She gave him a sideways glance.

"S'posed to be a big storm coming," she said. "We might have to lock up early—go home where it's safe—leave the local thugs to fart around on their own."

He swiped a few drops of soap from his slacks.

"Yeah, they say heavy rains and high winds—but I'm guessing they're wrong—they usually are. Probably nothing more than a summer squall. Either way, we have to record these reports and file them with the county. Maybe, after that, if everything is calm, we can knock off a little early. But first, put on a pot of coffee. I brought scones." He turned and started toward his desk.

"Some big spender win the lottery?" she said.

Deputy Jennette loved the triangular pastries, but she considered them too foo-foo—too expensive—when you could buy a dozen donuts from the Pick-n-Go for the price of three raspberry scones. Neil Edward checked his watch—eight o'clock—straight up. He counted.

"A thousand and one, a thousand and two—" Even though he expected the sound when the cell's iron door slammed shut, Sheriff Longcarver flinched.

10

Spike slid his right hand into his jacket pocket and wrapped his fingers around the cool metal. Every time he touched it, he felt a thrill, a sense of power—of control. He'd never fired one—never held one until now. But he wanted one. Someday, maybe soon. Maybe this job would land him enough cash for the fake ID to hide his record. Then, he'd buy one. Something bigger—more powerful. As for this one, he knew he'd have to put it back where he'd found it—under the spare tire, wrapped in the dirty sock. If he didn't get it exactly right, his brother would know, and his brother would beat the crap out of him. Well, at least his brother would threaten a beating. But the weight of the thing in his pocket was a rush enough to risk the wrath of his brother. He turned away from the hotdogs, faced the counter, and watched the ragged woman count out her change. Where did Travis get the gun, and how long did he have it? Maybe their old man gave it to him, or maybe he stole it—hell, maybe he stole it from their old man, or maybe he just took it. From the day their dad had started serving time—this time for life—Travis had assumed the role of head of the house. Not much to head up anymore, only them and their frightened mouse of a mother. Their mother, almost a ghost—slinking from shadow to shadow. But still, Travis was in charge, at least for the moment.

"Hey, you two guys. You buy something or get out."

Spike glanced at the clerk, then at Kevin.

Kevin stood with his mouth open, gaping at the man.

The clerk stepped from behind the counter and pointed one stubby finger at the NO LOITERING sign posted above the refrigerator case.

"I don't want you hanging around in here if you're not buying something."

"Spike, he saw our faces. Let's go," Kevin whispered.

"Fuck that," Spike said.

"But we'll be on the camera—the cops will see us." Kevin's face flushed pink, and a thin layer of sweat glistened.

Spike took a deep breath. He walked to the counter and pulled the gun from his pocket. He aimed at the closed-circuit camera.

The clerk shot his hands above his head.

"Wait! Wait! I don't want any trouble—take the money—take anything."

The woman turned, her eyes widened, her jaw dropped, but she didn't make a sound.

"Spike, what are you doing? We're not—"

"Shut up and get the cash."

Spike pointed the gun at the clerk.

"You get over there and keep your hands in the air. You wanna live? Then move it—now."

Before the man could step, Spike swung the gun toward the camera's blinking light and pulled the trigger. The bullet hit the concrete wall behind the counter. Shards of shrapnel sprayed the room.

The force of the blast surprised Spike. He fired again. And again, and the woman screamed, and Kevin screamed, and the clerk jerked forward and crashed into a rack of powdered donuts. He sprawled at Spike's feet. Blood gushed from his back and soaked his dirty white shirt.

11

Tyler looked up—searched for the Harley that backfired or the kids tossing cherry bombs. The store's door flew open—a woman raced out screaming. She dropped a plastic bag—a can of cat food fell from the bag and rolled onto the street. Glass cracked against the pavement—pale liquid splashed the sidewalk.

Seconds later, Kevin followed. He waved one hand while hitching his sagging jeans with the other. He grabbed the door handle—launched into the passenger's seat.

Tyler recoiled.

"Jesus, what's that smell?"

Spike came tearing out of the Always Open waving both hands. He clutched an empty pillowcase and his ski mask in his left hand—in his right, he gripped a gun. In one swoop, he flung the door open and dove into the back seat.

"Move it, asshole. Drive!"

Jake tugged on the bill of the ball cap, flipped up his collar, and hunched his shoulders. He hoisted the toolbox. A solid fifty pounds. A comfortable, familiar weight—a weight that felt good. He walked through the parking lot, careful to dodge eye contact with anyone, careful to refrain from swinging the metal box.

He approached the dock but avoided looking too closely at any of the children. The last thing he wanted was for Emily to spot him—for her to forget their/her idea of him "dressing up." If that happened, she might blow his cover.

He didn't have to worry, though. The children were busy removing their shoes and tossing them into the soft surge below the dock while their teacher frantically tried to control the chaos. What was a lucky break for him sure looked like a major headache for her. He felt bad for the young woman, and he wanted to lend a hand, but that would be way too risky. Jake kept his head lowered and slouched on through the circus of happy children.

When he arrived at the *Hattie Belle's* deck, he stopped and looked up. A tall, weathered fellow with pepper gray hair leaned against the cabin's outer wall. The man wore oil-stained jeans and a frayed, long-sleeved flannel shirt. He chewed a toothpick and grinned as he watched the shoe-tossing show. When he glanced down, Jake flicked a quick wave. The man smiled and motioned toward the boarding platform.

"Permission to come aboard, Captain?" Jake used the phrase he'd learned from the mechanic.

"Yeah, sure. Come on."

With one effortless swing, Jake hoisted the toolbox on the boat's deck—it landed with a dull thud. He leaped up the boarding steps after it.

"Dennis Thompson. Captain Denny to most folks. Welcome aboard." The captain held his hand out—made direct eye contact.

Jake sent up a word of thanks that he'd opted for the professional-grade, glue-on fake beard—no way, in this bright light, the other man would have missed the elastic string on the cheaper version.

Jake shook the man's hand.

"Thanks. Jake Burton." The moment he spoke, he cringed. He hadn't planned to use his real name. He'd intended to be as invisible as possible—get on board, pretend to monitor the engine, watch his daughter laugh and play with the other kids—and leave. With luck, his ex would never know. Nobody would know. But now, his luck seemed about as good as that teacher's—and it was too late to change it.

Denny eyed the toolbox.

"Dickerson called. Said he had a family emergency, and you'd be filling in for the first tour. Said you normally work in Port Angeles."

Although it might have been a good idea, the mechanic hadn't mentioned anything about calling in. That wasn't in the plan, and going against the plan made Jake uncomfortable. The fake beard itched like crazy—he forced himself not to scratch.

"The marina called me and asked if I could take an extra shift. They didn't say why."

The captain spat his toothpick overboard.

"Yeah, well, my guess? Not a family emergency. I'm guessin' Old Dickerson needed a little hair-of-the-dog to steady his nerves this morning. What that man really needs is an intervention."

The captain shifted his position. He looked across the water, then up to the clouds. Using one hand to shield his eyes, he mumbled something Jake didn't catch.

"Sorry?"

"Oh, no big deal—just taking note of the weather. NOAA ra-dar shows a squall on the way. Course, as you know, they're pretty typical this time of year."

"Your boat do okay in bad weather?"

Denny patted the *Hattie Belle's* hull.

"Nothing to worry about. She's solid." He pushed a sliding door and motioned for Jake to step inside.

Before entering, he paused and looked skyward again.

"Clouds are moving fast—storm will probably come and go quick. But push comes to shove? We'll head back in. No use tak-ing any chances."

Denny swept his arms wide.

"Here she is, my girl, in all her glory. The lovely *Hattie Belle*."

Jake knew the captain was being dramatic, but he heard genuine pride in the man's voice. Denny's tone and the immaculate appearance of the old boat were testaments to his caring and commitment to his vessel.

"So, I haven't worked on this kind of boat. She a tug?" Jake said.

"Nope, but a lot of people mistake her for one—she has that look. She's a trawler—was used for sport fishing—mostly freshwater, trout, and bass. But I like to be out in the open water, so I converted her. A lot of my buddies at the time were taking guys fishing, but I did the math and figured there would be more money in booking bigger groups to watch whales and other wildlife than hauling four or five guys at a time. I guessed those guys weren't really interested in fishing anyway—they only wanted time away from their wives—time to drink and lie to each other. It wasn't for me."

Jake didn't fish, but he'd been on plenty of party boats. His father-in-law chartered them for corporate events like fundraisers and team-building weekends. When the vessels weren't hauling large groups of foreign tourists around the Pacific Northwest waters, they were available for private parties. When Jake had been in the man's good graces, Marilyn's father had confided in him—the chartered cruise parties allowed him to monitor his guests and keep control of the situation. He said that boats bring out the best and the worst in people, and he liked having a handle on the personalities of his employees, his friends, and more important, his enemies.

As Marilyn's husband—and the favored son-in-law—Jake had been required to attend these floating galas. His ex-wife, of course, had basked in the attention the guests showered on her. After all, she was the only daughter of their wealthy and extremely influential host. And, like her father, she enjoyed showing off her war hero husband.

Those events weren't the worst part of the marriage, but they ranked near the top of the list. He disliked the long receiving lines where he and Marilyn, and her parents, shook hands and greeted special guests—CEOs of major corporations, university chancellors, governors and senators, and one time, the Vice President of the United States. Jake had hated the noise and the forced camaraderie. Reggae music and Jimmy Buffet tunes blared from speakers on every deck. Businessmen and women let their hair down in boozy flirtation, dancing, and maneuvering. Much like what Denny had said about the fishing boat business, the corporate party boat scene wasn't for him.

Sunlight poured through the *Hattie Belle's* windows and warmed her varnished teak walls. Handrails placed every four feet ran the length of the vessel. Benches welded to the gray steel floor ran parallel to the windows and two sliding doors, one on each side, allowed easy access to the deck. Framed posters identified the wildlife that whale watchers were likely to see. Three steel posts wrapped tight with thick rope supported the entire structure.

"Guests stay in here, or if they're adults and they don't mind a little spray, out on deck. Helm and my berth are forward." Denny said.

He pointed toward the stainless-steel wheel fixed on a thick wooden base to the right of the dashboard. A narrow mirror mounted over tinted windows gave a view of the back door and deck. Below the mirror, an array of instruments, mounted flush on a glossy teak panel, glowed and blinked. Some of their functions were obvious to Jake—compass, GPS, an electronic chart, a radio. But he could only guess at the rest of them.

The scent of teak oil blended with window cleaner and swirled through the cabin. A salt-water breeze blew in from the open doors.

"She's lovely," Jake said.

"Yeah, she's a good old girl. And she'd done right by me. Well, come on, let me show you my quarters. Then we'll head on down to the engine room."

Following the captain across the cabin, Jake noticed Denny favoring his right leg. A lifetime of physical training had given Jake a keen awareness of how people moved and what hurt when they did. It was a skill his commanding officer had encouraged.

Four stairs led down to a locked door on the left side of the dashboard. Denny fished a key ring from his pocket.

"It's small," he said, "but cozy. Until I met the misses, this was home."

Twin bed. Chest of drawers. Roll-top desk. Two bookcases. Metal screws anchored a deep maroon carpet. The desk chair was locked to the floor to keep it from rolling in rough seas.

"How did you cook?" Jake said.

Denny pointed to a cabinet with a brass plaque labeled GALLEY.

"Microwave. Instant coffee. Soup."

"Got it," Jake said.

He scanned the walls of Denny's room—framed charts of local waters, a large map of the South Pacific. A photo of Denny in a white captain's uniform standing next to a slender woman wearing a pale blue wedding dress. She held a bouquet of bright yellow daffodils.

"Not saying I don't like sharing a bed with my wife, but there are times I miss the quiet and the motion of sleeping aboard. You ever spend time at sea?"

Jake liked this man. He was the kind of man you could spill out your troubles to over a beer or a bottle of whiskey—he was a man who would listen. On a different day, under different circumstances, Jake could imagine himself making friends with this man.

"Nah, not really," he said.

"Well, if you ever get the chance—go for it. The best dreams you'll ever have are the dreams you have at sea."

Tyler stomped on the accelerator and careened away from the convenience store. He gripped the steering wheel and kept his eyes focused on the road. His lips pursed into a thin, tight line. Kevin slumped low in the passenger's seat and stared out the window. Spike sat up and stuffed his mask into his jacket, followed by the gun and the empty pillowcase. His pocket bugled. No one spoke until Spike spotted a red convertible by the side of the road.

"Butterfield, slow down. Check it out. Three girls with a flat. Let's go rescue us some babes."

Tyler responded by slamming the pedal to the floor and flying past the stranded car. Spike swiveled around to watch the girls waving at them.

"What's the matter with you, asshole? Did you even see that blond hottie? Three of them—three of us. Turn around, you idiot."

Tyler ignored him until he reached the exit for the last rest stop before the town limits. The trip from the west side of Port Angeles to Otter's Run should have taken forty minutes. They'd made it in under twenty. Tyler swerved off the highway and pulled into a spot between two rumbling semis. The big trucks provided cover for the old Toyota. He yanked the key from the ignition and turned to glare at Spike.

"You're the idiot, Drumthor. What the hell did you do? One minute you're in the Stop and Shop—supposed to be grabbing cash. The next thing I hear a shot—no, lots of shots—and you two come flying outta the store. And you're waving a gun. Seriously? A gun?"

Spike started to speak, but Tyler cut him off and turned toward Kevin.

"And what the hell is that smell? You reek, man."

Spike leaned forward and punched Kevin's shoulder.

"He stinks because he shit himself. Who the hell takes a dump in his pants?" He hit Kevin again.

Kevin rubbed his shoulder. His voice trembled.

"Well, who the hell shoots a guy? We were only supposed to fake like we had guns. You know, like scare the guy. You said it yourself, small-time crime if all we did was grab cash. And, and— maybe you killed that guy." He sniffled and reached for the door handle.

"I gotta go to the toilet because—"

"Kevin, wait. What's he talking about? You killed a guy?" Tyler turned his attention to Spike.

Spike's hand trembled as he smoothed his hair. He turned toward the pale reflections in the car's window—feigned indifference.

"Look, I don't know what happened. I was aiming at the camera because the guy was yelling at us to buy something or get out, and we didn't have time to put our masks on, so I figured—"

Kevin made a whimpering sound.

"There was blood everywhere. That guy was on the ground, and there was blood everywhere."

Tyler ignored him—trained his full attention on Spike.

"What are you doing with a gun anyway? Where'd you even get it?"

"When Travis loaned me the car—I looked around. You know, in case he had some weed or booze or something. Figured we'd party after we made the hit. All I found was his stinking gym clothes and his gun."

"You took his gun?"

"Your point?"

"You were only supposed to pretend you had a gun."

"I don't do pretend."

Tyler shook his head. "So, you shot the guy?"

"No, asshole. I already told you. I didn't shoot him. I aimed at the camera. Next thing I know, the guy falls over and starts spurting blood, and then—" Spike shrugged.

"We got outta there."

Kevin choked his words.

"We're going to jail for the rest of our lives. We're gonna be like your dad. We're gonna die in prison."

Spike leaned forward.

"Well, at least you don't have to worry. No one inside wants a fat bitch that shits herself when she's scared. And leave my old man outta this." He started to swing at Kevin, but Tyler grabbed his arm and stopped him.

"Shut up! Both of you. We're not going to prison. Look, we didn't steal anything, and maybe the guy's okay. Maybe the cameras weren't working. All we need to do is get out of here and lay low for a while." He pushed Spike's arm away.

"Just where the hell do you think we can go?" Spike said. "Travis wants his car back before his shift tonight."

"And I gotta get changed," Kevin said. He squirmed in his seat.

Tyler bit his lip and closed his eyes for a moment. Hailey. His chances with her were probably getting smaller by the second. They needed a plan, and these idiots were brain-dead. Opening his eyes, he looked at Kevin, and then he turned to Spike.

"He's right. We can't go anywhere with him stinking like a homeless camp. Think your brother's gym clothes would fit him?"

Spike snorted.

"Yeah, they're both porkers."

Kevin shot back.

"I might be fat, but I'm not a killer."

Spike leaned forward to strike Kevin but again, Tyler blocked his fist.

"Stop it! We don't have time for you to pick at each other like a couple of old ladies."

Tyler chewed on his bleeding finger. After a few seconds, he spoke.

"There's a marina not too far from here. We can leave the car in the parking lot, Kevin can change in the public toilet, and you and I can steal a boat. We can go hide out on one of the islands until we make a better plan."

"No, Travis needs the car for work," Spike said.

Tyler sighed.

"Look, we stash the car, and you call him and tell him where it is. He can figure it out."

"Easy for you to say—you're not the one on the end of an ass-beating later."

Tyler turned the key and started the car.

"Well, he'll be a lot more pissed if he has to bail your sorry ass outta jail again, right?"

He veered back onto the road, clipped a curb with the front tire, and cut off a silver Subaru. The other driver laid on the horn. Tyler screeched past. Spike stuck his hand out the back window and raised one finger.

15

Tyler and Spike leaned against a sun-warmed boulder at the marina's edge and watched Kevin stumble across the parking lot. The heavy-set teenager pulled at his drooping jeans and clutched the wad of clothing Spike had fished from the car's trunk.

"What a moron. That guy should be riding the short bus to the retard school. I don't know why they let him in the same building with us. Don't they have a special school for the 'tards?" Spike said.

Tyler followed Spike's gaze.

"Knock it off, man. He just wants to hang. Besides, I get that you don't care about being a nice guy, but picking on the slow kid is low, even for you."

"Look, Butterfield, maybe you guys went to kindergarten together or some shit like that, but he's gonna drag us down. I'm thinking we ditch him. We go now, and by the time he's done changing his diaper, we're in the next county. Besides, the guy is a total pig."

"Don't be so hard on him, Spike. It's not his fault he's a slob. You ever see where he lives?"

"Yeah, I went over there once. His mom was shit-faced at nine in the morning," Spike said. "She's a big fat drunk. I swear, she's the size of a bus—barely fits in that dump of a trailer. And the place is a sty. No wonder Kev's old man split. I mean, who could live like that?"

"Right. Kevin caught a raw deal. So, lighten up on the guy."

"Just 'cause you feel sorry for the loser don't mean I gotta pretend he's not a creepy retard." Spike pulled a new pack of Camels from his pocket and tugged the cellophane from the package.

Tyler dropped the subject and scanned the marina's lot. A shiny new Lexus and a late-model Subaru wagon rolled to the exit leaving behind an assortment of worn and battered vehicles—a couple of Chevys of indeterminate vintage, Travis's beater, an old Volvo station wagon, and one tired blue Ford pickup. An ancient trailer at the far end of the lot served as the marina office, a kayak and jet-ski rental business, and, Tyler figured, home to a maintenance guy or night watchman. The trailer sat permanently parked on gray concrete blocks next to a gray concrete building—the public bathroom. According to a chipped and faded sign painted on the wall, the building also functioned as a net-loft and storage shed—available to all registered boat owners.

Hailey's father owned a boat—a yacht—Hailey called it a yacht. Tyler guessed the judge didn't keep his boat—his yacht—in a marina like this one. He probably kept it in some fancy place with valet parking for boats, and a restaurant, and maybe a golf course or whatever rich people with yachts wanted. Tyler reached into his pocket for his phone—for a quick peek at that smile. Hailey's smile. No phone.

"Hey, I left my phone in the car." He stood and stretched.

Spike pushed off the boulder, and they walked across the lot. They didn't talk. The only sounds were the cries of the gulls overhead and the crunch of gravel underfoot. The breeze carried the scent of the sea and something musty. Tyler guessed it was the smell of the boats moored close to shore. Would Hailey agree to go out with him, or at least answer his texts, if he owned a boat or even a car? But cars and boats took money. Lots of money. He remembered why they were in the marina in the first place.

"Spike?"

"Yeah?"

"What happened back there? I mean, for real. Did you shoot that guy?"

"I didn't shoot him. I aimed at the camera, but I think—maybe—I hit the wall. Fucking gun. It's out of tune or something."

"Kevin says there was blood everywhere."

Spike hocked a loogie and spat the slimy glob on the ground. "He's a pussy and a drama queen. There wasn't blood everywhere—just some on the guy's back."

"Some?"

"Okay. A lot. But not everywhere. Some on his back and some on the floor—maybe."

Tyler stopped walking. He turned and faced Spike. "Do you think you killed him?"

Spike waited a beat—raked his fingers through his hair. The corners of his lips curled in a tight grin.

"I don't see how. Like I said, I'm pretty sure I hit the wall. Maybe a chunk flew off. But I'll tell you this, if I *did* mean to pop the guy, he'd be gone for sure. Anyway, what's it to you?"

"Jesus, Spike. If that guy dies, it's armed robbery *and* murder."

"Chill, Butterfield. First off, nobody dies from a chunk a wall hitting 'em. And second, we didn't get anything. Fat Ass didn't even swipe one a those dogs he was slobbering over. Misdemeanor—maybe."

Tyler continued walking. A few feet from the car, he turned toward Spike, this time shielding his eyes from the sun.

"What's it like?"

"What's what like?"

"The gun. How's it feel to pull the trigger?"

Spike stopped in front of Tyler—his body blocked the light. Slow and deliberate, he pulled the gun from his pocket. Slow and deliberate, he leveled the barrel at Tyler's heart. His eyes narrow, his smile thin.

"You wanna know how it feels? It feels good. Real, real good."

Silence until Tyler swallowed and forced a short laugh.

"Yeah, okay. You better put it away before somebody sees it and calls the cops."

Without moving, Spike scanned the empty parking lot. Even the gulls had vanished. He smiled again.

"Yeah, that's right. Someone might see it—call the cops." As slow as he'd pulled it, Spike slid the gun back into hiding.

When they reached the car, Tyler fumbled in his pocket for the key but paused when a sign at the far end of the parking lot caught his eye. Ads painted on weather-worn wooden planks touted adventure activities designed to entertain tourists and to introduce them to the beauty and natural environment of the Pacific Northwest.

"Hey, check it out. Whale-watching tours."

"So now you wanna play tourist and shit? Man, you are so fucking lame." Spike leaned against the car and flicked his lighter.

Tyler tried to ignore Spike, and he tried to ignore the pull of the fresh stream of smoke. Forgetting about the car and his phone, he walked to the sign.

Tyler read out loud.

"Four-hour tours. Enjoy views of the U.S. San Juans and the Canadian Gulf Islands while watching whales, seals, cormorants, and other native species. This is our way out of here." Tyler tapped the sign.

Spike peered at the once colorful, now faded depiction of islands and sea creatures. He squinted at the lettering and sounded out words.

"Straight of June D Fu ka? I don't get it."

"Juan de Fuca, you idiot. Strait of Juan de Fuca. We get on a tour boat, and when it gets to Canada, we hop off. Or maybe they stop somewhere for lunch or something, and we don't get back on. Whatever."

Spike frowned.

"You think we can just walk into Canada?"

"Yeah, I do," Tyler said. "Don't you remember that guy—that guy who had that bed and breakfast in that town right on the border. Shit, what's the name of that town?"

"Blaine?"

"Yeah, Blaine. It was all over the news. That dude used to rent out rooms to guys—mostly from Iraq or Arabia or places like that—whatever. Anyway, the guys checked in, but after a few days? Gone."

Spike squinted through the cigarette smoke.

"Yeah, I do remember something about that. They walked through the guy's backyard and crossed the border. Right?"

"Yeah. They escaped into Canada. And then they disappeared."

"But what the hell would we do up there? Do they even speak English—I mean good English?"

"For fuck's sake, Spike. Get real. It's Canada, not France. The point is, once we're in Canada, the U.S. cops can't hassle us. Right? We lay low for a week or two. Wait 'til things blow over, and then we hitch a ride back home."

Spike smacked Tyler's arm.

"You might not be as dumb as you look, Butterfield."

Tyler shielded his eyes again and turned toward the dock and to the *Hattie Bell*.

"Come on. Looks like that boat's getting ready to leave. Let's go watch some whales."

"How much does a whale-watching trip cost?" Spike said. "I only got a twenty, and I bet lard-ass doesn't have a cent."

16

Tamara stretched her arms wide—balanced—as the dock swayed. She turned to see two lanky males sauntering toward her. One looked about twenty. He wore a black leather jacket and a deep scowl. The other was younger, maybe eighteen—slender with wavy blond hair and impish blue eyes—the sort of guy she and her girlfriends might have called a total fox when they'd been in high school. Marina employees?

Looking back at the children, she clapped her hands for their attention.

"Okay, guys. Everybody holds hands with two other children. Everybody. Get in a line!" As the children grabbed hands, Tamara turned and walked up the dock to meet the newcomers.

The guy in the jacket started to speak, but his buddy stepped forward and offered what Tamara guessed was his signature smile, the smile that could melt the hearts of most high school-aged girls.

"Is this the whale-watching boat?" he said.

Tamara bit her lip. *The school sent boys? Maybe they needed the extra credit—or maybe make-up credit, but assisting with little kids? Didn't seem like the kind of assignment these two would want. Still, help is help—and at the moment, she needed help.*

She stopped in front of them, placed her hands on her hips, and frowned.

"You're late," she said. "You were supposed to be here early to help load the supplies. Where were you?"

The two guys exchanged a quick look then the blond kid moved closer to her—a little too close.

"We're sorry. Honest. We had some car trouble."

Tamara stepped back.

His friend chimed in.

"Ah—yeah, we had a flat."

"Names?"

"Tyler Butterfield." He held out his hand to shake, looked into her eyes, held her hand a beat too long.

She pulled back and glared at his friend. Up close, he looked older than twenty—face pockmarked and lined.

"You?"

"Spike."

"Spike, what?"

"Spike." He stared past her.

Tamara looked from the kid named Tyler to his friend and back to Tyler.

"Well, okay," she said. Her brow furrowed. "Stuff happens, I guess. But there were supposed to be three assistants. I specifically requested three helpers."

"There are three of us." Tyler glanced toward the parking lot. Tamara followed his gaze.

"Yeah. But Kevin had to take a piss," Spike said.

Tamara stiffened—shot a look at Spike but held her tongue.

A boy jogged across the parking lot, waving his arms.

"Hey, you guys. What's going on? What are you—"

"Kevin, shut up. We're trying to talk here," Tyler yelled over Kevin's question.

The boy paused a moment, scratched his backside, then continued toward the dock—now at an amble. Shiny polyester basketball shorts tugged at his thighs and crotch. A roll of belly fat sagged over the top of the shorts, and a white t-shirt stretched tight across his chest. Yellowed sweat stains ringed his armpits.

"That's Kevin," Tyler said.

Tamara pressed two fingers to her temple and breathed in and out, slow. She had hoped for three high school girls—girls who were better dressed and more professional looking. She had hoped to take photos of the assistants with the children—maybe display the pictures on the Events Board at the school—maybe impress her colleagues and calm the prickly headmaster.

She pointed at Tyler.

"Okay, you. You can help me get the children safely on board. And you two, unload the lunches and juice boxes from my car." She looked at Spike and gestured toward an old green Volvo wagon parked near the head of the dock.

"It's unlocked. Everything's in the back." She hesitated, then continued. "And, can you grab my sweater? It's on the passenger's seat." With that, she turned her attention back to the children.

"Hey, what's—"

Spike stopped Kevin before he could finish his question.

"Shut up. She wants us to unload stuff from her car, so move it. Now." He shoved Kevin and pointed to the Volvo.

Kevin simply shrugged and shuffled back up the dock.

Tamara turned to help Karlie zip her sweatshirt. As she bent forward, she caught a glimpse of Spike. He was watching her, making a lewd gesture, and grinning at Tyler. She felt a chill slide down her spine—tried to brush the feeling away. Just boys being boys.

17

At six-foot-four, Jake could stand in the engine room and rest his arms on the cabin floor above—his chest and shoulders easily cleared the hatch opening giving him a comfortable vantage point. Denny had to stretch to gain the same position.

"Okay, I'll leave you to it." The captain seized a thin metal rail and climbed up several steps to the cabin's main salon. He leaned over the four-by-four-foot opening and tapped the hatch cover.

"Most of the time, I leave this up," he said. "But with that lot, we better close it. You don't need any pint-sized assistants helping you top off fluids. Let me know when you're ready, and I'll fire her up."

Jake pushed back from the edge and crouched low. Denny kicked the hatch brace—a pneumatic tube whooshed and slowly lowered the cover into place.

The space looked like someone had loaded a paint sprayer with battleship gray and let loose on everything—walls, floor, shelves. A single bare bulb, protected by a metal mesh cage, lit the room with a harsh, clear light.

A flat pan underneath the engine caught a slow drip from an unseen joint or crack somewhere in the bowels of the machine. Even with the engine cold, the room was warmer than the boat's main cabin, and it smelled of diesel and grease.

Jake had expected to feel claustrophobic, but though the space was not much bigger than his truck bed, it was okay. Nice even. Maybe like that "happy place" the damn court-ordered shrink had told him to find.

He studied the engine for a couple of minutes. Topping off oil shouldn't be hard—hell, he'd dumped gallons of Pennzoil in his Honda Civic back in high school. He'd only have to locate an oil cap, search the cabinets for a can and a funnel, and then, job done.

But there were several caps—in various sizes—none of them labeled. Two hard plastic globes, the shape of thermos bottles, hung upside down from a tangle of tubes and wires—also unlabeled. After a few minutes, Jake gave up. With luck, the real mechanic kept the engine in perfect operating order—no one would know about four hours without a fluid top-off, and even if Dickerson did notice, for sure, he wouldn't say anything.

Jake sat on an overturned plastic recycle crate and dragged the toolbox next to the engine. He unlatched the clasp, rummaged through the box, and pulled out several tools. He laid them on the floor to look like work in progress.

Above him, the hatch cover rattled as the children clambered aboard the boat. He skooched the crate closer to the steps to hear better.

"I want a window seat!"

"Me too! Me too!"

"No worries, everybody gets a window seat."

"Okay, Conrad, please sit down—you can do your filming from your seat."

"But Miss O—"

"Conrad, please. Think of your chair as the press box. Can you do that?"

The young woman's voice stayed calm and gentle even though she had to be frazzled with the situation. Jake had never seen Marilyn calm and gentle with Emily. He worried that without him in the picture, Emily's life might consist of too many rules and not enough hugs.

Three sharp knocks—Denny raised the hatch cover and peered into the engine room.

"She about ready?"

Jake looked up and gave him a good-to-go gesture.

Denny held the hatch cover open and glanced over his shoulder at the minor pandemonium in the cabin.

"I'll let her warm-up for a few minutes. If you've got things settled down there, it looks like our teacher could use a hand."

Jake climbed out and kicked the pneumatic shaft.

18

Neil Edward dried his hands, crunched the paper towel into a ball, and tried for a hook shot. He missed. Shaking his head, he swooped down, grabbed the paper, and slam dunked it from a foot away.

And the crowd roared.

He smirked at himself in the mirror before leaving.

"Sheriff, while you were off having your morning constitutional, we got us some action down at the marina." Jennette hung up the phone and reached for her handbag.

"Yeah? What kind of action? Gull drop another load on Deputy Leone?" It was an old joke—private between the two of them. The only "action" Dwayne Leone, the marina manager and part-time volunteer deputy, ever saw was the criminal behavior of a particularly nasty bird who took aim at the deputy's bald head whenever possible. The bird was a better shot than Neil Edward.

Jennette snatched a set of keys from her desk. "Nope. Major crime in progress. Grand theft auto. I'll lock up."

He held up one hand, palm out.

"Hold on a minute. Details, please. Let's make sure we're both needed before we close the office. There might be more calls."

Jennette paused on her way to the door.

"Oh, come on. You know as well as me, nothin' ever happens around here. 'Specially not on a Tuesday morning. If I don't get to go to crime scenes once in a while, I'll lose my skills. And you wouldn't want that, would you?" She cocked her head and raised one eyebrow.

Neil Edward sighed. Among others, Jennette's skills included typing seventy-five words per minute, the ability to balance the trickiest of budgets, and survival—survival of a traumatic event. She'd lost her left leg in a motorcycle accident on her wedding night—sheared it clean off. When the paramedics found the leg, her lace bridal garter, stained red with blood, still circled her thigh. Her groom didn't make it.

Most women would have been devastated, but Jennette was a tough old bird, even when she was young. The docs fitted her with a wooden leg, and in no time, she was back slinging whiskeys and sliding beers down the bar. It's almost impossible to argue with skills like that.

"Okay, Jennette, you win. You can give me the details on the way."

Neil Edward parked the heavy black and white police vehicle close to a rusting dented Toyota on the far edge of the Mary Cove Marina. Deputy Leone stood rigid—his legs spread in a wide stance. Though he wore faded jeans, green rubber boots, and a denim work-shirt—Mary Cove Rentals embroidered on the breast pocket—the brass badge pinned to his shirt collar lent a certain authority. He pointed his hunting rifle at a man who leaned against the aging car. The guy held both arms up—blinked and squinted—the morning sunlight in his eyes.

Adjusting his sunglasses, Neil Edward strolled over to the men.

"Morning, Deputy Leone."

"Sheriff," Leone spoke through clenched teeth. His eyes remained fully focused on his prisoner.

"What's the story?" Neil Edward said.

"Caught him red-handed. Brazen criminal—right out in plain sight."

"Hey, I told you a hundred times, I wasn't stealing it. It's my damn car."

"Okay, thanks, Leone. You can stand down now. I'll take it from here."

Leone slowly lowered his gun and relaxed his stance, but Neil Edward saw the look of disappointment cross his deputy's face.

"But stay close, Deputy Leone. If I need backup, I want you ready," he said.

"You got plenty of backup, Sheriff. This perp isn't going anywhere." Jennette stepped next to Leone—the two deputies stood united—their collective adrenaline palpable.

Neil Edward forced down a smile. He turned his attention to the man next to the car.

"You can lower your hands now. Why don't you tell me what's going on here."

"I got the call from Dickerson," Leone said. "He was taking the morning off. Sitting in that truck over there—belongs to some friend of his. Was mixing a little whisky into his coffee when he saw this thug trying to break into the car. And I—"

Neil Edward stopped him.

"Hold on. Where's Dickerson now?"

"Sleeping it off in the net-loft."

"Great. Well, you can put everything in your report. Right now, I want to hear his side of the story." The sheriff focused on the other man, who now shielded his eyes with one hand and scratched his belly with the other.

"What's your name?"

"Travis Drumthor. And it's about time somebody listens to me," he said. "Like I told this idiot about a million times, this is my car. Look on the registration."

Neil Edward took a moment to study the man. He had the look of a tired, forty-year-old road construction worker, but the sheriff guessed his appearance was due to lifestyle choices rather than years of hard labor. He was more likely twenty-seven—twenty-eight at the most. Baggy, unwashed jeans hung low, and a dirty gray t-shirt stretched over his sagging beer gut. Judging by the man's stringy hair, the grime under his nails, and his serious need for a shave, it had been a while since the man had seen a shower.

"Alright then, Mr. Drumthor, where are your keys?"

"Fucking brother has it. One key. I only gave him one."

"I'd appreciate you watching your language," Neil Edward said. "There's a lady present."

Travis turned and stared at Jennette and the holster she'd strapped over her clingy yellow sweater. She gripped her firearm with both hands.

"She a cop?"

"She's one of my deputies."

"She don't look like a cop. What's with the skirt?"

"Not your business. She's earned the right to wear whatever she wants. Now, tell me again. Your keys?"

"My fu—my brother has it. He borrowed my car this morning—I gave him the key. He was supposed to get it back to the house so I could take it to work, but he called me—guess something happened, and he left it here. I had to hitch a ride all the way out here to pick it up. He was gonna leave the key on the front tire, but the asshole—he took it with him. I got a spare key in the glove compartment, so I was breaking in to grab it. That's when this yahoo scared the shit outta me. Pointing his gun at me and yelling and everything."

"Where's your brother now?" Neil Edward said.

Travis shrugged. "Hell if I know—it ain't my job to babysit him. All I know is he's gonna be real sorry when he gets home."

"Why don't you call your brother now? See if we can get the key from him or at least find out where he is."

"Um, well, I forgot my phone. I left it at home."

Neil Edward stood silent for a second. His gut told him the guy was telling the truth, but there was something else.

"Let's have your license to start," he said.

"Well . . . see . . . I mean . . . well . . . I have a license, of course. But I was in a hurry, and I forgot it—my wallet—it's on the table at home."

"With your phone?"

Travis looked down—didn't answer.

Jennette and Leone stared at him—neither moved.

Neil Edward slipped both hands into his pockets and looked at the ground. He kicked at a pebble—waited a beat. Then he looked back at Travis.

"Well, Mr. Drumthor, you say this is your car, and of course, I want to believe you. But we can't verify that unless we see some proof, and you don't have a key to get to that proof, so you see, I need to look around. That be okay with you? I mean, to verify your story."

"I don't give a crap—bust into it if you want. Look around. I got nothin' to hide."

"Thank you, Mr. Drumthor."

"Watch him," Neil Edward said. He turned and walked over to the cruiser, popped the trunk, and rummaged through a bag of tools until he found what he needed.

Six minutes later, Sheriff Longcarver and Travis stood to-gether next to the car and waited while Jennette fished around in the glove compartment. Leone flipped the latch and dug through the contents of the trunk.

"Expired." Jennette handed her boss a sheet of paper.

Leone completed his search, walked around the car, and stood next to the sheriff. Neil Edward tilted his head in question.

"Mostly the usual stuff—couple pairs of jeans, one stinky gym sock, box of tools, a few empty Budweiser cans. Only strange thing—four boxes of ammo—Speer 9mm Luger hollow points. Heavy duty. Found them inside a McDonald's bag, under a bunch of wrappers."

"Gun?"

"Nope, but I found this in the console." He handed a cell phone to his boss.

The sheriff took the phone and held it up for Travis to see.

"This yours?"

"Nope."

"We found it in your car."

"Well, it ain't mine."

"Since we found it in your car, we'll need your permission to look inside. Because of, you know, privacy laws."

"Hell, crack the thing wide open for all I care. Snoop all you want. It ain't my phone."

"Thanks for that, Mr. Drumthor. Now, where's the gun?"

Travis spit on the ground—narrowly missed Jennette's shoe. She scowled at him but remained planted firmly in place.

"I don't got no gun."

"No gun. Why the ammo? Four boxes. A lot of rounds for someone who doesn't have a gun," Neil Edward said.

Travis rubbed his eyes and shrugged.

"I don't know, man. It ain't mine. Maybe your junior wanna be cop-boy planted it."

Neil Edward turned to Jennette.

"Did you find the key?"

"No. Bunch of parking tickets, pack of cigarettes, a box of condoms—extra-large—and part of what I think was a Big Mac." She looked at Travis—let her gaze travel slow from his feet to his eyes.

"Would have taken you for more of a medium kinda guy," she said.

Leone snickered.

Neil Edward shot him a look before glancing at the registration. He read through it and then looked at Travis.

"Well," he said, "we have a guy—that's you—who's found breaking into a car, and he says he owns this locked car. But this guy doesn't have I.D., doesn't have a phone, the key that he says is in the glove compartment isn't there, and the registration of this car is expired. There is a cell phone in the car, but it doesn't belong to the guy who says the car is his." He waited a moment.

"Oh yeah," he added, "and there is the matter of four boxes of live ammo and no gun."

Travis scratched at his belly again. He didn't make eye contact with the sheriff.

"So, I guess we don't have much of a choice here, do we?" Neil Edward turned to Jennette.

"Cuff him and put him in the cruiser."

Travis clenched and unclenched his fists.

"Wait a god damn minute. You can't arrest me—I didn't do nothin'. You got nothin' on me. It's not against the law to have an expired registration. It's just a ticket or something."

"We're not arresting you. We're going to hold you until we can make some sense of your story. That's all."

"I get a phone call. I know my rights."

"Sure, sure, you'll get your call. Jennette?"

"With pleasure, Sheriff."

"Ah, Boss," Leone said, "that guy's twice her size. Do you think—"

"She'll be fine."

Neil Edward knew Jennette could handle Travis Drumthor without breaking a sweat. She had proven herself long ago at the Blue Balls n Beer when a drunken biker had tried to put the moves on her. Jennette, the feisty peg-legged bartender, was having none of it. When that old boy leaped on a stool and took a dive over the bar, she was ready. She'd leaned against the wall on her one good pin and swung that wooden leg with a force that not only knocked the lights out of the biker, it took out most of the top-shelf liquor and a row of beer mugs. Glass and booze and biker blood sprayed the old Blue Balls. When the whole thing was over, somebody noticed that, sure enough, that wooden leg still sported a pretty lace garter. Since then, as a show of respect, men brought offerings of garters in the hopes of getting a date or even a warm smile from Jennette. Neil Edward had no worries about his number one deputy—she could handle Travis Drumthor.

He turned his attention to the phone Leone had given him. The glass was cracked, but the photo on the lock screen was easy to see—a young woman—seventeen, maybe eighteen. Clear skin, silky shoulder-length hair, an all-American, clean-cut sort of girl. Her look didn't fit with the current trend of nose rings and purple dreadlocks. If he'd been a gambler, he'd bet she didn't have a single tattoo—not a small pink rose or tiny butterfly—anywhere.

He handed the phone to Leone.

"You ever see this girl? She looks vaguely familiar, but I can't place her."

The deputy squinted at the screen.

"Yeah, that's Judge Lynden's kid. Pretty girl. I recognize her from a picture in the paper not too long ago."

"Wasn't she awarded some kind of scholarship?"

Leone handed the phone back—shook his head.

"I didn't read the whole story, Boss. Only remember the face. Sorry."

Neil Edward took one more look at the smiling girl behind the cracked glass, then returned the phone to Leone.

"No worries. We'll get this sorted out at the station. Put this and the ammo in the cruiser. And one more thing."

He glanced at Travis.

"Mr. Drumthor, we'd like to take your vehicle to the station— with your permission, of course."

"What's in it for me?"

"Well, tell you what. You give us permission to tow your car to the station so we can make sure everything is in order, and if everything *is* in order, well then, we'll cut a new key for you. Sound fair?"

"Whatever."

"You heard the man, Leone. Give Jenkin's Tow a call. Have them haul this to the lot behind the station. Thanks."

Neil Edward headed toward the cruiser, then paused and turned back to his deputy.

"Leone?"

"Boss?"

"Good work today. Professional."

Sheriff Longcarver didn't wait for a reply before turning again and walking toward his vehicle. He knew that by eight that evening, the tale of the attempted "grand theft auto" would spill over the bar at the Blue Balls n Beer, and that by ten o'clock, Volunteer Deputy Dwayne Leone would have become something of a local hero.

Every time he saw his daughter, she looked bigger—at least taller. Emily's height, athletic build, and dark brown eyes came from him. Her pale blond hair and intelligence, he credited to Marilyn.

Emily squatted in front of a bench. The tip of her tongue poked from between her lips, her brow furrowed as she concentrated on the task of tying another child's sneaker—a pink and green plaid sneaker with Hello Kitty appliques.

"Hey, Lexie, if you cry, you'll get me all wet!" Emily formed an exaggerated pout as she wiped a single tear from the girl's cheek.

"Emily, you're so silly." Lexie giggled.

"There, all done!" Emily wrapped her arms around the other girl. After a quick hug, she stood and moved through the group toward a boy who'd put his vest on inside out.

The teacher knelt on the floor—her brows knit in deep lines. Biting her lower lip, she worked to buckle fidgeting second graders into bright orange life vests. A kid, a boy of about eighteen, maybe nineteen, knelt beside her.

"Hey, hold still, or I'll tickle you," the kid teased a small boy.

"Ryan, hold still. Let him help you get your life vest on so we can get going." The teacher shot a glance at the teenager.

"Thanks," she said.

Off to one side, two little boys struggled to unbuckle each other's life vests. Jake wove through the group and sat down on the bench next to them.

"Hey guys, whatcha doin'?"

One child ignored him and continued to fuss with a buckle. The other pointed at his friend.

"We can't wear these things. I, for sure, can't wear this thing if I'm filming. It will get in the way."

"Move around," his friend said.

The child twisted to one side giving his buddy a better grip on the buckle. He wore black and white saddle shoes, khaki slacks with cuffs and ironed sharp creases, a tucked white shirt, and a maroon bow tie. Who dressed this kid? And saddle shoes?

By contrast, his friend wore scuffed sneakers—one untied lace dragged on the floor—jeans and a faded blue t-shirt stained with something that could have been grape jelly.

Jake sat with his hands folded in his lap.

"Whatcha filming?"

The boy bobbed his head and waved a smartphone at Jake. "News. We're reporters. Well, Tristan is a reporter. I'm a photographer—a photojournalist—and we cover all the news whenever it happens."

Jake reached up and smoothed the fake mustache to hide his smile.

"Ah, I see. So, what's your name?

"Conrad. Conrad Huffington. The third. My dad is a famous photographer, too."

Again, Jake worked to hide a grin. He liked this kid, liked his attitude.

"Well, Tristan, and Conrad Huffington, the third, those are important jobs," he said. "But, say, don't those cameramen on foreign assignments have to wear camo jackets?"

Both children paused their efforts and looked at him.

"And, I remember seeing a reporter on television wearing a bulletproof vest when she was covering a riot." He rubbed his chin—tried to look thoughtful as he studied the boys.

"Yeah, I suppose those professionals have to wear the gear required for the job. But I guess since you guys are only pretending to be a reporter and a photojournalist, it doesn't matter if you wear the appropriate stuff or not. Right?"

He turned from the boys and scanned the rest of the group. When he made eye contact with the teacher, she gave him an appreciative smile and gestured toward the little boys behind him. Both children now helped each other refasten the buckles they'd undone.

Jake smiled. Pros—budding professionals. Those kids will lead the six o'clock news before they're out of college.

The *Hattie Belle* bobbed and swayed as two more young men plodded aboard. Both balanced cardboard boxes piled with smaller cartons, but one kid, sweating, overweight, wearing gym shorts and a t-shirt, stumbled under his load. Jake rushed to grab a box in danger of slipping from the kid's arms.

"Need a hand?" As he took the load, Jake detected the sour scent of unwashed hair, the not-so-faint smell of stale body odor, and something less pungent but more noxious.

"Thanks." The kid's face flushed pink. He pulled his t-shirt up, over his belly, and wiped sweat from his face.

Jake grimaced at the sight—this was the kind of young man who used to walk into the gym all flabby and unsure of himself. The kind of guy who would walk out, five or six months later, flexing his muscles, calling out jokes to his newfound team of bros, beaming with pride. Jake had always enjoyed the challenge of helping guys like this transform their bodies and, more important, their self-esteem. But reality? That opportunity probably wouldn't come—not for this kid, not for himself. At least not in the near future—maybe not ever.

The other guy wore a black leather jacket. Black leather jacket in mid-June. Too hot, even this time of day. Slicked back hair, black t-shirt, black jeans slung low. A pack of unfiltered Camels stuck out of the jacket's chest pocket. Sweat beaded across his brow, but he didn't seem to notice—a caricature of Fonzie—out of time, out of place. A chill spread up Jake's arms. Something about this guy reminded him of another guy—a guy he'd only met once at the gym. A guy he wished he'd never seen.

"Where do you want this shit?" The kid in the jacket called over to the teacher. Several children pointed at him.

"Bad word! Bad word!"

The teacher looked up and glared. She gestured toward a bench at the back of the cabin.

"You can put everything on that. And watch your language."

She turned from him in time to reach for a little girl who walked on the top of a metal bench—arms held wide—as if she were practicing on a balance beam.

"Amanda! No climbing! Get down from there!"

The guy in the leather started to respond, but Jake coughed and looked at him—made eye contact—only for a second. But in that second, Jake saw something dangerous—dangerous like oil in a hot pan too close to the edge of a burner, dangerous like containers stacked too high on a transport ship.

The guy broke contact.

"Whatever," he said. He moved toward the back of the boat and plopped his load of boxes on the bench.

Jake took a deep breath, held it for a beat, and exhaled. That one had an attitude, but as long as it didn't impact Emily, he didn't care—didn't care about him or his friends. *Not my rodeo. Not my clowns.*

20

Jake moved to the helm station and stood close enough to watch and listen but far enough back to avoid being included in any conversations. Emily sat in the captain's chair at the helm station. Denny had adjusted the seat so she could stretch forward and touch the wheel.

"What's this?" She pointed to the half globe of glass fixed on a bracket next to the wheel. Under a layer of clear fluid, a reedy blue needle, poised on a spindle, danced between numbers painted on a thin brass disk.

"Ah, now that's something as old as the art of sailing itself," Captain Denny said. "That, my girl, is a compass."

Emily tapped her finger on the glass and peered down at the needle.

"What's it for?"

"It's for telling us where we are and where we're going. A tool that keeps us from getting lost—something everybody should have."

"Like GPS!" Emily said. "Mom has GPS in her car. Grandpa says Mom couldn't find her way out of a paper bag without GPS."

Jake smirked at the comment. Marilyn held an MBA, yet somehow after three years in the same house, she still couldn't say for sure whether the Good-Health Pharmacy was on the way to, or in the opposite direction of, the Red Apple Market.

"Well, GPS is handy too. We have one of those on the boat, but I still like an old-fashioned compass."

The guy in the leather jacket joined Denny and Emily at the helm station.

"Where's the GPS?" he said.

"Here." Denny tapped a button on a small screen—a digital display lit up. He pressed another button.

"With this, we know our direction and our speed. We can also tap this, and it marks where we were at any point."

"Why do we need to know that?" Emily said.

"Well, let's say we see a whale."

"A whale! I can't wait to see a whale." Emily beamed.

"Me too," Denny said. "But sometimes, the whales are off taking naps or visiting their other whale friends, so we don't always get to see one. But, let's say we do see a whale, and we need to circle around—not get too close—because we don't want to scare it. We tap this button, and it puts a marker on where we were when we saw the whale. That way, we can move away, give the critter some room, and still get back to where we were when we saw him."

The guy in the jacket leaned in and studied the instrument.

"So, what if you wanted to go to, say, Canada. Could you figure out where it is with this?"

"Better than that," Denny said, "we can program the GPS and tie it in with the auto-helm—if we do it right, the boat will steer herself to where we want to go." He tapped the screen. A company logo lit up, followed by a black and white map.

"Old school," Denny said. "The new charts are in color, but they're three times the price, and this one does the job. Of course, in these waters, I don't use the auto-helm. Too much stuff out there—boats, crab traps, logs, rocks, sandbars—you name it. Only time I use the GPS is out on the open water."

"Huh."

Denny studied the guy. "Hey, son, once we're underway, if you want a turn at the helm, you just let me know. You're welcome to give it a try."

The kid scowled when Denny used the word "son" but he didn't answer. He simply continued to stare at the black and white digital chart.

"Can I try, too?" Emily said. "I don't wanna be a pirate anymore. I wanna be a boat captain!"

"Well, let's see. Think you can tell north from south?"

Emily pointed to the N on the compass.

"Great job!" Denny beamed. A gull dive-bombed the boat leaving a gooey smear of green and white guano on the front window.

Emily burst into giggles. "Ohhhhh icky!"

Boat captain. So right now, his little girl wanted to be a boat captain. What did she want before pirate or boat captain? Veterinarian? Teacher? How many kids wanted to be an astronaut or a firefighter? How many followed their childhood dreams?

The worst part of this divorce was that he'd been pushed out of the loop—he was missing all the day-to-day stuff of Emily's childhood. He'd been happy—watching Emily and the captain—but thoughts of the divorce made him remember the restraining order, which made him think of Marilyn, which made him tense up, which booted him straight out the door of that damned happy place.

"Okay, young lady," Denny said. "Time for us to shove off. You better go grab a seat with your friends. We can talk more later, and then I'll show you how to steer the boat, okay?"

He lifted her from the helm chair.

With a grin lighting her face, Emily found her way to an open spot on one of the benches. She wriggled in next to the girl with the plaid Hello Kitty sneakers.

Jake listened in as Captain Denny slipped into the role of tour guide.

"Now, children and grown-ups too, you've got to learn a few proper boat parts if you want to be sailors. So, listen up." The captain turned and faced the front of the boat. He let go of the wheel and pointed to his left.

"This side is the port side, and this side," he pointed to the cabin's right, "is starboard." He pivoted back to face the children. "We call the back of the boat—aft. And the back door there? That's called the companionway. Anyone happen to know what we call the front of the boat?"

Kevin thrust his hand up and blurted his answer.

"The pointy end?"

The children giggled.

"Ah, good guess. Lots of people call it that." The captain nodded to Kevin.

Kevin flushed and looked down, but Jake noticed a shy smile.

"Besides the pointy end, we call the front of the boat the bow. You can remember it this way." The captain bent over in a deep, theatrical bow, then straightened and smiled. His young audience applauded.

Jake tuned out Denny's lesson and focused on the young teacher. Pretty. None of the glamour or sophistication of Marilyn. Just pretty.

The blond teenager slouched at the far end of a bench facing the window. *Daydreaming? Zoning out?* He'd been helpful and polite, but other than that, Jake couldn't get a read on him.

The guy in the black leather had moved to a corner. He faced the group but held a cell phone pressed to his ear—when he spoke, his voice was too low for Jake to catch any of the conversation.

Across the cabin, Captain Denny held court in front of the teacher and her students. Sunlight splashed through the vessel's broad windows, bounced off the polished teak walls, and drenched the *Hattie Belle's* cabin in a warm, tawny glow.

The children sat cross-legged on the floor in front of the helm station wearing their orange life jackets. Jake couldn't help but imagine a small pumpkin patch. All that was missing was a skinny, stooped scarecrow and Captain Denny almost fit the bill.

"Okay, crew, listen up!" Denny clapped his hands with a sharp smack for attention and waited for the teacher to settle the children. He looked like a man who enjoyed his work—like a guy who would do the job even without a paycheck.

Tamara pressed one finger to her lips and shushed her class in a dated caricature of an old-fashioned librarian. After a few moments of jostling for places, the children quieted.

"Now we're about to get underway," Denny said. "Who wants to look for whales?"

Eight little hands shot up. The kid in the gym shorts had edged in as close to the group of children as possible while remaining on the sidelines. He started to raise his hand, but his buddy in the black leather shot him a look that brought that hand down fast.

Faking a scroll through his cell phone, Jake studied the guy in the leather. Black clothing, constant scowl—meant to intimidate but didn't. None of that mattered. Something about him brought up the memory of a guy with a hollow-eyed stare. A stare that had made Jake want to disappear, a stare that sent a shiver up Jake's spine. *Forget it.* Jake shook the memory and turned to watch the captain.

"All righty then, we'll hunt for whales!" Denny grinned.

A skinny, red-headed girl close to the captain held her hands out as if to stop him.

"No hunting!"

Jake smiled when he noticed she was barefoot.

"We love whales," she said.

"No whale hunting!" The other children chimed in, and the once quiet cabin returned to chaos.

"Whoa—hold on there! I didn't mean *hunt* for whales, I only meant *look* for whales. Hunt with our eyes. We all love whales, and nobody will hurt them."

Jake watched the children. *Nobody will hurt them.*

Captain Denny paused and scanned the group. The children resettled.

"Now then, Rule Number One—the most important rule. Stay inside the boat. No going out onto the deck, no sticking your heads out the doors or windows. If you're a grown-up, well, you can go out—there are jobs for grown-ups on the deck."

He looked at Jake and the two guys in the back and pretended to snarl at the children.

"But everybody under the age of sixteen—stay inside the boat. Any of you lot sixteen years old?"

The children laughed.

Jake glanced at the other two guys. Neither of them acknowledged Denny's comment about grown-ups on deck. The blond continued to stare at the water, the guy in the jacket sagged against the wall, hands in his pockets, eyes now closed.

"Alright then, what is Rule Number One?"

"Stay inside the boat!" A chorus of high-pitched voices, and one lower voice, called out the answer.

"Good job, crew. You're all going to make fine sailors. Now then, on to a few more important rules."

Most of them paid attention, but one child, a serious-looking boy with short-cropped sandy hair and thick-rimmed glasses, seemed preoccupied. He pulled something out of his jeans pocket, and after a quick peek, he slid it back into place. He did this four, maybe five, times. Each time he went through the routine, his glasses slid down his nose, and he paused to push them up before reaching back into his pocket.

Jake remembered some of the things he'd stuffed into his pockets as a kid and shuddered. *Boys.*

The girl who'd used a benchtop as a balance beam raised her hand.

"Why did you call the bathroom the head?"

"That's an old word the pirates used, but we still use it today."

"Jenny is a pirate girl," another girl said.

Jenny stuck out her bare feet and wiggled her toes for the captain.

"Ah, I see, so she is," Denny said.

"Will we see any baby whales?" Tristan asked.

"We might, but it's a little early in the season. If we do see a baby, it will be close to its mother. So, keep a sharp lookout."

"Do other boats look for whales too?" Conrad mumbled his question—eyes glued to his phone.

"A good question. Our ship, the *Hattie Belle*, belongs to a fleet—a group of boats. All the captains are friends, and we use our radios to share news and keep each other safe in emergencies." Denny turned to the dashboard and plucked a radio mic from its holder.

"Now, I'm going to call our friends out there, so everybody be quiet for a minute, okay?"

Heads bobbed. Kevin raised one finger to his lips and shushed the way Tamara had earlier. Emily giggled.

Jake tuned the captain out and turned his attention back to the kid in the leather. He chilled at the memory of those eyes. He'd seen them in the gym once and later in a police photo. Those eyes—hollow, haunted.

Jake brushed the back of his hand across his forehead and forced himself to focus, again, on the captain. But the spidery feeling in his spine remained.

"Attention the fleet, attention the fleet, attention the fleet. This is the *Hattie Belle* reporting in. Repeat. This is the *Hattie Belle* reporting in. Over."

Retorts crackled through the radio's speakers as several other vessels in the fleet checked in.

"*Steilacoom Witch* reporting in. Over."

"*Joggins* reporting in. Over."

"*Lady Blaine* reporting in. Over."

Denny muted the radio and placed the mic back in its holder.

"Now then, time for a couple more questions," he said. "Then we're ready to head on out. Who has another question?"

"What if pirates try to come onto the boat?" Kevin asked.

"I don't expect we'll see any pirates today. Except for our Jenny here. But if we do, we'll call our friends on the radio and get help."

Denny beamed at the children.

"Now, time for one more question. Who has the last question?"

Tristan raised his hand.

"Do you need any help driving the boat?"

The captain answered by pointing to Jake.

"No, I can drive the boat by myself, but I do need my trusty mechanic there to make sure the boat runs smooth."

Eight children, two adults, and one teenager looked back at him. Jake faked a cough and covered his face with his hand.

"Want to say anything to our guests?" Denny asked.

Jake shook his head, faked another cough, and waved him off.

"Okay then, we're ready to head out. Who wants to blow the whistle?" Again, hands shot up.

Denny looked over the forest of waggling fingers.

"Jake, could you and—" He pointed to Tyler. "You. Untie the lines? Thanks."

Jake straightened and slipped his phone into his pocket. He brushed his discomfort aside. Let that go. So what? Something about a guy in a black leather jacket sparks a memory.

No danger in that.

Jake jumped from the deck. Tyler climbed down from the boarding platform. The dock swayed. They both took a moment to find their equilibrium and to stare at the thick ropes holding the boat tethered to cast iron cleats.

Jake took a step toward the teenager and held out his hand. "Hey, Jake Burton."

The kid thrust both hands in his jeans pockets, looked down for a flash, then back up at Jake.

"Tyler Butterfield. So, you're the mechanic for these tours?"

"Nah. I work on big rigs in Port Angeles—same stuff, though. Diesel repair," Jake said. "The regular guy had some family issues—had to take the day off. I'm filling in."

He glanced at the teen. Clean cut. Jeans and a plain white t-shirt. No piercings or tattoos—at least none visible to Jake. He didn't seem to fit with the other two.

"Who are your buddies?"

"Ah, the fat guy, that's Kevin. He's a little slow, but he's okay. Guy in the jacket? That's Spike."

"So, the school sent you guys to help out with the field trip. Extra credit or something like that?"

The kid looked up for a moment and peered at a contraption at the back of the boat. A rubber inflatable hung from pulleys fixed on two metal davits.

"Yeah, something like that," he said.

"Must be close to graduation, right? A couple of weeks from now?" Things about these guys didn't add up—didn't feel right.

"Yeah."

"You know anything about boats?" Jake said.

"Not a damn thing. I know about cars and motorcycles. My stepdad is a mechanic. Sometimes I help him at the shop. But got nothin' on boats." He walked to the end of the dock and peered at the *Hattie Belle's* heavy anchor chain.

Although Jake wasn't jazzed about these "teacher's helpers," this kid was clearly interested in the vessel, and he had some mechanical experience. For sure, he had more experience than Jake, and he might have skills that would come in handy.

Tyler straightened, glanced at Jake, and then pointed to the ropes.

"How hard can it be? I think we just unwind 'em and throw 'em on the deck," he said.

"Yeah. Right." Jake said. "Let's do this."

Tyler remained at the head of the dock while Jake walked to the rear of the vessel. They managed to get the heavy lines off the cleats at about the same time, and with a quick look and nod to each other, they heaved the ropes up and onto the boat's deck. Immediately, the *Hattie Belle* drifted sideways, away from the dock. It took a few seconds before they looked at each other again—registered surprise.

Jake was closest to the boarding platform. He scrambled onboard without much trouble, but Tyler barely made it. He dashed the boat's length, leaped from the dock, hit the platform off-balance, and staggered back toward the water. Jake grabbed his arm and hoisted him onboard.

Catching his breath, Tyler grinned at Jake.

"Shit, man," he said, "that was close."

Jake looked toward the cabin. "You better not let the teacher hear you talk like that. You'll get detention."

Tyler flashed a smirk.

"She's kinda hot. I'd spend a couple of hours in detention with her. Yeah, I'd—"

His words were lost in the long, loud blast of the boat's horn.

23

Tyler squinted against the intense reflection of sun on water. He stood on the aft deck facing Spike.

"Spike, chill."

"I told you I don't like brats."

"Look, it's just 'til we figure out how to get off in Canada. Go with it."

"Fuck off, Butterfield."

Kevin clomped onto the deck.

"Hey, what are you guys doing out here? That teacher wants you to come back in and learn the boat stuff."

Spike spit over the rail.

Tyler looked toward the companionway.

"Maybe we should go in—figure out how to get a boat back from Canada."

Spike stared at the water roiling behind the *Hattie Belle's* stern.

"Travis is gonna pick us up."

"You talked to Travis?" Tyler said.

"Left a message on his phone."

"That's lame, Spike. You know your brother—he'll space us out."

"I told you, Travis will pick us up. Drop it."

Kevin's face scrunched into worried lines.

"Wait. What do you mean—get back from Canada? What are you guys talking about?"

"Sorry, buddy. Everything happened so fast we didn't have time to tell you," Tyler said.

"The thing is, we've gotta get out of Washington for a while. Until things blow over. You know, because of the thing with the store."

"I don't get it, Tyler. Why Canada? And . . . and . . . for how long?" Kevin bit his lip.

"Long as it takes," Spike said.

"Not long," Tyler said. "But we gotta go to Canada. The cops can't touch us there. You get that, right?"

"No!" Kevin flushed—shook his head. "If I go to Canada then . . . well then, what about my mom? She's sick. She needs me."

Spike laughed.

"Sick? She's a damn drunk."

Kevin hung his head and mumbled.

"Jerk."

Spike took a step toward Kevin.

"What did you say, asshole?"

Tyler pushed between the two, then paced the width of the deck.

"Butterfield?"

Tyler stopped and slipped his hands into his jeans pockets.

Spike moved closer to him.

"Butterfield, do I have to babysit those brats *and* both of you?"

"Kevin's got a point. I didn't think about my folks when we came up with this plan. If they start to worry, they'll—"

"It's a good plan," Spike said. He spit over the transom again. The wind caught the glob and flung it back to splat on his sleeve.

Kevin jammed his hands into his armpits and hugged himself. "He's right, Spike. We have to go home. Besides, next week is graduation, and Tyler's gonna give Hailey a present."

Spike snarled at Kevin. He wiped his sleeve on the railing—turned to Tyler.

"That Hailey bitch? You think she even knows you're alive?"

"She invited me to her birthday party. At her parent's house."

"You moron. Give it up, man, cause she ain't going to. Least not for you."

Tyler stared at Spike. Shoved his hands deeper into his pockets. Turned away.

"Look, Butterfield, forget her. You wanna get some? I'll take you to the rez. Lots a young puss out there—real, real young. Get 'em ripped—they do anything. But we go back now? We got cops on our ass. They're gonna be lookin' for whoever was in that store. Maybe the camera wasn't working, but sure as shit, somebody saw us."

Kevin waved his arms.

"Like that lady at the counter."

"Yeah. That bitch at the counter." Spike glared at Kevin.

Tyler bit a fleck of skin from his thumb. He stared at the raw flesh. It had seemed so logical at the time—all that adrenaline, the gun shots, the high-speed race up US-101. It seemed to make sense then. He turned to Spike.

"Look, maybe we screwed up. Maybe we're in more trouble than the store thing."

Spike shook his head.

"Here's the deal, Butterfield. You're in, or you're out—your choice. Make it."

"Well, you guys never told me about Canada. I don't wanna go there. I'm gonna help the teacher, and then I'm going home." Kevin turned.

Spike grabbed his arm and pulled him close, face-to-face.

"Listen to me, you ugly piece of shit. You think I give a fuck what you do? I don't care if I ever see your fat face again. But you say one thing about that store—or about Tyler, or about me, or my gun—and that skank you call a mother? I'll make damn sure she wishes you were never born."

Kevin twisted out from Spike's grasp and bolted through the companionway into the cabin.

"Why do you have to be such a jerk?" Tyler said.

Spike spit over the side again—this time straight down. "He's a fucking scared pussy. What about you, Butterfield? You scared?"

24

Kevin wiped his arm across his eyes as he brushed past Jake. He plodded through the cabin and settled down with the children. Jake couldn't be sure, but the kid looked like he'd been crying.

Except for Conrad, the children sat on the benches chattering to each other and pointing at the wildlife and scenery Captain Denny had described. Conrad stood braced against the hull, holding his phone to the window.

Emily pointed to several shiny black birds diving into the waves.

"Look, you guys! One time, my dad and I saw some birds like that sitting on poles in the water. They had their wings spread out like this." She stood and stretched her arms, spread her fingers wide, and made slow fanning motions.

"My daddy said they were drying their wings in the sun." She looked over at Jake and wiggled two fingers in his direction—their secret wave. He glanced around—saw that the others focused on the captain—and returned the private gesture.

"Your dad's right," Denny said. "And look over there." He pointed across the water toward the shoreline where two bald eagles soared in sweeping circles.

"Those eagles are super strong. They can grab a salmon right out of the water and carry it all the way up to their nest on the top of the tallest tree."

The boy with the glasses slid off the bench and pressed his nose against the window.

"My dad says that eagles are sky-rats cuz they'll eat anything." He pushed his glasses up his nose.

"Well, I wouldn't call them sky-rats, but they will carry off cats and small dogs if they get the chance."

"They eat puppies?" A slender girl with straight black hair and almond-shaped eyes burst into tears.

Before Denny could react, Kevin jumped from his seat and rushed to kneel in front of the girl.

"He's kidding," he said. "They don't eat puppies or cats either. They eat fish and crabs and stuff."

The child sniffled, rubbed her eyes with her fists, then leaned against the little girl seated next to her. Kevin stood and moved to the edge of the group.

Denny scratched his head.

"Okay, now, forget the eagles. Let's look for harbor seals. They are the cutest critters. They look like—" He stopped himself. "Harbor seals are super cute, and they love it if you wave to them."

Now distracted, all the children, even the girl who'd been crying, jumped off the bench and joined Tristan in pressing their noses and hands against the glass.

Jake knew he could coax the kids into sitting again, but he hung back—Denny and the teacher were in charge. He looked around for her and realized he hadn't seen her in a while.

He walked to the captain and spoke in a hushed tone.

"What happened to the teacher?"

Denny pointed toward a door with a brass sign that read HEAD.

"She's been in there quite a while now," he said. "Bad place to be if she's feeling woozy. Could you check?"

Jake started across the room, but before he reached the bathroom, the door swung open, and Tamara stepped out of the closet-sized space. She held onto the door handle with one hand and wavered. She held her other hand over her mouth. Her coloring had gone from a healthy pink to a pale greenish tint. Jake looked back at the captain, and from the expression on the other man's face, Jake knew he'd noticed the color shift too.

"Go outside on the deck, take a few deep breaths, and look at the horizon. You'll feel better fast." Denny said. To Jake, he added, "Go with her. She looks a little dizzy, and I don't need anybody falling overboard."

Jake crossed the cabin to the teacher. "Here, take my arm," he said. "I'll help you."

She looked up at him for a second but turned her head away. Jake guessed she was working hard to hold onto whatever she'd had for breakfast.

As they made their way through the cabin, she muttered.

"My students. I shouldn't leave them."

The children had gathered in a circle between the two benches, and in the center of their group, Kevin acted out the motions of a seagull with a clam in its beak. He held his arms out wide and dipped and swooped. He made a strangled *caw caw* sound that reminded Jake more of a crow than a gull, but the children didn't seem to notice or to mind.

"Drop the clam! Drop the clam!" they chanted.

At the wheel, the captain looked on and laughed at the show.

"I think they're in good hands, don't you?" Jake gave her arm a soft squeeze for encouragement and continued to move through the cabin toward the door.

Jake helped Tamara step over the threshold between the salon and the aft deck, then paused to give her a moment to breathe in the rush of fresh, salt air. When she nodded, he nudged her onward, grasping the railing with his left hand and holding his right arm bent for her to grip as they made their way along the narrow passage toward the bow. The *Hattie Belle* rose and fell with a smooth, even cadence.

Although it had been a long time since he'd been at sea, the motion didn't bother him. In truth, he was surprised at how comfortable he felt moving along the rolling deck. Jake wondered if walking on a boat might be a bit like riding a bicycle—once you get the rhythm of the sea in your bones, you never forget it.

25

Jennette pointed to the side of the building where a skinny figure dressed in lavender tights and a baggy Seahawks sweatshirt stood on tiptoes peering into the office through the now locked window. Spears of scarlet neon hair poked out from under a rhinestone-studded baseball cap.

"Check her out," she said.

Neil Edward grimaced.

"She's early," he said.

Most weeks, Anita Anderson waited until Wednesday to launch her citizen concerns or sound her alarms. As far as he could remember, she'd never had a legitimate issue to report or a concern worth even noting, but if he or Jennette didn't follow up, Anita would file a written complaint with the mayor's office. The mayor would then issue a reprimand, which would result in the sheriff being forced to write an apology letter to the annoying busybody. And, if the mayor—one of Jennette's many suitors— didn't follow up with a reprimand, Anita would bump her complaint up the food chain until she got the satisfaction she sought. One time, she went all the way to the governor's office with her complaint. Although he'd been grateful Anita hadn't come after him on that particular occasion, Neil Edward felt sorry for the head of the Public Works Department who'd naively chopped down a dead and diseased maple tree without first calling for a public hearing. Anita was particularly fond of public hearings, so she'd been especially miffed by that breach of protocol.

Jennette smirked.

"It's your turn."

"I know, I know." Neil Edward parked the cruiser and turned to Jennette.

"Let's get this guy into the cell, and while you process him, I'll handle our concerned citizen. Make sure you log the ammo and see if you can get one of the kids from the high school to come by to take a shot at getting into that cell phone. We've got permission, so we're legal—or close enough—and I have a feeling we can clear up this 'grand theft auto' case once we get into that phone."

Forty-five minutes later, Neil Edward dropped his hat on his desk and ran his hands through his hair.

"What was the old looney up to today?" Jennette held a clipboard in one hand and a pencil in the other. She looked at a small pile of items on her desk and made a note on an intake sheet.

"Her neighbor's security alarm was buzzing. They're away visiting grandkids, and she was sure their home was being burglarized."

"And was it? Being burglarized?" she asked.

Neil Edward walked over to the coffee pot and poured a cup. He broke off a corner of the one remaining scone, popped it in his mouth, and swallowed.

"Nope. Family of mice made a nest in the attic—seems they were chewing on the wires and set the alarm off. I shut it down and called Port Angeles Animal Control—they're sending some-one out this afternoon. Case closed."

"Well, that was an easy one." Jennette squinted at something on her desk and pulled back. She made another note on the form.

He tipped his coffee cup in her direction and took a sip.

"Yep. And the next one is yours. So, what's been happening here while I was off fighting crime?"

Jennette looked up from the clipboard.

"Actually, a lot. Right after you left, I got a call from my friend in the Clallam County Sheriff's Office. You know that convenience store outside of Port Angeles—the one right before you get on the 101?"

"The Stop and Go?"

"The Always Open Stop and Shop," Jennette corrected him. "Well, there was an armed robbery this morning—around eight. Clerk got shot."

He sat his cup on the desk. Deep ridges creased his brow.

"Is the guy—"

"He's alive, but according to my friend, barely. They've got him in intensive care at Mercy. Apparently, the guy has a heart condition."

"Shooters?"

"They don't know yet. Cops found one old guy in the store, but he ducked down behind a rack when he heard the clerk yelling about not wanting any trouble. He didn't see the shooter. Or shooters."

"Wow, that *is* a lot."

"That's not all. I managed to get into the mystery cell phone. I know who it belongs to—and I know about our friend in the holding tank."

"Are you telling me you got into the phone?"

Jennette stepped from behind her desk and bent her one natural leg enough for an exaggerated curtsy—her voluminous black and yellow skirt billowed around her.

"Resident computer geek, at your service, Sheriff."

"How? I mean—"

"Online class in IT. I'm in my second term."

The lines on the sheriff's brow deepened.

"You're not thinking about leaving law enforcement, are you? I mean, if it's the hours or the money—if you need a raise—"

"Aww, Sheriff Longcarver. Can't live without me? That's just plain sweet." She walked back around her desk and plopped into her chair.

"No, I would never think of leaving you, Boss. I thought that maybe if I picked up some new skills, I could do more around here—or score some side gigs. But, if you're serious about that raise, well—"

Neil Edward exhaled. "So, how'd you do it? How'd you get into the phone?"

"To be honest, breaking into a cell phone—even if you have permission—takes technology Neah County doesn't have, so I used something more powerful."

He twirled one finger—hurry up.

"Women's intuition. The kid has a senior photo of Judge Lynden's daughter on the lock screen. I did a Google search— her name is Hailey. So, I tried Hailey1234 and bingo—we're in."

Neil Edward stared at Jennette and shook his head. Women. He pulled a metal folding chair next to her desk and sat down. "Okay, whatcha got?"

"Well, first off, I ran the plates on that car. It does belong to Travis Drumthor. But, as we already knew, the registration is expired. And, Mr. Drumthor's license was revoked—seems like he has a little drinking problem. First DUI, he got a warning. Second time he got popped going sixty-five in a school zone—that was a major hassle for our man back there. The third time he drove his car right through the front door of the Sugar Shack in Sequim. From what I learned, no people were hurt, but he took out a row of soft serve machines. Turns out the things explode if you run a car into them." Jennette made a clicking sound.

"What I would give to watch all that strawberry swirl dripping from the ceiling," she said.

Neil Edward's back ached, and he longed for that massage, but something told him it was going to be a long, long day.

"Okay, that's good stuff. What about the ammo and the phone?

Jennette picked up the cell phone.

"Nothing on the ammo yet, but this belongs to Tyler Butterfield—clearly a friend, maybe the best friend, of one Eugene Francis Drumthor, aka Spike."

"His brother?" The sheriff gestured toward the other room.

"Yep, younger brother." She handed the phone to him.

Neil Edward punched in the code and the Recent Calls screen popped up. There were several calls to and from Spike, a few 800 numbers, one to someone named Kevin, and one to Fat Mama's pizza delivery. The sheriff skipped to the text messages. Again, several to and from Spike—mostly short confirmations regarding plans to hang out, mostly answered with emoji. Only one text from Spike caught his attention—*Get the car back by 2 or Travis will kill me.* Three emoji's followed—all angry red faces covered with symbols. He held the phone out to Jennette. "Means?"

"Serious swearing," she said.

"Got it."

He continued to scroll through the texts. There were several miscellaneous messages from politicians pleading for votes or salespeople pitching products. There were no texts to the boy named Kevin. But there were four to the girl on the lock screen—one an invitation to see the latest action movie, two requests for a chance to talk—maybe after school. The last message simply said that he really, really liked her and wished she'd at least talk to him. She had not responded to any of the texts.

In the photo app, snapshots of teenage boys doing things teenage boys do—goofy faces, moon shots, a couple of photos of the pretty girl on the lock screen—both taken from a distance—both candid. Lots of selfies of a good-looking kid with a broad smile next to a scowling boy with slicked-back hair. The kid with the scowl wore a black leather jacket in every shot, and he seemed, to Neil Edward, older than the others.

He set the phone on Jennette's desk.

"Tell me what you know about these kids—Tyler and his pal, Spike." He pressed back in his chair and waited.

Jennette leaned forward, and her eyes twinkled—a sure sign she was about to launch into some juicy news.

"Well—" Although there was no one else in the front office, and the door to the back room was closed, Jennette looked around and lowered her voice.

"The blond boy, Tyler? Nice kid. I asked around. Decent grades, graduates this month. Comes from a fairly normal family, parents still together, one older sister—married with two babies—she moved to Seattle a couple of years ago. Tyler and his parents live in a small house in Port Angeles out in one of those suburbs on the east side. His mother is in a quilting club and volunteers at the senior center and the foodbank. His father works at the refinery in Anacortes—he's a fly fisherman." She paused for a breath.

Neil Edward scratched his head. He'd been gone less than an hour, and during that short time, Jennette had processed a suspect, figured out the password to a stranger's cell phone, and dug up enough dirt to fill a dossier. The woman really did deserve a raise.

"What about the heavy-set kid? Anything on him?"

"Not much. Kevin Woods. Lives with his mother in a trailer somewhere in the county. Got a DUI and driving without a license. Was held back a grade. That's about it on him."

"And the snarly looking kid? The one in the jacket?"

"Ah, yes. The real interesting guys are the brothers Spike and our guest, Travis. Turns out both of them have been in and out of jail several times. The youngest, Spike, dropped out of school in the tenth grade. Seems he has some sort of learning disability—affects his reading."

"How old is he?"

"That's what's weird. He's twenty-two, but he hangs around with those two teenagers. As far as I could find out, they're his only friends."

"What about the older brother?"

"When we first got to the marina, I thought I remembered him from somewhere, but it took me a while to put two and two together. He's fatter and dirtier than the last time I saw him. At that time, he was at the courthouse—in the gallery. His father was being tried for assault and manslaughter. I expect the public defender asked the family to clean up some for the trial."

"When was this?"

"Two, maybe three years ago. They lived in Forks at the time. Later, I think they moved to Sequim. I can look it up if you want."

He shook his head.

"No. Go on."

"So, Travis and Spike. Their father, Clive, is one mean son-of-a-bitch. Angry man. Everybody knew he pounded on his sons—well, at least on the older boy, and he was well-known for slapping their mother around too. Her name is Joyce. One night he got over-the-top drunk—or maybe high—and he killed a guy. Then he battered the guy's wife. I heard that Drumthor completely lost it. Word is, he went home and beat Joyce so bad the EMTs called the coroner when they first saw her. My friend says she sees Joyce at the grocery store from time to time—she looks like the walking dead—according to my friend, that is."

"What about him? Clive?"

"He's serving life—no parole."

Neil Edward pushed the chair back and stood up. He glanced at the small pile of objects on Jennette's desk.

"So," he said, "Did we learn anything from what he carries in his pockets?"

"Well, we know he smokes weed." She used the tip of her pencil to push a half-smoked joint from the pile.

"And he doesn't have much money." Again, she used the pencil, this time to tap on a folded ten-dollar bill.

"We know he's superstitious. Carries a good luck charm." She jabbed the pencil point through a jump ring attached to something covered in white fur. She dropped the object in Neil Edward's open hand.

He peered at the thing for a moment.

"What is this? Rabbit's foot?"

"Nope—kitten's paw. Clive Drumthor is one mean son-of-a-bitch. And, I might be going out on a limb here, Boss, but it looks like his boys didn't fall far from the tree."

26

Jake steadied Tamara as she struggled up the sloping exterior walkway between the hull and the cabin. She leaned into him, and while he knew it was simply for support, he liked the soft pressure of her body against his. A lot of time had passed since he'd been this close to a woman—and for a moment, a longing and a sadness washed over him. It wasn't so much the sex that he missed—although he did miss that—it was more the feeling of being part of something, someone else. The connectedness of taking care of someone and having them take care of you. The trust—the knowing that someone had your back and that you had theirs. The connection didn't have to be with a lover—there were others.

His Commanding Officer had said that the bond between brothers-in-arms is tighter and more lasting than the bond between any husband and wife—critical, at times, to save your life and theirs. The CO was right. Marilyn left him over a difference in dreams. Richard would have given his life.

Tamara clasped her hand over her mouth.

"Take a deep breath," Jake said. "You're okay. We're almost to the front—it's more open up there, and you'll feel a whole lot better."

Tamara didn't look at him, but she pushed on.

As they made their way past the salon, Jake peered through the windows and searched for Emily. The children, and Kevin, now gathered on the starboard side—their noses pressed against the glass—their backs a wall of bulbous orange canvas. Emily's blond ponytail swung from side to side as she pointed at something on the water. *She's happy, doing well.* There will be hell to pay if Marilyn ever finds out about his breach of her rules but seeing Emily with other children—hearing her laughter—totally worth the risk.

When they'd moved beyond the cabin, Jake turned, lifted Tamara's arm from his, and placed her hand on the railing. Her fingers clutched the carved wood—her eyes shut tight—her breathing shallow.

"Try to take a deep breath," he said. "No shame in heaving over the side if you need to—don't worry about that. But try to fill your lungs with fresh air if you can. And, like the captain said, look to the horizon."

He stayed close, but to give her some privacy, he turned his head and gazed into the distance.

They'd motored across the Strait of Juan de Fuca and were traveling in a north-easterly direction around the southern end of Vancouver Island. The island was on Jake's places to explore list, but since moving to Port Angeles, he hadn't even made it off the peninsula. He shielded his eyes to cut the glare and tried to get a better look at the Canadian coastline. Without clearing customs, they'd have to remain in U.S. waters, which meant they wouldn't be able to motor close enough to get an intimate view of the island. Still, he could see that the land was as rich in forests and beaches as its neighbor to the south.

Now, at a little past eleven in the morning, the breeze blew fresh and crisp. Jake followed the advice he and the captain had given to Tamara and sucked in several deep, cleansing breaths. For a moment, he wished he'd moved upwind of the woman in case she did need to spew overboard, but the space was tight, and he didn't want to jostle her. Taking his chances, he stayed put and leaned against the rail.

Out here, far from the shore, the water was a deep teal with diamonds of sunlight winking on its surface. As the *Hattie Belle* pushed through low waves, she carved curls of white foam that cascaded into aquamarine pools on either side of her bow. Sparkling rainbows shot up from the swirling froth. *Wouldn't Emily be delighted if her father could hold her safe and let her lean out over the railing to see the waters dance?*

Behind and off each side of the *Hattie Belle,* several similar-sized boats plowed the water's surface or dug into rolling waves. The fleet Denny had described—the group of vessels who'd reported in to let the others know they were ready for the day—the group of captains, all working together, all looking to provide their passengers with a memorable adventure on the water, whales or not. They probably shared a close camaraderie—most likely met at a neighborhood pub for beers after a long day, swapped stories, and looked after each other. For the second time that morning, Jake started down a familiar rabbit hole but forced himself to stop his mental trajectory. He figured it must be the rolling of the boat beneath him and the gleam of the water. He needed to forget it, or at least block it out—for now. He coughed and then stood straight.

After a long stretch, Jake pressed his back against the cabin—its wood now warmed by the sun. Through half-closed eyes, he studied Tamara's profile. More alert now and obviously more comfortable, her forearms rested on the railing, the breeze tugged at her tangled mass of black curls. Though they'd been outside only a short while, the greenish tint of seasickness had disappeared, and her pale skin had begun to glow from the sun. Tamara was about a foot shorter, and he guessed maybe three or four years younger than him—early thirties at most. Slender. Earlier, he'd looked for a ring—an old habit—didn't see one, but that didn't mean anything. She dressed simply and, to Jake's thinking, appropriately for the occasion—white t-shirt, khaki capris, white trainers. Marilyn would have dressed differently for a trip on the water. She would have worn pressed white slacks, a white silk blouse, a navy jacket, and designer deck shoes. She would have outfitted Emily in a dress reflecting the same theme. She would have spent half a fortune to fashion a nautical look for a four-hour trip.

Tamara turned her head and smiled at him.

Jake pushed himself away from the cabin wall.

"Well, somebody's feeling better," he said.

She held out her hand.

"Tamara O'Dwyer. And, thanks. I appreciate your help. Guess I'm not very good at this boating thing."

"No worries. I like getting out on deck now and again. Clears the brain."

Tamara's brow furrowed.

"The truth is, I've always been anxious on the water, and this isn't my first go-around with *mal de mer*."

"Everybody gets seasick at some point. Even Captain Bligh."

Her face softened.

"I did think about taking Dramamine, but the last time I tried it, I fell asleep on a ferry heading to Victoria. Didn't wake up until they blew the whistle at the dock. I can't risk nodding off today. Especially not with these assistants." She made air quotes at the word assistants.

Jake tilted his head.

"Sorta begs the question, doesn't it? I mean, why take a group of kids on a whale-watching tour if you—their teacher—are afraid of the water and are prone to seasickness?"

"Yeah, I know, it sounds weird. But I'm not really afraid, more nervous than anything. And I want these little guys to love nature—the animals, the forests, the water, and, you know, the whole thing. Their parents pay big bucks to send their children to Ruth Hudson Elementary. These kids are the privileged ones—the ones who'll hold important positions in society, decision-making positions. I hope they'll make decisions based on a love of the planet rather than a love of money."

A breeze swirled around her and carried the faint, clean scent of Ivory soap and coconut oil. Jake breathed in—held her fragrance—lingered with the scent until he had to exhale. Then he turned toward the sea.

They leaned against the rail and gazed across the water without speaking until Jake took a long breath.

"Think we should get back to the kids?" he said.

"Let's give them a few more minutes," she said. "You were right back there, in the cabin. They're doing great. And that one guy—the kid in the shorts—I was so busy getting everyone organized, I didn't catch his name."

"Kevin."

"Kevin. He's doing a great job with the children, but I feel sort of sorry for him. He seems to crave attention and affection, and it's obvious he has some developmental challenges. I've seen kids like Kevin before—even in the private school. Always the focus of teasing and cruelty. It breaks my heart." She paused. "And those other two, I wonder about them as well. The kid who helped you with the ropes—he seems a little out of place. And that guy in the jacket? I don't trust him. What do you think?"

"You know kids," Jake said. "They're just boys trying to figure out where they fit in. Don't overthink it."

An eagle flapped toward a Douglas fir on the far shore, made a single turn into the wind, and settled on a bare branch.

"Maybe you're right. Maybe I'm over-analyzing things. Still—" she chewed her lower lip. "I wonder why the school sent boys. Girls. I thought they'd send girls for sure."

"Probably some politically correct policy," Jake said. "Don't sweat it."

Tamara waited a moment, then turned to face him. She touched his arm—a quick, light touch.

"Okay, so, tell me about you, Mr. Mechanic. Mike, the Mechanic?"

27

Vera Johanson pressed her back into the chair, held her arms straight, and flattened her palms on well-worn oak. One of three cell phones lying face down at the edge of her desk rotated as it vibrated against the wood. Another announced an incoming text with a sharp ping. On the far wall, a stately antique clock chimed the half-hour. Vera closed her eyes for a moment and tried to will herself to some other place—some other time. She opened her eyes and stole a glance at the locked cabinet under the bookshelves. It wasn't even noon, but Principal Vera Johanson longed for a swallow of liquid memory loss. With a sigh, she looked up at the three girls standing in a loose row in front of her desk.

The shortest girl, the one with bright green nail polish and silver nose-ring, pointed at the pinging phone.

"Ah, Ms. Johanson? Can I get that text? It could be somebody important."

Vera leaned forward.

"No, Kaitlyn, you may not touch that phone. Not now and not for several hours. The three of you are spending the rest of the day in detention."

"Come on, Ms. Johanson. I mean, like, what were we supposed to do?" A slender girl with long purple streaks in pale blond hair scrunched her face into a pout. She twisted a lavender strand around two fingers and rocked back and forth from foot to foot.

Vera leaned in further and pointed one finger at the girl.

"Willow, you know very well what you were supposed to do. You were supposed to meet Ms. O'Dwyer at the marina. You were supposed to help her take eight children on a whale-watching trip. You were supposed to—"

The third girl interrupted her.

"Hey, it wasn't our fault the tire got popped."

Vera pushed the chair back. She stood—ramrod straight. Her dark gray suit, maroon blouse, and single strand of black pearls were selected to give an air of intimidation and authority, but the girls didn't seem to notice.

"Aiysha, do not interrupt me. If you do that again, you'll remain in detention until you graduate—if you graduate."

Vera kept her voice low and steady—she glanced down at her desk.

"It may well not have been your fault—about the tire. But I'm looking at three cell phones, all of which appear to be working. Not one of which, to my understanding, was used to call me, or the marina office, or Ms. O'Dwyer. A simple phone call to explain your problem would have been the responsible thing to do. The thing a *responsible*, college-bound senior would have done."

She paused for dramatic effect. After a moment of silence, she continued.

"Now, who was driving the car? And who's car is it?"

Willow let out an exaggerated sigh, stopped rocking. She slumped to one side.

"It's my dad's car, so of course, I was driving," she said.

"Well, Willow, tell me, how did you get the flat?"

"Like I think you already know, we hit a pothole. Like Kaitlyn said, it wasn't our fault."

The principal pressed her lips together to keep from saying something she'd regret. It was clear her lecture on responsible behavior hadn't fazed the girls. She tried a different tack.

"What did you do to fix the flat?"

She honestly didn't care, but she'd have to provide documentation—for the detention and for not awarding them the extra credit they'd applied for. This close to retirement, she didn't want to do anything against the myriad of new rules imposed by the current culture. Besides, she'd have to do some significant apologizing to the young teacher who'd worked so hard to arrange the outing. Not to mention the explanation she'd need to present to the tetchy headmaster at Ruth Hudson Elementary.

The center phone pinged again. Aiysha leaned forward—her fingers stretched toward the desk.

"Can I—"

"No. You may not." Vera pulled on a handle, and with one smooth scoop, she slid the phones across the desk and dropped them into the waiting drawer.

"Hey, you can't—"

"Yes, I most certainly can."

Aiysha straightened, crossed her arms over her chest, and glared at Vera.

Vera ignored her.

"Now, let me ask again, what did you do to fix the flat?"

"Well, we did try, but we didn't know how," Willow said.

"And some guys went by us, but they didn't stop," Kaitlyn added.

"Jerks," Aiysha muttered.

Vera held herself back from glancing at the tempting locked cabinet again.

"So?" she said.

"Well, we called my dad, and he called triple A, and some old man came out and fixed the tire for us." Willow braided blond and lavender strands together.

Vera cleared her throat.

"And was your father upset? Was he concerned that you were going to be late for your community service assignment?"

Willow looked up from her braid and tilted her head as if she didn't quite understand the question.

"I, uh, don't think so. He asked how the car was. He wanted to know if it was scratched or anything."

Vera looked at her watch and then up at the clock.

"It couldn't have taken long for the auto club to fix the flat. What have you been doing for the past, say, two or two and a half hours?"

Aiysha and Kaitlyn looked at Willow. Willow looked at Vera, and then, without any outward semblance of embarrassment or apology, she shrugged.

"So, we did *think* about going to the marina—to check it out. But we knew we were already too late, so we figured, what the— you know. So, we came back to town and went to the mall and ate lunch, and, you know, we hung out." She shrugged again.

"Well, you're going to hang out some more. This time in the detention hall. I want each of you to write a letter of apology to the teacher you were supposed to assist. You can show me your work after the final period. Come back here with your laptops. I'll check your work before you email those letters to Ms. O'Dwyer. You may leave now." She looked toward the door.

"Ah, Ms. Johanson, we need our phones."

Vera fought a smile.

"You can pick them up when you come back this afternoon."

"But, there's no Wi-Fi in the detention hall."

"No," Vera said, "I suppose there isn't. Better get going on those letters now." She sat down and feigned attention to a stack of folders on the desk.

Grumbling, the three girls left the office and shuffled down the hall.

Vera stood. She walked around the desk, closed her office door, and turned the lock. She plucked a small brass key from a bowl of paperclips on the desk and crossed her office to the bookshelves and to the locked cabinet. She had an apology and a phone call to make, but first things first.

28

Jake blinked and swallowed. Avoiding her eyes, he continued to scan the sparkling water and dark beryl shoreline. Long stretches of emerald forests veiled any hints of civilization. In some places, evergreens marched down to the water's edge. In others, trees rooted on top of slate-colored boulders at the head of rock-strewn beaches. Now and then, a stand of ghost-white birch punctuated the gloom, and every so often, a sensuous red ma-drone beckoned.

"Jake. Jake, the Mechanic. Not much to tell." He reached up to scratch under his chin, stopped short, and dropped his arm to his side.

"I keep the engine running. That's all. Pretty boring."

"Kids?" she asked.

She was still looking at him—he could feel that, but he stayed focused on the scenery. For some reason, maybe it was the endorphin-drenched morning, or maybe plain old loneliness, he wanted to spill his guts to her. Wanted to tell her about the agony of the past several years, how he'd lost everything, how much he missed his daughter's laughter, how he craved—

"Naw," he said. "Married for a while. Didn't work out. Just me now."

"Oh," she said.

"What about you? Kids?"

Tamara turned from him and faced toward the bow—her eyes closed. The wind blew her hair back. She gulped the air and then let it out with a slow exhale. She opened her eyes but continued to face forward.

"No, she said, "My husband and I wanted kids, but it didn't work out."

"Hey," he said, "I don't mean to pry. It's just that, well, you're so good with kids. Maybe—"

"Maybe we could adopt, right?"

Jake stood still and didn't speak. She'd share her history if she wanted to—if she needed to—only a matter of time.

After a few minutes, she turned toward him.

"The thing is, we might have if I'd acted better. But—" She blinked and looked down.

"You don't want to hear my sad little story."

"The engine's humming, and that's my only job. Tell me."

Tamara looked up and across the water. She shielded her eyes for a few seconds before turning again to face Jake.

"We lived in Wisconsin, and we were on our way to visit his parents in Michigan. I was seven months pregnant. The roads were icy, and Craig, my husband, was driving. And we were arguing—we were always arguing." She took in a breath and let it out in a slow sigh.

"I don't even remember what the issue was that day. Anyway, he got distracted and didn't see the brake lights ahead of us in time to stop. We plowed into the back of an eighteen-wheeler. We were both injured, pretty banged up, but—" she looked down. Her hand drifted over her belly.

"Airbag?"

"Didn't deploy. Manufacturing defect or something. Craig wanted to sue—he was so angry. But I went into a deep depression. I couldn't perform—the school had to let me go. That made Craig even angrier, but I didn't care about my job. I could hardly move. I could barely breathe. To be honest, I didn't want to breathe. Sometimes I blamed Craig. Other times, I blamed God. Most of the time, I blamed myself."

"You get any support?"

"Craig gave it his best—I know that he tried. It was the first time in our marriage that he made an effort to, well, to care. He said we should try again. He said we should adopt, or become foster parents, or even quit everything, move to Europe, and start all over again. But I couldn't function, and finally, he couldn't stand to be around me anymore, so he left."

"What happened then?"

She looked down at the water, reached out, and ran her hand across the varnished rail.

"So, there I was, with no job, no husband, and no baby. I don't know what I would have done without my brother. He's a family-law attorney—lives in Seattle. He's one mean son-of-a-gun in the courtroom—at least that's what I've heard. But he's a great judge of people. He knew I needed to be around children again, and he knew I needed to get away from the Midwest. He wanted me closer to him, wanted to give me support. So, he found this job for me and helped me move. My brother made a good call—like I said, he's one mean lawyer, but he's a kind brother."

They stood quiet for a couple of minutes until Jake pushed back from the rail and stood straight.

"So, now you're a teacher at this fancy private school. You happy?"

"This is the end of my first school year at Ruth Hudson, and even though there's a lot of pressure from the administration to perform to some pretty high standards, I love it there. And these kids—they saved me. So that's it. That's my story." She pushed back from the rail and ran her hand through her curls.

Jake wanted to wrap his arms around her, protect her, block the pain and the sorrow that haunted her. But he couldn't do that, so he did what he could.

"I'm sorry," he said.

"Thanks."

They stood side by side and watched gulls swoop and play in the wind. Finally, Jake changed the tone.

"So, what's up with those little boys with the cell phone—the reporter and the photojournalist? Photojournalist. That's a pretty big word for second graders, isn't it? What's that about?"

Tamara smiled.

"Yeah, they're a pair, aren't they? As you might have guessed, Conrad is the leader. His father works a camera for Channel Five News, and Conrad can't wait to grow up and be a famous photographer like his dad."

"That's cute," Jake said. "What about the other kid, the reporter? Does his mom report the news?"

"No. That's Tristan. He pretty much goes along with whatever Conrad says. When Conrad's dad told him that all news photographers worked with reporters, Conrad had to have one. So now, we have the news team of Tristan Whiting and Conrad Huffington."

"The third," Jake said.

"Yes, Conrad Huffington, the third." Tamara pointed to a harbor seal a few yards away. With its sleek gray and black speckled head, long, bristly whiskers, and big round eyes, it looked more like a puppy than a creature of the sea.

Jake followed the animal a moment.

"What happens to the news stories?" he said.

"Oh, it's pretty cool. I managed to talk the principal into letting me set up a private channel for the school. Everything gets uploaded from the student's phones. There's a computer in the teachers' lounge, and we all take turns monitoring the posts. Parents can view the videos, but nothing goes out to the kids until a teacher okays it. It's a safe way for kids to practice social media skills."

Did Emily post videos? Could he watch her day-to-day activities this way?

"Do all the kids post videos?"

"Not all the kids have cell phones—only the ones with parents willing to foot the bill. Also, while most parents can afford it, some don't think their kids should have cell phones. We have a video component in the art class, though, and a few of the other children use that time and equipment to make videos, but mostly, it's a few regulars like Conrad and Tristan. Still, I figure if it bolsters the future career of even one of my students, it's worth the time and trouble."

The seal blinked twice and dove under. Remembering the captain's faux pas with the puppy-eating-eagle story, Jake now understood why Denny hadn't compared harbor seals to small dogs.

Tamara straightened.

"Actually, some of the videos are pretty darned funny. Kids are smart, and they're more insightful than you'd imagine." She brushed a strand of hair from her face. The wind blew it back.

"Sometimes, after a long day, I log in from home, curl up with a glass of wine, and watch their posts. It's relaxing and renews my faith in the future." She paused for a moment, then continued.

"Of course, they aren't available to the public—like I said, only parents and teachers have access."

Yet another thing Marilyn kept from him. Jake sucked in a deep breath of clean sea air—forced himself to push his anger away. He focused on the gulls soaring overhead, on the dappled light playing hide and seek between dark green trees on shore, and on the buttons of foam the *Hattie Bell* left floating in her wake.

A rough scraping jolted them as Captain Denny slid a door open and leaned out.

"Teach," he said, "you better get in here. We have an incident."

29

Now, steady on her feet, Tamara led the way back to the cabin. Spike and Tyler were gone, and the aft deck was empty. A chorus of crying and quarreling greeted her and Jake as they stepped through the companionway.

"Lemme see. Lemme see."

"No! It's my turn. I get to hold it now."

Two little girls huddled on a bench, hugged each other, and made soft sobbing sounds. With considerable pushing and jock-eying for position, the other children pressed around a boy who held something his cupped his hands for them to see. Spike, Tyler, and Kevin leaned over the children and peered at the object.

Tamara rushed across the cabin.

"Ryan! What *is* that?"

The children stepped aside to give her room. The boy held his hands up—showed her his treasure.

"Harvey. My turtle," he said.

Tamara stooped to examine the lumpy object, flinched, and jerked back. The turtle lay still in the child's hands—its shell about the size of a silver dollar, the color of mold. The smell of rotting flesh, overpowering.

"Why isn't he moving?" she said.

The boy shrugged.

"He's dead."

The girls on the bench sobbed louder.

Kevin moved to join them. The rumpled teenager spoke to the little girls in a soothing, sing-song voice.

"Lexie, Amanda, don't cry. It's okay. Everything is okay. The turtle is with Jesus now."

Tamara took a deep breath and exhaled. She turned her attention back to the little boy.

"Ryan, why did you bring Harvey with you today?"

"He's a turtle. They like water."

"But, didn't you say he's dead?"

"Yes," Ryan said. "I'm going to bury him at sea."

"Don't you think it might be a good idea to bury him at home? Maybe in your backyard? Maybe your parents could help you dig a nice grave for Harvey?"

The child pursed his lips, closed his hand around his pet, and crossed his arms over his chest.

"No. Harvey wants to be buried at sea. It was my daddy's idea."

Of course, it was your father's idea.

"Well, let's put Harvey away now and maybe after we eat, we can put him in one of the lunch boxes and have a ceremony. Do you think Harvey would like that?"

The boy seemed to consider her offer.

"Promise?" he said.

"Promise."

"Okay." He started to slip the turtle into his pocket when Tristan reached to grab it.

"Wait! I didn't get to hold him yet."

Ryan jerked his hand out of Tristan's reach.

"Grab hold!" Denny called out.

A wave crashed against the hull and rocked the *Hattie Belle*. The children squealed. Ryan tumbled forward. The turtle flew from his hands, hit the window with a resounding crack, and landed on the floor, upside down. It spun three turns, then stopped.

Ryan scrambled to his feet.

"Harvey!"

Tamara bolted for him, but before she could reach the child—or the turtle—Spike bent down and scooped the creature up. He turned it over and drew back. A thick gray gum oozed from a crack along Harvey's back.

"Gross," he said.

Ryan burst into tears and punched Tristan.

"It's your fault. You made me drop him. Now he's hurt!"

Tristan yelped.

"Miss O. He hit me!"

Amanda let out a long, piercing wail.

Tamara started to speak, but Spike nudged two children aside and knelt by Ryan.

He placed the animal in Ryan's hand.

"Here," he said. "Don't worry about your turtle. He ain't hurt. Once you're dead, you don't feel nothin'. That's the whole point a dyin'." Spike stood and gave Ryan an awkward pat on his head.

"Miss O. He said, ain't." The barefoot girl pointed at Spike.

Tamara jumped in.

"It's okay, Jenny. He's a grown-up."

A look of confusion crossed Spike's face.

"But my mom says only ignorant people say ain't."

"No, it's really—"

Spike straightened. His expression changed.

"Screw all of ya." He turned, pushed Jenny aside, and stomped out of the cabin.

"Great," Tamara said. She looked at Jake.

"I'll talk to him," he said.

She mouthed thanks and then focused on the children.

"Now, let's all sit on the benches and look for those whales, okay?" She turned to Tyler.

"Could you and Kevin grab the juice and the boxes? I think lunch might be a good distraction."

30

Jake crossed the aft deck. Guy with a lousy attitude—humiliated by an eight-year-old. *Calm things down—deescalate.*

Spike glanced at him and glowered. He fussed with his lighter—tried to get it to stay lit long enough to ignite the cigarette dangling from his lips. He kept clicking and clicking, but the wind was strong and blew the flame out.

Jake leaned against the railing and faked disinterest. There were NO SMOKING signs all over the boat, but he figured this wasn't the time to point them out. Finally, Spike crouched down behind a solid wooden panel on the boarding ladder gate and managed to get out of the wind long enough to light the cigarette. He took a deep draw, straightened, and blew a stream of smoke aft. Glad to be upwind, Jake avoided making a face or saying anything about smoking.

The two of them stared across the water, not saying a word until Jake looked skyward. The puffy white clouds were gone. A canopy of heavy gray shapes now darkened the sky.

"Does the wind feel cooler to you?" he said.

Spike spit a speck of tobacco. "Can't tell."

"Yeah, bet that jacket is warm. Looks like one I saw at the Harley dealership. You ride?"

Spike took another hit, tilted his face upward, and tried to blow a ring, but the wind snatched the smoke from him. He looked at Jake. For a second, the two made eye contact. A chilling stare. Spike looked away.

"No," he said. "I just like it."

Before Jake could add anything, Denny stepped through the companionway and crossed the aft deck, his jaw set hard.

"Hey," he said. "Get rid of that. No smoking onboard. Can't you read?" Without waiting for Spike to respond, he spun around and went back inside.

"Fuck." Spike flicked the butt over the transom—it disappeared in the boat's wake.

31

Jake rotated his shoulders forward and back, let the tension drain from his muscles, and let the cabin's warmth relax him.

Kevin held up a juice box.

"Who wants grape?"

The children clamored around him.

"I do!"

"I do!"

"I want cherry!"

Kevin placed small, waxy cartons in their outstretched hands.

"This is like being Santa Claus," he said. "I always thought it would be fun to play Santa Claus—at the mall or someplace like that."

Tyler looked up from the clipboard Tamara had given him.

"Maybe. But I don't think Santa has to hassle with all these allergies." He squatted in front of a plastic bin packed with cardboard takeout type boxes and scanned the board.

"Lexie Wilson?"

"Here!" One of the girls crying over the dead turtle a short while earlier snatched the box from Tyler's hand and twirled back to her seat.

Tamara had been right about food being a good distraction. She and the two assistants had the whole lunch thing under control. Figuring his help wasn't needed, Jake made his way to the helm station.

Denny checked several instruments and jotted notes in a logbook. He looked up briefly, then resumed his work. After a few minutes, he closed the book and scanned the horizon. Dark clouds blotted the once clear morning sky, and frothy white caps rode increasingly large waves. Heavy drops of rain splattered against the windshield, only a few at first, then many, then a steady percussion.

Denny frowned and looked eastward.

"Here it comes. Squall. I was hoping we'd be out of the path by now. You might want to take a look at those fuel filters. Dickerson was having some trouble with the port filter last week. Don't know if he got it cleared up or what. Probably won't be an issue, but to be on the safe side—"

"On it," Jake said.

"I'll go have a word with the teacher. Those little tykes need to be sitting down—holding on."

"You're sure about the boat?"

Denny patted the wheel.

"This old girl is used to heavy seas. Anyways, these things usually blow in fast and leave as quick. I don't think we need to head back early. But truth is, for a while, it's gonna be rough."

Jake didn't have a clue how to check the condition of the fuel filters or even what fuel filters looked like. At least now he had the port and starboard thing down. With luck, Dickerson would have fixed any issues, and the engine would continue to purr along without a problem until they made it back to the marina— to safety.

He glanced at his watch. They'd been out over two hours, with two more hours to go. The captain had faith in his boat—good enough. And the kids would be physically safe. But the roar of the wind and what was sure to be some hard rocking and rolling—well, fear can do a number on anyone's psyche. Tamara's discomfort on the water couldn't help. Jake wasn't sure he agreed with Denny. Maybe cutting the trip short—heading back to the marina early—would be wise.

Tamara, Kevin, and the children sat in a circle on the floor with their lunches and juice boxes placed on sheets of paper toweling. Despite the growing gloom outside, the cabin remained well-lit and, though cooler than it had been earlier, still comfortable.

When Jake had first seen the children at lunch, it had occurred to him that maybe eating, with the prospect of rolling seas on the horizon, might not be the best of plans. He frowned at the thought of eight children—and maybe a couple of adults—seasick on this small vessel. But no one in the circle, including Tamara, appeared concerned with the change in the boat's motion—or maybe they were all too preoccupied to notice.

"Look, Ryan, peanut butter and jelly. And Pringles! What did you get?" Amanda rattled a red tube of chips.

"Same as every day. Stupid old turkey sandwich and apple."

"Here, I don't want my whole sandwich—you can have half."

Tamara grabbed the sandwich before the little boy could take a bite. She handed it back to Amanda.

"No! Amanda! Ryan! No food trades."

Amanda placed her hands on her hips. She puffed her lips out in a pout.

"But Miss O, he always gets boring stuff. This is supposed to be a fun day. I want to share my fun stuff with him."

Tamara stood. The boat rolled slightly to port, and she stumbled. She grabbed the top of a bench and steadied herself.

"Children, listen up! Everybody—listen to me." She waited until all of her students, and Kevin, looked in her direction.

"Thank you, Amanda, for wanting to do something nice for your friend, but this is like school lunch. No food trades. No sharing. Some of us have food allergies, and some of us have special meal guidelines. So, everybody eats their own lunch, okay?"

Amanda grumbled something Jake couldn't hear, but she returned to her peanut butter and jelly.

Karlie raised her hand.

"Karlie?"

"Miss O, I hafta go potty."

Tamara sighed.

"Again? Okay, Karlie. But remember to hold onto something at all times. We don't want you falling."

Kevin raised his hand.

"Kevin?"

"Ah, Miss O, I can eat anything, so if somebody doesn't want their lunch—"

Tyler braced against a wall as he consulted the board again. Making a final check, he leaned over and handed it to Tamara.

"Join us," she said.

Tyler peered across the room to the forward windows. Jake followed his gaze.

Rain lashed Spike as he crouched against the bow railing, huddled into his jacket, head down. His frame made a thin black silhouette against the slate sky.

"No, thanks," Tyler said. "I'm not hungry." He looked away from the windows and back to the cabin.

Jake grabbed the handle and raised the hatch cover. He caught Tyler's eye and gestured toward the opening.

"You wanna check it out?"

"Yeah, okay." Tyler straightened and stretched, but he stumbled as the boat rolled first to one side and then to the other. He grabbed a handhold. Gripping the rail, hand over hand, he made his way through the cabin toward Jake.

"I think it's getting rough out there," he said.

"I think you're right."

Jake waited until Tyler lowered into the engine room, then he dropped into the small space and closed the hatch.

32

The small, now hot room smelled of diesel and warm oil. Despite its volume, Jake found the low rhythmic rumble of the engine somehow calming. He pointed to hooks where ear protection, headlamps, towels, and two pairs of oil splattered bib overalls swayed with the boat's motion.

"Earmuffs if you need 'em."

Tyler waved him off and lowered onto the overturned crate.

"I'm used to engine noise," he said.

Jake flipped another crate, and the two of them sat watching the giant machine for a few minutes. The liquid in the pan under the engine sloshed back and forth, mixing sheen with water.

"This is pretty cool," Tyler raised his voice—not to a shout— but loud enough for Jake to hear.

"Lots of power," Jake said. He immediately winced—his comment sounded lame, probably showed his lack of knowledge, but Tyler continued to stare at the engine.

"Wish I knew more about diesel," he said. "It would be fun to work on one of these babies."

Jake took a chance.

"Well, here's an easy start for you. The captain says the regular mechanic was having some issues with the port fuel filter. Why don't you see if you can find it and figure out if there's an issue and, if there is, how to fix it?"

Tyler leaned forward for a closer look.

As the *Hattie Belle* rolled from port to starboard, several of the tools Jake left out slid across the engine room floor.

"I'm not so impressed with the regular mechanic," Tyler said. "I mean, like, who leaves tools around? Even in the shop, we put 'em back after we use 'em, and in here, with this boat rocking, his tools are sliding all over the place. Bet a couple of 'em slipped behind the engine. Won't see those again."

He grabbed a wrench as It skidded past his foot and dropped it into a drawer in the toolbox. He gathered several more tools and placed them in the box. Then he shut the drawers and clicked the lid closed.

Jake pretended to study the back of an oil can to hide his embarrassment.

"Yeah, I know. But I haven't had a chance to clean up his mess yet."

A moment later, Tyler turned to Jake and pointed to the two inverted bulbs.

"These are the fuel filters, right? Red liquid, so they've gotta be diesel. Right?"

"Is that what you think?"

"Well—they both look clear to me. I don't see a problem, and the engine sounds steady. So, maybe leave it until there's a real problem?" Tyler tilted his head and waited.

"Nice work," Jake said. "You're talented—know what you're doing." The heat in the engine room had turned both their faces ruddy, but Jake saw Tyler flush as the kid turned away.

"Serious," Jake said. "You could probably get your own shop. Set up a good life for yourself."

Tyler leaned down and stared at the ripples in the pan.

"Wonder where this stuff is coming from? Don't think it's transmission fluid—too clear. Would be more like, you know, milky if it was mixing with water." His question wasn't directed to Jake—more like muttering out loud.

Jake cleared his throat and shifted on the crate. He pressed his knuckle against the mustache.

"Unless you've got other plans."

"Oh, sorry—got distracted. Naw, no plans. A shop would be cool, but you gotta have bucks to start your own business." Tyler kept his eyes on the engine and scanned the hoses, one by one. He reached out and tugged on a clamp. Without looking up, he continued.

"I can't even get enough cash to take Hailey out to dinner. Best I can do is McDonald's—with a coupon."

Jake didn't ask—he waited. You can't rush a guy who's got something to say. You have to wait for it to come out in its own time. It didn't take long.

"Something's burning," Tyler said. He leaned down, dipped one finger in the liquid, and held it to his nose for a sniff. Nodding, he looked over at Jake.

"I'm guessin' you have your shit together. Nice wife, big house, new truck. Of course, I want all that. But Hailey—her old man is rich as God. I don't know why, but her folks, they're nice to me. Well, they were that one time—at her graduation party. You should see their house."

"Hailey is your girlfriend," Jake said.

Tyler didn't respond. His brow furrowed as he stared at the fluid in the pan.

"Her parents would be impressed if you started a business, right?"

"Yeah, maybe. But even if I could set up my own business, Hailey probably won't want to marry a grease monkey. I bet she'll go for a doctor or maybe a judge, like her old man." He straightened and turned to Jake.

"There's a leak somewhere, but I don't see it."

"Good job. I was hoping you'd catch that. Alright, go back up on deck, and I'll take care of this." Jake lifted his ball cap and scratched his head.

"Though, on second thought, things are about to get rough. Might make sense to hold off until we're docked—let the regular guy handle it. Hard to troubleshoot when you're rocking and rolling."

"Maybe. But if it was my boat—maybe that mechanic is like Travis—drives his beaters into the ground and then dumps 'em. Travis—he doesn't care about cars. I don't get it."

"Who's Travis? Is that Spike's real name?" Jake said.

Tyler rolled his eyes.

"No. Spike would kill me if I ever said his real name out loud. I don't even think he knows I know it. Nope, Travis is Spike's brother. Total waste case, but Spike thinks he walks on water." He reached over, touched a pipe, and jerked his hand back.

"Shit! That's hot. Man, they should wrap that with something." He stuck two fingers in his mouth and squeezed his eyes shut.

"You okay?"

Tyler nodded yes but kept his eyes closed for a moment.

"So, what's so great about Travis? I mean, for Spike?"

Tyler opened his eyes, looked at his fingers, and fanned his hand back and forth. He glanced at Jake, then focused on the engine again.

"Beats me. Travis is a dirt bag, just like their old man. Except their old man's in for life."

"Life?" Jake asked.

"Yeah. He robbed a couple at gunpoint. Had a baseball bat too. Old people—you know, in their fifties or so. Of course, he was high. When he got home, he was so fucked-up he beat the crap out of their mother. Wasn't the first time, but that time she almost died."

"She press charges?"

Tyler studied his burned fingers.

"She never did. She just took it. But the guy he beat up? He was some city councilman or something. Big guy in town and had friends in the police force. Spike's old man had a public defender—didn't stand a chance. They popped his ass for life. That's just how those guys are—always doin' some stupid move."

A life sentence is a lot for a beating—even a severe beating. Didn't seem right, but then again, Jake had first-hand knowledge of how a slick lawyer can tilt the scales either way.

"So, I'm guessing Spike made some stupid move already today. Right?"

Tyler jerked his head up and frowned.

"Hey, I gotta get outta here. Too hot." He stood, pushed the hatch open, and scrambled up the metal steps to the cabin. He let the hatch cover close behind him.

A thin bead of sweat rivered through Jake's fake facial hair. He pressed his knuckle to his chin. Tyler probably wished he hadn't said so much. And Spike wasn't just some guy in a counterfeit biker jacket rebelling against the world. Whatever he'd done recently—that morning—whatever he'd dragged his two friends into, wasn't over.

33

A wave smacked the hull sending a fine mist over the aft deck. Tyler rubbed his arms and shifted from one foot to the other.

"Damn, it's cold out here. I'm freezing."

Kevin looked over his shoulder at the circle of children. Most of them continued to munch on sandwiches, chips, and apples, but one little girl looked up from her lunch. Kevin lifted his arm to wave to her but dropped it when another spray of cold water drenched his t-shirt.

"Let's go back inside," he said.

Spike squeezed his eyes tight—smoke from his cigarette swirled around his face. He took a long drag, then tossed the butt over the transom.

Tyler edged back from the rail.

"I agree with Kev—what are we doing out here in this shit?"

Kevin extended his hand to Tyler for a high-five.

Tyler turned away.

Spike hunched his shoulders—raised his jacket collar. He scowled at his friends.

"I can't believe I have to spell everything out for you two. This ain't rocket scientist. We're not going in until we get our plan straight."

"It's science," Tyler said, "rocket science."

"Whatever." Spike reached into his pocket. He pulled out the pack of cigarettes. Another wave hit the hull, and a spray of salt-water slicked his jacket.

"Fuckin' boat," he said.

He swiped his hand over the leather. Jamming the cigarettes back into his pocket, he turned to Tyler and pointed through the veil of rain toward a long dark shadow.

"Listen. I was checking out that map on the screen, and I think we're close to Vancouver Island. I think it's over there. We gotta get the captain to stop and let us off." Spike pointed across the water to a stretch of dark land.

Tyler blew into his cupped hands and shivered.

"I don't think he will," he said. "That mechanic guy says the captain is gonna turn around and go back. He's afraid the kids will puke or something. I think we're hosed."

"Yeah, and most of those other boats are already gone. We're practically the only ones out here now," Kevin said.

Spike shook his head.

"No way. We're not going back. Not until we find out what happened—"

Kevin pressed against the window and wrapped his arms around himself. His teeth chattered.

"You mean, not until we find out if you killed that guy."

Spike stepped toward Kevin.

"Shut the fuck up."

Tyler pushed between the two.

"Stop it, you guys. Just stop it."

Spike grumbled but took a step back and reached for the rail. His hand slid along the wood.

"Did you guys touch anything in that store?" Tyler said.

Spike shot a look at Kevin.

Kevin looked at his shoes.

"No. Why?" Spike said.

"Well, so, nobody except that clerk saw you guys. Nobody was around when I was in the car. Those security cameras? The videos are probably too fuzzy to see anything. And, I saw that old lady

run out—she didn't look so reliable to me. So, I say we go back."
Tyler wiped a slick of spray from his brow.

"He's right, Spike. We should go back. I already told you, I don't
wanna go to Canada. I only changed my mind cause Tyler—"

"I told you to shut up. I'm not gonna listen to you snivel about
your fat-assed mom anymore. And, Butterfield, are you out of
your fucking mind?" Spike spit over the side.

"No. Listen. We go back and act like we don't know any-
thing—didn't even hear about that store. If anybody asks me or
Kevin where we were, we say we skipped school—got a pizza.
Nobody's gonna wonder where you were. We could—"

"No!" Spike stopped him.

"You were in on the plan. And you were the one who wanted
to sneak on a boat and go to Canada. But first sign of trouble?
You wanna run back home. That's your idea of workin' a job?"

"Spike, we've gotta go back," Tyler said.

"We go back? We go to prison."

"But—"

"And a pretty boy like you, Butterfield? You are *not* going to
like prison."

"Even if we don't, how are we gonna—" Kevin said.

"Listen, you dumb fucks. We're goin' in there and tellin' the
captain that you—Fat Ass—got hurt or something. You need to
get off the boat cause you gotta go to the hospital. Emergency
room. All the captain does is pull over and let us off."

"But I'm not hurt," Kevin said.

Spike took two steps toward Kevin, grabbed his arm, and
twisted it behind his back.

"I'll show you hurt. I'm gonna break your fucking arm. That's
hurt." He leaned into Kevin and yanked his arm upward.

Kevin yelped.

Tyler shoved Spike's chest with open palms.

"Jesus, Spike, cut it out. You're not breaking anybody's arm. Let him go."

Spike gave Kevin's arm a hard upward tug and then released him.

Kevin scuttled to the corner of the deck—as far away from Spike as the small space would allow—his lower lip quivering.

Spike jerked toward him with both fists clenched.

Kevin cringed—pushed his back against the railing.

Spike laughed.

"Pussy."

"Forget it, Spike," Tyler said.

Spike turned toward Tyler.

"Okay, Butterfield. You got a better plan?"

"No," Tyler said. "But your idea—it might work. Not about breaking his arm, but maybe we could say he's seasick. Say we gotta get him off the boat before he gets spews."

Spike looked at Kevin.

"You think you can manage to play sick for a while? I mean, it shouldn't be too hard—I saw you eatin' all that shit the kids were givin' you."

Kevin rubbed his shoulder.

"What if that captain won't do it? What if he's got stuff to cure seasickness?" he said.

Spike patted his jacket pocket.

"I got this under control."

Tyler glared at Spike.

"You asshole. I thought you got rid of that goddamn thing. I thought you left it in the car. Shit, man."

"We didn't go back into the car, remember? Besides, you're gonna be real glad one of us thinks ahead," Spike said.

"Damn it, Spike. Right now, nobody knows it was us at the store. But they find that on you, we *will* go to prison. Get rid of it."

"What are you guys talking about?" Kevin glanced from Tyler to Spike, then looked down—avoided eye contact with Spike.

"Toss it overboard," Tyler said.

"Listen, you little pussy. Just 'cause you don't have a pair doesn't mean I gotta freak out. I got this."

Tyler balled his fists.

"I said get rid of it, Spike."

"Or what?"

Tyler and Spike glared at each other—rain slicked their hair and skin.

"Hey, if you two don't stop it, they'll bust us for sure." Kevin glanced at Tyler, then looked down again.

Tyler exhaled slow and unclenched his fists. He took a step back.

"So, where do you think he'll pull over?" he said.

"How the fuck would I know? There must be places he can land. Maybe a marina or some beach or something. He's a captain—it's what he does."

Spike glowered at Kevin.

"So, can you do it? You only got one job—act sick. Can you do it?"

Kevin looked at Spike and swallowed hard.

"*You* only had one job at the store, and look where that got us," Tyler said.

"Hey, fuck you, Butterfield." Spike swiped at his rain-splattered jacket again. "Come on, let's do this. The sooner we get off this goddamn boat, the better." He turned and stepped into the cabin.

Tyler and Kevin stayed put until Kevin spoke.

"Tyler?"

"What?"

"He's still got the gun, doesn't he?"

Tyler thrust his hands in his jeans pockets and hunched his shoulders.

"Yeah. He's still got the gun."

34

In the short time he and Tyler were below, the cabin had shifted from a warm, light-speckled room to a damp space heavy with salt-tinged air. The sky had darkened to slate, and the wind now tossed puffs of dirty foam over the surface of the confused charcoal sea.

Jake searched for his daughter. The children no longer ate, or laughed, or crowded by the window to watch wildlife and scenery. Now they huddled together, holding onto benches and to each other. The *Hattie Belle* rolled and lurched through the water.

Tamara moved among them. She knelt before each child and spoke encouraging words. She'd buttoned a baggy green sweater over her t-shirt and had pulled her unruly curls into a ponytail. Conrad and Emily bumped heads together as they watched something on his phone. Emily didn't look frightened at all—Emily was fine. But not all the children were handling the situation as well.

"I don't like this. I wanna go home." The barefooted girl whined.

"I don't feel so good, Miss O." Another child held her hands over her belly.

Jake stepped closer to the group—Tamara looked up at him.

"I think we've had enough. We should go back now. I'm going to speak with the captain." Her voice stayed soft and low but wavered. *A tinge of panic?*

"Here." Jake offered his hand to help her stand. He touched the ceiling for stability as the two of them made their way, carefully, haltingly, across the cabin to the helm station.

Spike, Tyler, and Kevin stood next to the captain. Kevin now wore a scrunched-up black wool cap, and all three were soaked. Probably been out on the deck, in the wind—and spray—probably smoking cigarettes.

Denny stared through the front window as he moved the wheel in small, wedge-like motions. Waves snarled, twisted, threw clumps of foam at the *Hattie Belle*, and smashed into her hull.

The radio crackled to life.

"*Hattie Belle, Hattie Belle, Hattie Belle.* This is the *Steilacoom Witch*. Come in. Over."

Denny leaned forward and grabbed the mic from its holder. "*Steilacoom Witch*, this is the *Hattie Belle*. Over."

"Hey, Denny, looks like you guys are rockin' and rollin' as much as we are. We're heading back in before my passengers get queasy. Besides, we won't see any wildlife in this soup. *Steilacoom Witch* over."

"Yeah, I hear ya, Clint. You giving refunds? *Hattie Belle* over." Denny's eyes flicked from the front window to the instruments on the dashboard as he spoke.

"Nah." The voice hissed.

Denny bent forward again and adjusted a nob on the radio.

"I'm giving 'em coupons for food and ten percent off drinks at the Balls. Or, if they want, they can reschedule for half-fare. You heading back? *Steilacoom Witch* over."

"What about the others? They leaving too? *Hattie Belle* over."

"Yeah. *Joggins* left first. And *Lady Blaine* turned. So, what do you think? *Steilacoom Witch* over." The radio hissed and sputtered.

"Yeah, I'll swing around now. Was hoping to show these little guys a whale or two, but there you have it. Mother Nature. You guys have a safe trip back, and if you've got time, let's grab a beer once we get everyone settled. First round's on me. *Hattie Belle* over and out."

"Roger that—on the beer. You guys be safe too. See ya later. *Steilacoom Witch* over and out."

Denny returned the mic to its holder, checked a gauge, and turned the wheel to starboard. Waves slapped the hull, and the *Hattie Belle* shuddered as she fought her way into the wind.

35

Jake waited until Denny completed the turn and stabilized the *Hattie Belle.*

"Good call," he said.

Denny glanced at Jake, and refocused on the waves.

"Not much of a choice at this point. Won't take us long—we've got the current. Hey, thanks for working with the passengers—not in your job description, but I appreciate the help. Join us for that beer when we get back."

Jake grinned.

"Thanks."

Tyler stepped next to the helm.

"Captain, Sir. We have a problem."

Denny glanced away from the water long enough to give Tyler a quick look.

"I'm a little busy right now, as you might guess. I'm trying to get us closer to shore where the water will be calmer. Better ride for everybody."

"Well, that's actually good," Tyler said. "Getting closer to shore. Because our friend is seasick, and we think we should get off the boat and get Kevin to a doctor. We must be pretty close to Canada now, right?"

Spike moved closer to Denny.

"He's right. We gotta get off cuz, Fat As—I mean, Kevin, he's like, real sick. Bad."

Denny continued to stare at the sea.

"There's some candied ginger in the head. Give him a couple of those and get him out on deck. He'll be okay."

"No, see. You don't get it. He's gonna start hurling chunks pretty soon. All over the boat. All over those kids. It's not gonna be pretty." Spike gestured toward the children.

When Spike mentioned the children, Tamara sucked in a breath.

"We can't go to Canada. We'll be back in port soon—already made the turn. So do like I told you—give him some ginger and get him out on the deck." Denny glanced past Spike to Kevin. "Besides, he looks fine to me."

Jake agreed. Kevin didn't look the least bit sick. Instead, he seemed preoccupied with sneaking looks back toward the children.

"Listen, old man—" Spike started to speak, but Jake stepped forward.

"Let's tone it down a little," he said.

"I don't have to tone it down for you or nobody." Spike shot a glance at Jake.

Jake tensed.

Tyler intervened.

"Look, just let us off here—or close to here. In Canada. After that, you guys can go back and—"

"And nobody gets hurt," Spike said.

"Miss O! Miss O! Amanda is throwing up!" Conrad pointed to the thin, dark-haired girl who bent forward, both hands on her stomach. Her lunch, and most of her breakfast, gushed out onto the clean, painted floor.

"Oh, Honey." Tamara stumbled across the cabin and knelt next to the little girl.

"Miss O. I don't feel so good either," Tristan slapped his hand over his mouth.

The sour smell of vomit hit Jake in a gust. He looked at Denny.

"We better get rid of that before everybody gets sick. You have something to clean it up?"

"There's cat litter in the engine room. Dickerson uses it to soak up spills. Starboard side, I think."

"Shit," Spike spit the word.

"I'll get it," Jake said. He crabbed as fast as possible across the rolling boat. When he reached the hatch cover, he grabbed the handle and gave a quick pull. A thick cloud of smoke rolled out from the engine room.

Two little girls screamed. Conrad jumped up and down and yelled.

"Miss O—the boat's on fire! The boat's on fire!" The *Hattie Belle* bowled to port and sent him sprawling.

"What the—" Tyler gaped, open-mouthed, as thick smoke billowed from the engine compartment and clouded the cabin.

"Get the children toward the back! Now!" Denny yelled to Tamara. He spun around and pointed at Spike.

"You. Hold the helm steady." He raced to a fire extinguisher mounted on the dash, ripped it from its holder, and pulled the safety lock. He thrust the extinguisher at Jake.

Jake squinted through the fumes—didn't see flames—ignored the steps and jumped through the open hatch. Tyler followed him into the smoke-dark hole.

36

The rag he'd tied over his face muffled Jake's words.

"Smoke. Tell the captain—no flames, just smoke."

Tyler curled his elbow to his mouth and breathed against his shirt. He coughed once then called up to Denny.

"Just smoke—no flames."

"Got it." Denny pulled back from the hatch.

"Grab the headlamps." Without turning from the engine, Jake pointed toward the pegs on the wall.

Tyler pulled two lamps and a towel from a peg. He handed a lamp to Jake, wrapped a towel around his nose and mouth, and squatted.

Jake and Tyler strapped the lamps around their head before leaning toward the great blackened engine. Around them, smoke swirled faster and faster in an upward spiral as the roar of an exhaust fan competed with the engine's rumble.

"He flipped the blower," Tyler said, "we should be able to find the problem now. I still don't see any flames, so that's good."

Jake coughed and moved back a foot. His eyes watered, and he could barely see. His throat burned from the smoke he'd inhaled.

Tyler crouched low and used the headlamp to flood the engine with light from the base upward. He pointed to a thin dark line in one of the rubber hoses.

"Look," he said.

Jake shifted forward again and leaned in.

"There's gotta be a crack," Tyler said. "I'm thinking oil. And it's gotta be dripping on a hot pipe—probably the manifold." He pulled the lamp from his head and directed the beam to the hose.

By now, the smoke in the engine room was a light haze leaving only a ghostly spiral drifting up from the center of the engine.

"I should have seen that," Jake said.

Tyler paused in his search and looked over at Jake.

"Yeah, well, yeah. But it happens. The guy who should have caught it was the regular mechanic. That's his full-time job. You ask me, that guy's a loser."

Jake shifted to his knees.

"Let's do a quick repair and get out of here—we need fresh air."

"Yeah. He must have some electrical tape around here—that should hold it for a while." Tyler pulled a drawer open.

Jake started to move toward the closed cupboards and to a bank of drawers on the starboard side, but the boat jerked to port, and both he and Tyler lost their balance—Jake landed on his rump.

Tyler fell sideways. Something flew through the open hatch, smacked his shoulder, and dropped to the floor. It rolled out of sight.

"Shit!"

"What happened?"

Tyler grit his teeth.

"Fell on my elbow. Damn, that hurts."

"You okay?"

Tyler rubbed his elbow.

"Yeah. But that thing that hit me fell under the engine. You see it?"

"No. But I can look."

"Forget it. Let's tape that crack and get the hell outta here. I feel sick."

37

Jake pulled the rag from his head and shoved it into a back pocket. Tyler's face and arms were grimy, and when he rubbed his eyes, he left two smudgy gray circles. Jake guessed his own face, at least the half above the rag, was just as filthy. A layer of black soot clung to their clothing. They swayed in place as they hung onto the overhead rail, struggling to gain purchase on the rocking vessel.

"Look!" Karlie squealed. She pointed across the cabin.

Tamara had moved her class to the corner closest to the back deck. The children now huddled together and stared at Jake and Tyler.

"You look like monsters!" Jenny giggled.

"Yeah," Conrad added. "King Kong!"

Tristan waved his hands. "No, no. Big Foot!"

"Big Foot! Big Foot! Big Foot!"

Tamara pressed her finger to her lips and made a shushing sound.

"Okay, now, children, that's enough. We need to thank Mr. Mechanic and Tyler for putting out the fire." She shot a questioning look at Jake.

He gave her a thumbs-up.

Tyler growled at the children. They laughed and squealed as he lurched and stomped in circles imitating the mythic Big Foot. The children joined him by tottering around and acting out various monsters.

Jake exhaled. Tyler's sudden playfulness broke the tension—at least for a moment.

"Sit down! Everyone. I don't want you falling over and getting hurt. Now sit down!" This time, Tamara's voice carried a tone Jake hadn't heard from her before—a harsh tone.

"Are you okay, Miss O?" Emily's face scrunched into worry lines.

Tamara's cheeks flushed beet. She glanced at Jake and then back at the children.

"Yes. Yes, I'm fine. Thank you, Emily. I'm just worried about all of you in this storm. It's important that everyone sits down and stays close together. Okay?"

Seven heads bobbed yes, but Ryan sat alone, by the open companionway. His small shoulders hunched into the puffy life vest. He whispered into his cupped hands.

The boat rose on a wave and slammed back down. As he gripped the handrail tighter, Jake remembered Tamara's promise to help the boy bury his small pet, and it occurred to him that this might be a promise she couldn't keep.

"Now, the grownups need to talk, so everybody be quiet, okay? Maybe play Telephone—stay close to each other and pass a secret message."

"Miss O, will you start the secret?"

Tamara glanced at Jake again, and when he nodded to her, she knelt next to Lexie and whispered something in the girl's ear. Lexie burst out in a giggle and turned to the child next to her to pass along the message.

Jake waited until Tamara settled the children and then offered his hand to help steady her. Together they stumbled to the helm.

"How bad is it?" Denny asked. He'd taken the wheel from Spike, and though the storm continued to toss the boat, he'd smoothed the motion.

Jake gestured toward Tyler. "Not serious. He found the problem—a cracked line. A small drip of oil on an exposed section of manifold. Hard to find it in all that smoke—good catch on his part."

"Yeah, we did a temporary fix, but that hose needs to be replaced, and those pipes need rewrapping," Tyler said. The thick layer of grime hid any acknowledgment of Jake's praise. He scratched his cheek—streaks of pale flesh slashed the soot.

"And, to be honest, that whole engine needs an overhaul."

"Is what he says true?"

"Yeah. He knows his stuff," Jake said.

"Damn Dickerson. I've asked him a hundred times if we should pull the engine. I've been thinking we've been past due for a couple of years now. But he always insists everything is perfect—no need to fix what isn't broken."

"Yeah, well, your guy is wrong. Like Tyler here said, the first thing you do when you get back to port is book an appointment to pull that beast and get it overhauled. If you don't, you could have a lot more trouble than a cracked line."

"Thanks, guys. Beers on me when we get back." Denny looked at Spike and said, "You too. Pretty good boat handling for a first-timer. Choppy, but again, first time and—"

Tamara interrupted. Her voice shook.

"Guys, I'm grateful to you two for jumping down there and fixing things. And to you, Spike, for driving the boat during all that mess, but now we need to get back home. Amanda fell on her way to the bathroom and dropped her inhaler into the engine room. She's already stressed out, and without her inhaler, she'll have serious breathing problems."

Tyler snapped his fingers.

"That musta been what hit me. Something smacked my shoulder and rolled under the engine."

"I'll go back down and look for it," Jake said.

"If it's under the engine, it'll be filthy." Tyler looked at Tamara, then at the floor.

"I shoulda grabbed it. Sorry."

Tamara's frowned.

"How much longer until we're back at the marina?"

Denny checked an instrument on the dash. "We're on the right heading, and we've got the current, so we should—"

"Wait." Spike stepped closer to Denny.

Jake tensed. Something had shifted.

Tyler edged between them.

"Like we said before, Kevin is sick, so we need to get off in Canada. We must be pretty close now, right? I mean, we can see Vancouver Island from the boat. We can't be too far, right?" he said.

Denny peered at the chart.

"We're close to the San Juans and not too far from the Gulf Islands—they're Canadian, but nobody's getting off the boat. You'd have to clear customs and immigration to step on Canadian soil, and besides, there's no place to tie up."

"We don't have to tie up," Tyler said. "Let us off at the beach. We can hitch a ride to the hospital. Or something."

Denny rolled his eyes.

"Don't be absurd. We can't get anywhere near the shore—too many rocks and sandbars—but we'll be docking in an hour, maybe a little longer. He can wait." He tapped the compass. "Why don't the three of you go out on deck, get some fresh air, and look at the horizon. He can puke overboard if he has to."

"We're getting off in Canada," Spike said.

He pushed Tyler aside.

"I know you're worried about your friend, Spike, but Kevin will be fine." Tamara's tone was now measured.

"Kevin, do you think you need to throw up?"

Kevin's face flushed deep pink. He hung his head.

"Kevin?"

"He's too sick to talk. We gotta get him off this fucking boat." Spike's tone dropped low and deep.

Jake moved closer to Tamara.

"Spike, I need to make sure you get back to the high school." Tamara pushed away from the support beam she'd leaned on but stumbled when the boat slammed to starboard.

As he'd done before, Jake offered his hand and helped her regain her balance, but he kept his focus on Spike.

"Look, we're all a little queasy right now—mostly because we're nervous and scared. But we're all going to be fine. Getting help for Amanda is our first priority." She reached over and touched Spike's arm.

He jerked back.

Tamara lowered her hand.

Jake stepped in front of her.

Spike faced Jake and Denny—his eyes narrowed.

"You guys aren't listening—"

A high-pitched screech from the back of the vessel stopped him.

"Miss O! Miss O! Ryan is outside the boat!"

All attention turned to the companionway and to the top of the aft railing, where a shivering little boy balanced. The wind whipped at his hair and short pants. He held onto the flagpole with his left hand. He gripped something in his right fist.

"Ryan!" Tamara screamed.

Jake pushed her aside and sprinted through the cabin. He'd almost made it to the companionway door when Ryan flung his turtle into the turbulent waters churning at the stern of the *Hattie Belle*. He let go of the flagpole—waved goodbye with both hands. A split second before Jake reached him, the child plummeted off the high railing into the swirling, frigid sea below.

38

Tamara screamed.

Denny raced to the helm and rammed the gear shift to neutral.

"Throw the ring! Keep your eyes on him. Don't let him out of your sight!"

Tyler pushed past Spike and raced to the stern.

The *Hattie Belle* pitched and yawed and threw wailing children to the deck.

Kevin reached for them.

"Tristan! Jenny! Grab my hands."

Jake ignored all of it—Tamara's screams, Denny's shouts, the cries of the children. He didn't think—didn't hesitate. He grabbed the railing, leaped over the gate, and plunged into the sea.

In the seconds he sank, he became clear about two things—even in June, the waters of the Strait were icy—hypothermia would stun a body in minutes. And, below the crashing waves, away from the howl of the wind and the anger of the storm, the world turned calm, silent, surreal.

The beat of peace exploded as Jake surged to the surface. He shook his head, flung droplets from his face, and twisted to the left. Salt stung his eyes. He scanned the roiling sea—couldn't make out anything but churning waves and piles of froth. Pumping his legs, he spun to the right. He held his arms wide for balance—wished he'd worn a life vest.

"Ryan!" A wave pushed Jake under, roared over him, and filled his mouth. He kicked and pushed to the surface, coughed, and spit. He tasted salt and the sour contents of his stomach. Squinting, he flailed from side to side—searching. Only mid-morning, but the storm had turned the day to twilight, and waves hid the horizon.

Yards away, something white splashed the surface. It sank under—burst upward, and dropped back into the waves. Jake started toward the life ring. A dozen strokes—then, in the distance, a flash of orange against the dark sea. The blot of color became a speck drifting farther and farther from the boat—farther and farther from the life ring.

"Ryan!" The storm drowned his voice. Decades of weight training had stunted his agility but built his strength. And now, weighed down by heavy canvas coveralls and sneakers turned to solid blocks, strength was paramount. Jake cut into the waves with broad strokes, but they were not clean strokes—the water lifted him, and dropped him, and made each of his attempts choppy, clumsy. He switched to side strokes—tried to glide over instead of through the waves. Jake didn't register the numbing cold or the ache in his lungs. He gulped foam and saltwater. Adrenaline drove him, and he kicked harder. No thoughts—he concentrated on the smudge of orange—nothing more. But his muscles felt the memory of another time—another time in churning water, a time when fear drove them—pushed them to the edge of their limits and still on to do more. This muscle memory evoked pain—so much pain that Jake frightened himself when he heard his voice screaming.

"Richard! Richard!"

One final, long stroke—he reached the boy. Jake grabbed at the vest, caught a strap, and pulled.

"Ryan! Buddy!" His words half laugh, half sob. "You're okay. It's all right now. I gotcha."

The child wriggled and thrashed until he grasped a handful of Jake's hair.

Treading water, Jake stayed vertical while he disentangled Ryan's fingers.

"Let go of my hair—hold onto my shirt," he said.

"I-I-I-I'm in tra-tra-tra-trouble," Ryan wailed.

"No, you're not, Buddy. You're okay. You're not in any trouble." As he spoke, he twisted toward the boat—were they too far away?

The *Hattie Belle* steamed toward them—stern first.

Ryan hiccupped—his voice raised to a higher pitch. "You, you, you don't understand. I-I-I lost my g-g-g-g-lasses."

"What?" Jake pulled away from the little boy enough to look at his face. The child's lips were pale blue, his skin almost translucent. He shivered so hard his teeth chattered.

"I-I-I lost m-m-my glasses," Ryan repeated. "Whe-whe-when I fell. I-I-I lost my g-g-g-glasses. My d-d-d-dad says if I, if, if I lose a-a-a-another pair of g-g-g-glasses, I-I-I'll be, I'll be, be in for it."

Jake drew the boy close, held him tight.

"It's okay, Ryan. We'll get you new glasses. Don't worry. We're gonna swim back to the boat now."

Ryan's stick-thin arms wrapped around Jake's neck. He spoke into Jake's ear.

"Wh-wh-who's Ri-Ri-Richard?"

Jake missed a kick. He blinked. His eyes stung with salt—not all from the sea.

"An old friend, Buddy. Just an old friend."

With one arm around the boy and the other in a sidestroke, Jake moved them toward the bouncing white patch in the distance. Again, he kept his eyes trained on a bright spot in the dark sea. The life ring tugged against the line, bouncing and slapping the water. Could he catch the ring and hold Ryan at the same time? His arms and legs were numb with cold—disorientation crept closer. His energy was draining, and in one terrifying flash, the weight of the child became the weight of a man—the weight of an old friend. Dead weight.

39

Jake screamed to jolt himself. He screamed again. The second time his mouth filled with salt water. He spat the frigid drink and gagged—his stomach knotted with pain, but the screams had done the trick.

He looked up, saw three silhouettes at the stern of the *Hattie Belle*. They waved and cupped their mouths. He knew they were yelling at him, but the wind ripped their words.

Jake grabbed for the life ring. Twice it jumped from his grasp, but on the third try, he looped his arm through the ring and slid it over the boy.

"Okay now, Buddy. I've got you, and I want you to hold onto this. Can you do that?"

Ryan let go of Jake's shirt and wrapped both arms around the life ring. Despite his violent shivering, the child appeared calm, composed, sleepy. Hypothermia—they didn't have much time. Jake held tight to him with his right arm and clung to the ring with his left. He stretched flat and kicked—never taking his eyes from the *Hattie Belle*.

Only a few more yards—a few more yards to reach Denny and Tyler, who knelt on the platform. Together, they pulled the line, hand-over-hand drawing Jake and Ryan closer. Kevin stood by. No Spike.

When the ring touched the steps, Denny leaned down, scooped Ryan up, and pulled him over the platform's edge. Jake exhaled as Denny pressed the almost comatose child into Tamara's embrace. Wrapping his arm around her shoulders, Denny helped her into the cabin. Kevin followed them.

Jake felt Tyler reach under his arms, felt him pulling. Too weak now to use his arms, Jake gave one last kick—upward momentum. With a final tug, Tyler dragged him from the water and stretched him out, face down. Jake gasped for air. Sharp pain pierced his gut, and with a heave, he vomited.

"Shit." Tyler took a step away. The boat rose and crashed down. Tyler lost his footing and slammed against the cabin door frame. He grabbed at a rail and pulled himself up.

Jake tried to push to his knees.

"Here." Tyler held onto the rail and offered his hand. Jake grabbed it, and with a grunt, Tyler hoisted him to his feet. A wave hit the starboard side and sent a heavy spray over the two of them.

"Let's get inside," Tyler said. He grabbed at the door frame and stumbled into the cabin. Drenched and shaking, he plopped down on the aft bench.

Jake stood in the companionway—he grasped the door frame to steady himself—a lake drained from his clothing and pooled at his feet. He swayed but managed to maintain balance as he focused on the group of children huddled around Tamara and Denny.

Ryan wore Tamara's green sweater like a bathrobe, a spot on the front showed the faint outline of his wet underpants. Jake let out a long breath. The trembling boy looked cold, tired, and frightened, but he was alive, and he would recover.

Conrad crouched against a bench and filmed the scene from a low angle. Denny's flannel shirt was dark and wet. Tamara's soaked t-shirt clung to her skin. Emily stood by Kevin's side. She, and all the others, stared at Jake. No one spoke until Denny took two steps forward and shoved a handful of paper towels at him. Jake grabbed the toweling and mopped his face. When he pulled his hand away, Tamara gasped. A child let out a cry.

"What?" Jake glanced down, expecting to see a stain of blood, but instead, he saw what looked like a dead spider curled in the wad of wet paper. He dropped the toweling to the floor and felt his face. Except for stubble—real stubble—it was smooth. No beard. No mustache. He looked across the room to Tamara—her expression both startled and hurt.

"Look, I'm—" Jake said.

"Daddy!" Emily pushed past the other children and ran to him with arms wide. No more pretending, no more deception.

Jake hesitated, then fell to his knees and wrapped his arms around his little girl.

40

Leslie Brody stood in the frosty air, wrinkled her nose, and sniffed.

"I think it's about time we organize a clean-up committee for this fridge," she said. "I'm not kidding you guys—small colonies are growing in these dishes. Some of them are so old that the people who stashed them don't even work here anymore."

Plucking a plastic container from a shelf, she gave it a shake. Something green and gelatinous sloshed. She read the smeared words printed on a strip of masking tape.

"Evie Karns. See what I mean? Evie retired last January." She closed the heavy door and scanned the room.

Dirty, smudged windows filtered sunlight across stacks of tattered magazines and dog-eared textbooks. Piles of worn romance novels cluttered sagging wooden shelves. The curling brown tendrils of a dead philodendron drooped down the side of a dented microwave, and an open cabinet spilled craft supplies—crayons, pots of paint, tubes of glitter, glue. An abandoned Christmas tree slumped in a far corner—faded construction paper ornaments dangling from dusty aluminum limbs.

"This entire lounge is a mess. We should get our act together and clean the place."

"Naw—leave it." Chris Lenser waved her off without taking her eyes from the four letters lined neatly in front of her.

"We only have to live with it for two more weeks. The summer janitorial crew will come in and nuke everything in sight." Her face lit up as she picked each of the tiles from the small wooden rack and placed them, one by one, on the grid.

"Ziam! Double letter score. Triple word score. Ziam for seventy-five points. And that's the game!" She whooped and raised her arms in victory.

"Ziam? Chris, is that even a word?" Susan Tye eyed the letters and reached for the *Official English Language Scrabble Dictionary*.

Amy Silverton, the youngest teacher at Ruth Hudson Elementary, clicked keys on a dated computer. She drummed the edge of the keyboard with her fingernail as she waited for the clunky relic to open to the school's private YouTube channel. Once in, she leaned forward and studied the video.

"You guys have gotta come see this!" She continued to watch the screen as she waved her fellow teachers over.

"This is too stinking cute. Tamara's kids are having a blast on that field trip."

Amy turned up the volume and pointed to the performance of a high school-aged boy acting a role in the middle of a ring of laughing second graders. Flapping his arms in slow motion, the chunky teenager galumphed between the children as he wove a pattern of hop and twirl. The children clapped and called out, "Drop the clam! Drop the clam!"

"Wonder what that's all about?"

"My guess is they're learning about seabirds." Having given up on finding lunch in the refrigerator—or organizing any sort of clean-up action—Leslie joined the group.

"Is that guy one of the teaching assistants Tamara got from the high school? He doesn't look like any high GPA senior I've ever seen."

Chris stretched her arms over her head and yawned. "High school kids are casual these days. I'm surprised his pants aren't halfway down his butt. Gotta hand it to her, though, Tamara has major ambition. I don't have the energy to organize a field trip this late in the year."

"Same here," Susan added. "It's all I can do to put up with the parents and their constant hovering around their precious babies. Besides, who wants to argue with you-know-who about dipping into the sacred school budget."

Amy looked up from the screen.

"Speaking of helicopters, Ryan's mother should be here any minute. She's bringing cookies for the afternoon snack. We should look busy."

A muffled bump caused the teachers to glance up in time to see a lavender, yoga-panted rump push the lounge door open. A squat woman turned toward them. Her face shone slick with sweat—damp curls flattened against her face. She carried two plates of cookies covered with plastic wrap.

"Hi, Mrs. Webber," Chris waved to the woman.

Puffing, she waddled across the room to the group.

"Hello, ladies! Brought the cookies. And, so you know—" she paused to catch her breath. "It's not easy finding a recipe that has no gluten, no nuts, no white sugar, and no dairy products. But I did it. Hope the kids like them."

She gripped the plates with one hand and swiped beads of moisture from her forehead with the other.

"Whatcha watchin'?"

"Your son's field trip. They're out on the whale-watching boat now. Conrad Huffington is filming the trip. He's our very own photojournalist."

"Conrad Huffington, the third," Chris corrected. "My husband and I know his parents. They're both extremely proud their son wants to follow in his father's career."

"Here, you can have my seat." Amy stood and offered her chair to the newcomer. Lydia Webber sat down, balanced the plates on her lap, and leaned toward the monitor.

In one scene, a thin boy with thick tortoise-shell glasses sat cross-legged on the floor. A strip of lettuce dangled from his lower lip. He chewed in lazy open and closed, open and closed motions while gazing into the camera with a slow blink.

"He's imitating Harvey, his turtle." Lydia giggled. "He loves that turtle." She paused and tilted her head.

"But gosh, I don't remember seeing it for—what? Three, maybe four days now. I wonder what happened to Harvey?"

They continued to watch as clip after clip—some more steady than others—flashed across the screen. In what looked like a panoramic shot, a row of children pressed palms and noses against a panel of windows and pointed at something splashing in the water. In another, the class sat in a circle and dug through lunch boxes for sandwiches and treats.

Leslie yawned and checked her watch.

"We've got fifteen more minutes. I'm gonna get another cup of coffee and finish grading papers before the bell."

"Wait." Amy touched her colleague's arm. She pointed to the screen. "Look."

In a still shot, a slender woman dressed in white trainers, khaki capris, and a green sweater stood next to an older man and two high school-aged boys. Her brows knit into deep furrows and her lips pursed tight. The man rested one hand on the boat's wheel and pointed at the teenagers with the other. Although the teens faced away from the camera, Leslie and the other women could see that one young man—the one wearing a black leather jacket—held both fists clenched.

Amy leaned in again and released Pause.

"Guys, I think something's wrong. Maybe we should call her. To check—you know, see if she needs anything."

"Oh, my God!" Leslie slapped her hand over her mouth. Her eyes widened. She stared at the monitor and the new scene.

On center screen, a large man with eyes shut tight held a young girl close. She clung to him as his arms circled her. Her head pressed against his shoulder. Dark hair plastered flat against his skull. Water drained from drenched workman's clothing and pooled at his feet.

A few yards away, the young teacher, now in a soaked t-shirt, knelt on the floor and embraced a skinny, shivering child dressed only in what looked like a wet wool sweater. The little boy's teeth chattered, and his lips were a pale blue.

"Ryan!" Lydia screamed. She dropped the plates—shards of splintered glass and cookie crumbs scattered across the teachers' lounge.

41

Neil Edward drummed a rhythm on the steering wheel with his thumb. He replayed Jennette's warning as he wove the cruiser around a traffic circle and onto the long uphill stretch to the Ruth Hudson Elementary School.

This doesn't sound good, Sheriff. The headmaster—well, you know how crabby he can be. He was about to pop. Said something about a video, and little kids in trouble, and law enforcement responsibilities, and he started rattling on about calling the school's attorney. My guess? He smells something amiss—maybe something that might upset those rich folks who send their kids there. He's covering his behind.

Neil Edward turned into the drive, parked, and took a minute to stare at the imposing vine-covered building. The place had always given him the creeps. As a child, he'd listened to stories of people being dragged—screaming and biting—into the asylum, never to be heard from again. Tribal people, mostly tribal women, were lost forever once they passed through the heavy oak doors.

Jennette had pleaded to be allowed to join him—the whole thing sounded, in her words, "too juicy to miss." But he'd refused her request, arguing that they'd already left the phones unmanned that morning, and besides, what if Anita returned with a follow-up or even a new complaint? And there was the guy in temporary custody. He should be watched. Now, looking at the dark entryway and the narrow windows mounted at the third-floor level, Neil Edward wished he'd let his gutsy deputy ride along.

He took a deep breath and exhaled. After adjusting his hat, he stepped out of the cruiser.

A tall woman greeted him and offered her hand.

"Leslie Brody—Science and Social Studies. Thanks for coming so quickly, Sheriff. I'm guessing there really isn't much of a problem. Some sort of misinterpretation. But with little kids involved . . ."

She continued to chat as she escorted Neil Edward to the teacher's lounge. She occasionally paused to point out displays of student artwork tacked to bulletin boards or to peek into classrooms through two-way mirrored windows. When they passed a thick, smoky-gray glass door, she whispered.

"The headmaster is in his office. He's calling the school's attorney. Something about liability." She rolled her eyes. "He's the most over-wound person I've ever met."

Neil Edward liked how she carried herself—steady, graceful, calm—even in a time of what might be a minor crisis in her workplace. He wondered why he'd never seen her around town. He glanced at her left hand through force of habit and found himself disappointed when he saw the single gold band.

"Here we are," Leslie said. She pushed a swinging door open—the smell of microwaved lunches made his stomach growl. Except for that one bite of scone, he'd missed breakfast.

"Sheriff, you're here!" A young woman rushed forward, grabbed his hand, and whisked him away from his guide. "I'm Amy. Come see the videos. We think there might be a problem on that boat, but we can't reach her. Can't reach Tamara—the teacher in charge. We can't get through on her cell phone. Maybe they're out of cell range?" She finally ran out of breath and stopped. Several others took up the frantic buzz.

"Okay, everybody, let's all settle down and have a look." Neil Edward tried for the calming sound of gentle authority.

The cluster of women huddled around the aging computer quieted and made room for him. Once settled, he and the teachers watched a half dozen or so video clips of children laughing, eating, and goofing around in the cabin of a small vessel. Neil Edward recognized the boat's interior from the glossy marketing materials the Chamber of Commerce dropped by the station each spring. He'd viewed the vessels in the Otter's Run whale-watching fleet from the shore and the dock, though he'd never been inside any of them. He'd never asked to take a tour. Boats made him nervous. But this one looked pleasant, looked like a clean, bright environment filled with cheerful, happy passengers. Until the final clip.

In the scene, the children no longer looked cheerful—they sat huddled together, and they appeared frightened and disoriented. The video was hard to watch because it jerked and bounced as the boat lurched and rolled from what had to be a storm—the predicted bad weather that had not yet reached the land.

Two of the kids Jennette had identified from the phone photos stood together—they leaned against a bulkhead for stability. One of them, the blond-haired boy, appeared almost as frightened as the children. His clothes were wet, and his face and arms were covered in something dark, maybe soil or soot. His companion, the kid in the leather jacket, looked angry. The third teen sat on the floor with the children—he seemed oblivious to his friends or the adults. Neil Edward waited until the clip ended and then held up his hand.

"Can we see that one again?"

Amy clicked a couple of keys, and the video restarted.

He pointed at the screen.

"There. Stop it there."

Again, Amy clicked the keys. Neil Edward leaned closer to the monitor and studied the grainy image. "Who's the big guy?" he asked. He pointed to a muscular man bracing against a doorframe. The man appeared exhausted and maybe ill. His clothing was drenched—he stood in a puddle.

Leslie bent forward and tapped the screen.

"That's Jake Burton. He's one of the parents. We don't see much of him. In fact, I think it's been over a year. But he's a super nice guy. Genuinely caring—only wants the best for his daughter.

Though," she paused a moment, "I seem to remember something about him having a restraining order—if that's the case, this might be worse than we thought."

Chris chimed in.

"If he does have a restraining order against him, I can guess who filed for it. The poor guy is unlucky in love. That ex-wife of his is one piece of work."

"Nasty woman with way too much money and way too much time on her hands," Susan added.

As if on cue, the door to the teacher's lounge swung open so hard it smacked against the wall.

"Mr. Longcarver?"

Neil Edward stood and took a moment to assess the new-comer. Tall, slim, meticulously colored blond hair—pressed navy-blue slacks with matching jacket, white satin blouse, and black flats. He didn't know much about women's clothing, but he guessed her outfit cost more than he made in a week—maybe a month. He offered to shake.

She swatted his hand away.

"I've seen the video. Everyone in town—probably everyone in the county by now—has seen the video. Once that nosy news photographer saw it, he violated the privacy rules. He released that video to the public. I *will* be retaining council."

Leslie broke in. "Oh now, Mrs. Burton. I'm sure—"

"I wasn't talking to you." The woman snapped at Leslie.

Leslie pulled back—blinked.

"And you saw that big gym rat, right? Well, he's my ex-hus-band, Jake. He's violating a court order and endangering my daughter's life. The lives of all those children. I demand that you arrest him immediately. If you don't, you'll be working as a cross-ing guard before the end of the year."

"Maybe I forgot or didn't hear proper, but I don't think I caught your name, ma'am." Neil Edward drawled his words in the tone he'd discovered could frustrate and fluster angry white citizens. He didn't use the trick often, but this seemed like a good time to play country bumpkin sheriff.

She huffed.

"Marilyn Davenforth Burton. I'm sure you've heard of my father, William Davenforth. I can assure you, Mr. Longcarver, if you don't get my daughter back here immediately and arrest my ex-husband, you will *never* forget my name again."

"Well, ma'am, we are looking into this as we speak. Best thing you can do is go home and wait by the phone, so we can call you straight off when we get news."

"I'm not going home. I'm going to my father's office. You'll be hearing from his attorney soon." Marilyn glared at Neil Edward and scowled at the group of teachers.

She pointed to Brody.

"And you people are also in trouble—shame on you for letting an inexperienced teacher take a group of children out on a rickety old boat. That's not what I signed up for when I sent in that permission slip. When I'm done with you, you'll all be looking for new jobs." She spun on one foot and headed for the door.

Leslie Brody started to respond, but Neil Edward shot her a glance. She pursed her lips.

"Well, yes, ma'am. We all understand. You do whatcha gotta do." He touched the brim of his hat. "'Fore you go, though, I do have one question."

Marilyn paused, turned back to him, her expression dark—frigid.

"What?"

Neil Edward dropped the charade and spoke in a low, measured tone.

"Do you have any idea why your ex-husband might be on that boat during a school field trip?"

"Not a clue," she said. She started for the door again.

"Mrs. Burton. One more thing," he said.

"Now what?" Marilyn whipped around and glowered at him.

"It's Sheriff Longcarver. Sheriff Neil Edward Longcarver."

Marilyn didn't speak—she marched to the swinging door, shoved it open, and stomped out of the lounge.

Neil Edward heard a couple of snickers and someone's soft clapping.

42

The storm's roar competed with the sound of waves smashing against the hull and the rumble of the *Hattie Belle's* engine. The acrid scent of smoke clung to glass, and wood, and clothes, and the temperature in the cabin dropped to a chill. Ryan's wet underpants had soaked through the wool of Tamara's sweater leaving a dark stain, but the child's violent shivering had changed to mild shaking and a case of hiccups. Tamara knelt, wrapped her arms around him, and drew him close to her. *This should never have happened.* Even though she'd been only a few feet away and even though she could easily see them—if only she'd been watching more closely—he wouldn't have fallen overboard. He wouldn't have gone outside. She looked past the children to the drenched man kneeling on the cabin floor. His eyes were closed, he clutched his daughter. If it hadn't been for him, Ryan would have been lost forever. Tamara trembled and hugged the little boy tighter. Whatever this man's story—whatever was behind that fake beard and false mustache—whatever was behind his lies to her, he had saved Ryan's life, and she would never forget that.

Tamara and the others remained still and silent—all eyes focused on Jake. Finally, Denny stepped forward.

"Get up," Denny said. He stood with his legs wide, his hands on his hips. A scowl darkened his face.

Jake looked up and took a deep breath. He pushed his shoulder against the doorway, stumbled slightly, and braced against the back wall.

Tamara gave Ryan a quick squeeze and stood. She started toward Jake, but Denny held his hand up—signaled for her to stop.

"He's weak," she said. "And he needs help."

Denny shot her a look—eyes narrowed, jaw set.

Tamara took a step back.

Jake continued to hold tight to Emily. She clung to him and pressed her face against his shirt. It was clear she was getting wet, but if she cared or even noticed, it didn't show. Tamara flinched— Emily was her student, her charge, but Jake was Emily's father.

Jake lowered his face—brushed his lips across Emily's hair, lifted his head, and made eye contact with Denny. The two men stared at each other for a moment—didn't move—until Denny snapped his fingers.

"I know who you are," he said. "You're the guy with the gym—the gym where that kid was killed. What the hell are you doing on my boat? Are you even a licensed mechanic? 'Cause if you're not, we're running illegally. I could lose my certification— maybe even my captain's license."

Jake leaned over and lowered Emily to the floor.

"Go stand with your teacher, Honey."

Emily didn't move.

"It's okay, Em. You'll be alright." Jake said. "We'll both be alright. Now, go stand with your teacher. That's a good girl."

Tamara kneeled again and held her arms wide. Emily stumbled across the pitching boat—her head down, her hands at her sides.

Tamara let out a small gasp when Emily pressed against her. The girl's clothes were wet and cold, and she trembled.

"Oh, Sweetheart." Tamara wrapped her arms around the quaking child the way she'd done with Ryan, but she kept her eyes on the two men.

Jake coughed and hacked foamy phlegm into his hand. Still pressing against the wall, he straightened and wiped his hand on his soaked overalls. Again, he made eye contact with Denny.

"Look, man, I'm sorry. The thing is, ex won't—well, the thing is, I just wanted to spend time with her. I wanted to see her playing with other kids—to see her happy."

Tamara held her breath. Denny seemed to hesitate—for a moment, his stance softened. But then, his expression hardened, and he took a step closer to Jake.

"Look, I'm sorry for your problems—whatever they are. But I'm not risking my boat or my license for you."

Denny turned to face Tyler.

"And you. Well, you did good back there. Some good thinking. But now it's time to get this boat home to port."

Tamara gave Emily a quick squeeze as she'd done with Ryan, before standing and locking eyes with Denny.

"Are we—"

"Yes," he said, "we're heading back now. We're on course. Shouldn't be long. A little over an hour or so."

Spike sat on a bench, alone, away from the group. Though he hadn't helped them pull Ryan and Jake to safety, his jeans were wet, and salt hazed his leather jacket. White crystals dried and glinted in the zipper teeth.

"Wait a goddamn minute," he said.

Tamara tensed.

Spike stood. He took a step toward her.

"I don't give a shit what you—"

A musical ringtone interrupted him.

"Miss O. Your phone is ringing." Ryan giggled between hiccups.

Spike glared at the child and Tamara.

Tamara bent down and gave Ryan's shoulder a light pat. She retrieved the cell from her sweater pocket and straightened.

"That's weird," she said. "It's the high school principal." She held up one finger and pressed the phone to her ear while still eycing the men.

Despite the tightness of their expressions—the set of their jaws, Denny and Tyler stayed quiet. They held onto the back of the bench and balanced. Jake slid down the wall to a squat and closed his eyes. Spike stood legs apart—rigid—fists tight.

The boat continued to pitch from side to side, plunge up and slam down, and quake. Still holding the phone to her ear, Tamara lurched to one of the wrapped poles and grabbed on.

"Tamara O'Dwyer."

"Vera Johanson here. Right off, Ms. O'Dwyer, I want to express my most sincere apologies. Things like this shouldn't happen. I swear, even after forty years in this field, I still can't understand what goes on in the minds of teenage girls."

Tamara pressed the phone tighter to her ear.

"I'm sorry. What?"

"You should have had those three assistants we promised, but the girls had a flat tire on the way to the marina, and instead of calling me—or you—they, well, they skipped."

Tamara straightened, her eyes widened. She stared at Tyler and Spike. *Who are these boys? These imposters who'd been spending time with my students?* She looked back at the children. Ryan and Emily huddled together off to one side while the others sat in a tight circle close to the port hull. Kevin appeared to be teaching them a modified version of shadow puppets without the shadows. Despite the rolling and pounding of the hull beneath them, and despite everything that had happened so far, the children looked happy—unharmed. *Maybe this could all be—*

"Well, Mrs. Johanson, these things happen. And as it turned out, the crew members have been a big help, so don't go too hard on those girls, okay?"

"That's so lucky! I was afraid you'd have to cancel the field trip. What can I do now? Shall I call the headmaster? Tell him the situation? Offer my apologies?"

Tamara closed her eyes for a second and pinched the spot between them. *She should expose these boys—now. Get help. Even if it meant her job—the children might be at risk. But then again—*

She looked at Tyler. He leaned against a bench and bit at a hangnail. *A kid out on a lark. Mixed up, but not malicious. And Kevin, he's kind, and he's trying his best.* She glanced at Spike, felt his stare, his eyes cold, almost empty. Not good, but still, maybe this could stay quiet. Maybe she could turn things around.

"That's kind of you, but don't bother. I'll take care of everything when we get back. We're heading in now, so it won't be long. Don't worry about it anymore."

"You're so understanding. Maybe, if you ever decide to leave Ruth Hudson, you'll consider us—teenagers can be difficult, but you seem to have a real understanding of young people."

"That's so kind of you, Mrs. Johanson. Thank you. Now, I have to go. It's snack time."

"Well, again, thanks for your understanding. And please be safe out there—this weather is horrible."

"Yes. And thanks again. Bye now."

Tamara touched her thumb to the screen and ended the call. She slipped the phone into her back pocket and glared at Spike and Tyler.

"That was Mrs. Johanson, your principal—that is, if you even go to Port Angeles High. She called to apologize because the assistants she sent to help me didn't make it. Something about a flat tire. Who are you?"

Tyler stared at the floor.

Spike smirked.

"I mean it. Who are you and why are you on this boat, and most of all, what are you doing with my students? It's against every rule at the school—no unauthorized persons are allowed near any of the students." She glanced at Jake but remained focused on the teenagers. Her voice rose as she stomped her foot.

"I demand an explanation. Who are—"

Denny stepped in front of her. His eyes narrowed, and he zeroed in on Tyler.

"Let me handle this," he said. "Look, I don't know what your story is, and frankly, I don't care. But what I do care about is that you don't have permission to be on this boat. You didn't pay for the trip, and you're not part of this group." He gestured toward Tamara and the children.

"Captain, Sir, we didn't mean anything—it was a mistake." Tyler looked up. His voice was pleasant—conciliatory—but salt spray had smeared the soot on his face and arms, and his clothes hung like dirty rags. Tyler had boarded the boat looking charming and trustworthy, but now he resembled a shabby, threatening-looking street person. "We didn't—"

Denny stopped him.

"You're stowaways—all of you. Sneaking aboard a ship—any kind of ship—is illegal. I'm guessing you'll all get fined and maybe do jail time." He glared at Jake and pointed one finger. "As far as I'm concerned, you should all go to prison, but it's not for me to decide."

"Just a damn—" Spike said.

Denny kept going.

"The Coast Guard will deal with you bunch when we dock. I'm calling them right now. They'll be waiting for us when we arrive." He scowled and started toward the helm, but Spike stepped in front of him.

"You ain't callin' nobody. You're gonna get us to Canada. I don't give a shit what you do afterward, but now, you get this fucking boat to Canada."

Tamara sucked in a breath and held it—a cold chill snaked down her spine. She jumped when Karlie tugged on the hem of her t-shirt.

"Miss O. I hafta to go potty."

"Shush, Karlie. You need to hold it for a little more, okay? I need you to go back and sit down with the others. In a couple of minutes, I'll take you to the bathroom. Can you do that for me?"

The little girl pouted but turned and wove her way back to the circle. Tamara glanced at Kevin. He was still entertaining the children and didn't appear to notice what his friends were doing—totally absorbed in his role as a teacher's assistant. *Good.*

Denny looked as if he were studying Spike. When he finally spoke, his tone was low, his words deliberate.

"Maybe you didn't hear me before. Maybe you don't understand how maritime law works. So, I'll spell it out for you. We don't have the proper documentation to clear Canadian customs on these tours. Even if we did, we couldn't take minors across the line without parents or legal guardians on board. So, we're going back to port where the kids will be safe. You and your buddies can work things out with the Coast Guard."

Spike leaned in—his face inches from Denny's—his tone a growl.

"I don't give a shit about your boat laws or these brats. My friends and me—well, Tyler and me anyways—we're getting off in Canada. You do whatever you need to do to land this boat, and nobody gets hurt."

"Now look, son—"

Spike pushed Denny's chest.

"I ain't your son. Shut the fuck up and get us to Canada."

Denny curled his fists and pulled his arm back to strike the younger man, but Spike jammed his hand into his jacket pocket, pulled the gun, and pointed it at Denny's chest. Denny stopped short—raised his hands above his head.

"Stop!" Tamara's eyes widened—she stared first at the gun and then into Spike's eyes. *Diffuse. Distract. Whatever it takes. Nothing matters but the children.*

"I get it," she said. "You have to go to Canada. We'll get you there." She turned to Denny. "Forget the rules. Do what you need to do to give them what they want."

She turned back to Spike and pointed at Jake.

"But that guy over there—he doesn't look so good."

Jake had slipped to a sitting position against the wall, knees drawn up, arms wrapped around his legs. His head flopped backward. His eyes were closed.

Denny lowered his arms, stepped around Spike, and walked to Jake. He squatted down and stared for a moment.

"I've dealt with this before—hypothermia. We have to get him warm and dry, or he's going to die. That will be on you." He stood and glared at Spike.

"What do you wanna do with the guy?" Spike waved the gun at Tamara.

Tamara swallowed—forced herself to ignore the weapon— pretend it wasn't there.

"Well, I think we should—"

"I'll take him to my cabin—get him warm." Denny reached for Jake, but Spike raised the pistol and pointed it at Denny's head.

Denny stopped in place. Spike kept the gun trained on Denny.

"You ain't goin' nowhere but that wheel. Butterfield, you handle this."

"But, I don't know—" Tyler blinked.

"Take him to my cabin." Denny pointed to the locked door near the dashboard. He tugged a ring of keys from his pocket.

"Here. It's the small brass one. Get him out of those wet clothes and into the bed. There are more blankets in the sea chest. Get some fresh water into him and some hot coffee. Use the microwave—there's soup in the cupboard—the one marked GALLEY. He won't fit into my stuff, but there are some spare bib-overalls in the engine room."

Spike swore, pointed at Tyler.

"You drag his ass down there and get him fixed up. But don't waste any time. If he dies, he dies." He narrowed his eyes and scowled at Denny.

"You. Turn this boat around and head to Canada. And you fuckin' well better not try any tricks." Spike glanced back at Tyler.

"Don't just stand there, asshole. Move it."

43

Rain slashed the windshield, and the cruiser cooled. When he stopped at the town's only traffic light, Neil Edward flipped the heat switch and stared at the bay. Waves snarled and twisted into frothy whitecaps. A single gull fought against the fierce wind. Despite the warm air now blasting from the vents, Neil Edward shivered. As much as he'd like to think otherwise, he felt sure he would travel across that angry sea before this cold, wretched day was over.

The light changed, and as the cruiser rolled through Otter's Run, Neil Edward flashed on a day when the sea had been calm and smooth as polished stone. The temperature had been so perfect he couldn't tell where the air stopped and his skin began.

He'd been seven. Out for a ride in his grandfather's canoe. The only sounds were the soft whoosh of the paddle as it dipped into the sea, the ancient call of a great blue heron, and the sharp crack and hiss when his grandfather punched triangles in the tops of aluminum cans.

The fragrance of fir, pine, and warm sand, floated from the land and blended with the pungent scent of saltwater, cedar wood, and the tang of beer.

When the sun slid behind the curve of the earth, Neil Edward's grandfather maneuvered into a kneeling position and sent a steaming stream into the still water. When he'd finished, he leaned back against the curve of the bow and closed his eyes. Soon, his snores rippled across the water.

Neil Edward had also needed to pee. He'd desperately wanted to follow his elder's example, but what if he fell from the canoe?

What if his grandfather didn't wake? What if he couldn't make it to shore? The deep water would be cold.

He'd crossed his legs and had debated how to wake his grandfather when he saw the gleaming, black fin rise silently from the sea. The fin came closer, moved slow and with grace. Neil Edward froze with fear. This was the fin of a blackfish—an orca—a killer whale. A killer whale swimming straight to his grandfather's canoe.

Sheriff Neil Edward Longcarver shook his head—shook the memory away. A long time ago, he'd vowed to forget about the whale. Promised himself he'd forget what had happened that day. And he wasn't about to break that promise now.

44

Tyler and Kevin struggled to drag Jake into a sitting position, to heave him to standing, to half-drag, half-pull him across the rolling cabin to the bow.

"Can you hold him while I unlock the door?" Tyler said.

Kevin grunted.

"Yep. But hurry—he weights a ton."

With Kevin breathing heavy and both of them sweating, they managed to get Jake down the three steps and into Denny's quarters.

"Hold him up. I'll get his clothes off." Tyler pushed Jake against Kevin and unclipped the buckles on Jake's coveralls. He peeled the wet canvas to the floor.

"We gotta get him on the bed to get his shoes off." Tyler ripped the bedding to one side. He grabbed Jake's arms and helped Kevin push the listless man onto Denny's narrow bunk.

Jake slurred his words and flailed his arms.

"What's happening?"

Kevin grabbed one arm and lowered it to Jake's side.

"Nothin' man, we're just getting you dry so you don't die on us." Tyler answered through gritted teeth.

They pushed Jake—now naked—onto his back and pulled the bedding over him. Tyler found the sea chest and hauled out two wool blankets.

"Here," he said. He tossed the blankets to Kevin and scanned the room until he saw the cabinet marked GALLEY. Within minutes, Tyler had a mug of tomato soup turning in the microwave.

"Give him some water, and when this is hot, make him drink it. I'll go find some dry clothes. Think you can handle this?" He paused at the door and waited.

"Kevin. Can you handle this?"

Kevin didn't answer.

45

Jake's eyelids fluttered open. He groaned. Muscles stiff, fingers numb. Kevin's blurry form morphed into clarity.

Kevin unfolded a blanket and spread it over Jake. He reached for a second one.

"Don't worry. You're gonna be okay, Mr. Mechanic. I saw your little girl hugging you. She's doing great, and we're gonna take care of you so you can take care of her." Kevin stood and walked to the cabinet.

The kid's words jumbled together, but Jake understood— Emily was alright. He exhaled, then shivered, licked his lips—dry and salty. He struggled to focus, to watch the young man work.

Kevin hummed a tuneless song as he pulled a mug from the microwave. After a slow, careful trip back to the bunk, he set the mug on the floor. He helped Jake sit and propped him against the bulkhead. He pushed the cup into Jake's hands.

No flavor—only warmth. The shivering slowed. Jake looked up when Tyler pushed the door open and clamored down the steps.

"Oh, good. He's alive." Tyler dropped a pair of dry bib-overalls on the foot of the bunk.

The smell of oily smoke on the clothing stirred Jake's memory.

"Spike is bitchin' about me not helping him. You okay with this?" Tyler mounted the stairs without waiting for Kevin's reply.

"Um, Tyler?"

Tyler's fingers touched the door handle. "What?"

"Are we going to prison? I mean, like Spike's dad? Are we gonna die in prison?"

Tyler turned and faced Kevin. He wiped his mouth with the back of his hand—shook his head. He lowered his voice.

Jake strained to hear.

"Honestly? I don't know. Yeah, well, maybe. Spike—he's—well, you know."

"But what about your girlfriend's dad? Isn't he some big-time judge or something? Can't he help us? I mean, if they catch us?"

"Sorry, Kev. That ship has sailed. She wasn't really my girlfriend, and I probably never had a chance with her anyway."

"But you said you went to her house. For her birthday party. You said her parents liked you."

"Yeah, well, she invited half the senior class to that party. And her parents were nice to everybody. I was hoping—you know. But nope, we're on our own. The only thing we can do now is go along with Spike." Tyler wiped the palms of his hands on his jeans and licked his lips.

Jake knew the look of fear. The fear crossing a recruit's face when he stands flattened against a dusty wall in a dark alley, trying to avoid a sniper's bullet or the shred of a grenade. The fear pulling the corners of a guy's mouth as he struggles under an over-weighted bar at the press. And the fear of desperation skittering across a teenager's eyes when he thinks the odds are hopelessly stacked against him, but he also thinks—for a dozen rat-scratching-like reasons—that he can't back down.

"What's Spike gonna do, Tyler?"

"He's pretty sure Travis can help us once we get to Canada."

Canada? Jake pushed himself to focus, to remember. *Canada?* He tightened his grip on the mug—felt its heat flow through his fingers. He forced himself to sit straight. Forced himself to focus on the boys.

"But, Travis—"

"Yeah, I know. He's a jerk. But we don't have any other options." Tyler said. "Look, I'm sorry I brought you along today."

"No worries, Tyler. I'm okay. We're having an adventure—like what friends do. Right?" Kevin's face lit with a smile.

Tyler stared at Kevin for a moment. He brushed filthy blond hair from his forehead.

"Yeah. Right. An adventure. Like what friends do." He pulled the door open, and paused. "Know what? You better stay down here. With him. You know, to keep an eye on him." With that, Tyler pulled the door open and left.

Jake slumped back against the bulkhead.

Kevin reached for the mug and peered inside.

"I'm gonna make you some more soup, okay?"

"Okay." Every move hurt, but Jake felt the warmth returning to his core and the fog in his brain clearing. He watched Kevin open a second can of soup, pour it into the mug, and hit Start on the microwave. All the while, the boy hummed a song Jake couldn't place.

"Hey, thanks. I mean, for helping me get down here. I'm pretty heavy—musta been a big job." Jake coughed—his voice scratchy from salt.

"No worries." Kevin made his way back to Denny's bunk. He halted every few seconds—balanced as the boat rolled and jerked. When he reached the bed, he sat on the edge.

"Here, it's not too hot." He handed the mug to Jake.

"Thanks."

"It's chicken noodle. For when you're sick. Well," he closed his eyes for a beat. "Like, I know you're not sick. I mean not sick, sick. But I thought—"

Jake looked into the mug. A red ring crusted the edge of the watery, yellow broth. He took a taste.

"It's great, man. Perfect."

They sat in silence while Jake sipped the warm liquid and sucked down soft noodles. Finally, Kevin spoke.

"So, ah, you're a Marine, right?"

Jake swallowed a clump of limp pasta and titled his head to one side—he felt the pain receding.

"Navy. Why?"

Kevin pointed to the tattoo spread wide across Jake's chest.

"I thought that was the Marine's thing."

In another time, another place, Jake would have huffed—made some demeaning comment about the Marines not having their own ships or something equally macho. But that time had passed.

"Nope. Navy. Whole different game."

"Wow." Kevin blew out a deep breath. "That's like, awesome, man. Like, thanks for your service, bro."

Jake stifled a smile—forced a stern, reflective look.

"Thanks, bro. I appreciate that." He tried a stretch—felt strength returning to his limbs.

"I better get dressed—something tells me they're going to need us up there." He passed the empty mug to Kevin.

Kevin flushed.

"Okay, here's the stuff from the engine room. I'll turn around. I would leave, but I gotta stay here on account a Tyler. He thinks somebody should stay with you."

Jake tugged at the mechanic's spare overalls. The pant legs stopped at his calve—the bib almost covered his chest. Dickerson was a full head shorter and half Jake's size, but at least his oil-stained and smokey work clothes were dry.

Kevin sat at Denny's desk with his back to Jake.

"You dressed?"

"If you call this dressed."

Kevin spun the chair around and gaped at Jake.

"Man, you look like the Hulk busting out of his clothes. If you get seasick and turn green, you will be the Hulk."

Jake shot him a quick grin and stood. He gripped a handrail, tested his balance, felt dizzy.

Kevin scratched his head.

"Um, if we're gonna go back up there, we should do it before Spike does something crazy."

Jake sat back down on the edge of the bunk.

"Yeah, okay. But give me a minute."

"Alright," Kevin said. "Tell me about the Navy. Tell me about your missions."

Jake gave the boy an intense stare.

"There are things I can't tell you. You know. Secrets. But someday, when this is over, we'll go out for beers. Two buddies. I'll tell you some stuff—some stories, okay?"

"Yeah. Secrets. I get it. Yeah." Kevin bobbed his head. He paused, scrunched his face.

"But, you know, I'm not twenty-one, right?"

"Don't worry about that, man. I'll take care of that. But now, I need you to help me get some things straight because that cold water messed with my head. What did you mean about going to prison? When you were talking to Tyler?"

Kevin lowered his head and covered his face with his hands. Then he dropped his hands and looked up at Jake.

"It's all a big mess," he said. "A big old mess. We were gonna rob the place—that's all. The store—it's the only place open all night. They sell a lot of booze and smokes, and we figured at the end of the night shift, there'd be a bunch of cash in the register. The plan was we—me and Spike—would go in, pretend like we had guns, and scare the guy. We were gonna grab the cash and get outta there. Tyler had the car running. Easy."

Jake stayed still. Pieces were falling into place—an ugly place.

Kevin went on.

"Tyler, he was in on it because he has this girlfriend. Well, he *wanted* to have Hailey as a girlfriend. She's cute, and he likes her—a lot. He wanted to buy her something for graduation, but he didn't have any money. So, when Spike came up with the plan about the store, Tyler was in."

"What about Spike? Why'd he rob the store?"

"Spike, he's such a jerk. I don't even think he cared about the money. Maybe he was trying to impress his brother. Who knows?"

"And what about you? You got a cute girlfriend?"

Kevin snorted and blushed.

"Naw. I knew it was a stupid idea from the start—pretend like we're bad guy robbers. We're a bunch of losers. But Tyler, he's my only friend. So, I thought it would be cool, you know, to do something with the guys. Even if it was a stupid idea."

"Yeah, guys doing stupid guy stuff."

"Right. So it shoulda been fun. But that jerk, Spike. He had to bring a gun—a real gun. His brother's gun. From his brother's car." Kevin closed his eyes and squeezed his hands together.

Jake sat up straight—fully alert now—all dizziness gone.

"What happened?"

Kevin opened his eyes.

"I don't even know. One minute we were over by the hot dogs, and the next minute Spike shot the gun, and the clerk was on the floor, and there was blood all over him, and there was blood all over the floor, and all over some donuts and stuff."

A chill iced through Jake. He flashed on the police photo of the guy with the hollow eyes—eyes like Spike's.

"What about the clerk? What happened to him?"

"We don't know. We just ran outta there. And drove and drove and drove. And I—my pants—I was so scared. I couldn't help it." He looked up—pleading.

"It happens," Jake said. He tried to sound kind, but his brain buzzed. *Emily.*

"So now you guys are trying to get away from the cops by going to Canada, right?"

"Yeah, that's Spike's plan," Kevin mumbled. He stared at the floor and picked at a scab on his knee.

"What about your parents? Won't they be worried about you?"

Kevin shook his head.

"Tyler is gonna call his folks from Canada. Tell 'em he's on a field trip or something. Spike's mom, well, she'll be glad he's gone for a while. He's mean to her."

"Do you want to go to Canada, Kevin?" Jake leaned toward the boy. He wanted to move on with this—to get upstairs. He needed to protect the children—to protect Emily. But he needed the whole picture.

Kevin dropped a piece of scab on the floor.

"No. Cuz my mom—she's not so good—she's sorta sick. She needs me. If I go to Canada, well . . . what about my mom?" He glanced up—his face flushed.

"Come on," Jake said. "Let's go upstairs. Spike isn't the only one with a plan."

"And later, we can go for a beer and talk about the Navy, right?"

"Yep. Later we'll go have beers and talk about the Navy." Jake waited a beat. "Ah, one more question, buddy. Where's the gun now?"

Kevin stared at Jake.

"Don't you remember? Spike pulled it on the captain. Right after we got you out of the water. Remember? Spike told the captain he had to take us to Canada, and the captain said he couldn't, and so, well, Spike pulled the gun on him."

Jake tensed. Spike was young, in his prime. Despite the hypothermia, Jake knew he'd be stronger than Spike, but not as fast. And Spike held the gun.

46

While he'd been watching amateur videos, the storm made land-fall. Fierce winds pushed Neil Edward forward, and heavy rain pelted his back as he dashed across the lot to the station.

Usually, he'd leave the cruiser in his official parking spot in front of the building. He'd park beside Jennette's pride and joy—a fully restored, bright turquoise, polished-to-a-shine 1955 T-Bird. But now, his spot was occupied by Anita Anderson's weather-bleached, be-stickered 1985 Toyota Camry. The Camry's collection of bumper art promoted decades of liberal, and a few conservative causes. Anita didn't discriminate—any organization that issued free decals earned representation on her ride. Probably a good thing, too. Neil Edward guessed that if even one of those stickers ever peeled off, that Camry would crumble into a pile of rust.

"About time." Jennette didn't give him a chance to shake the rain from his jacket before she lit into him.

"While you were over at that school watching home movies and chatting up teachers, I've been slammed. The phone hasn't stopped ringing for more than a minute."

"Wait, how did you know—"

The station's phone cut him off.

"Otter's Run Sheriff's Office. Can you hold a minute? I've got another call coming in." Jennette pressed a button and answered the second line.

Neil Edward rushed to his desk and picked up the first caller.

"There's a group of little kids on a boat out there. You gotta do something."

"Yes, we know. And we've got that well in hand."

"I'm worried," the caller said. "That storm is going to get worse. My brother-in-law he says—"

"Don't worry. We're working on—"

"But what are you going to—"

"We have the situation under control. Thanks for calling." He and Jennette hung up at the same time.

"Been crazy in here. Between the storm causing outages, and flying branches, and that video of those kids—" Jeanette took a quick look toward the other room.

"Plus, our guest is demanding his phone call. Crazy, I'm telling you—major crazy."

"Wait a minute. Back up. What about the video? And why is Anita parked in my spot?"

Two more calls came in, and then another. When they finally got a quiet moment, Neil Edward repeated his questions.

"What did you mean about the video? How do you know about that? And, again, why is Anita in my spot? Where is she anyway?"

"She's in the back—lecturing our guest on hygiene."

"She's what?"

"Yeah. She came in here to report some downed power lines, went back there to use the toilet, heard him hollering for his phone call, and started in on him. Meanwhile we got a slew of calls about that video."

"Tell me what you heard about the video."

"Some parent saw a video of her kid on a whale-watching trip, and I guess she freaked out. She called other parents, and they got freaked out too. And a parent who works for Channel Five saw the video and put it on the air. Like I said, it's been crazy. So, what happened at the school?"

Neil Edward sat on the folding chair by Jennette's desk. He ran his hand through his damp hair.

"Well, I saw that video too, and I don't feel good about this, Jennette. A guy with a restraining order on a boat with a bunch of little kids. And even though all those teachers seemed to like the guy—summed him up as a gentle giant—he's still breaking the law. Not to mention that boat is spitting distance to an international border. And there are two teenagers who don't seem to belong where they are, and one skinny little kid who looks like he's gone for a long swim in a cold sea. Things aren't adding up."

The phones started ringing again. Neil Edward moved to his desk to help with the calls as Anita left the back room, slamming the door behind her. She plopped down in the chair the sheriff had occupied moments before.

"No, I'm sorry, Mrs. Wilson, we can't come out to restart your pilot light." Jennette tapped her finger on the desk. "I know. I know. But you can call the gas company." She frowned—glanced at her watch. "Well, look it up—"

"Sound Natural Gas. Takes 'em about twenty minutes to respond." Anita rattled off a phone number.

Jennette gave her a puzzled look, repeated the number and wished the caller luck. She hung up only to pick up again a moment later. She rolled her eyes.

"Darned if I know, but you can Google it." She stood and paced behind her desk as she listened. "No, I have no idea who the best tree trimmers are or if they can come get the branches. Besides—"

"Northwest Toppers," Anita piped up. "Here's their number." She grabbed a pencil and scribbled on a notepad. Jennette mouthed thanks as a roll of thunder rattled the windows.

When the phones went silent again, Neil Edward turned to Jennette.

"I'm worried about the fleet, and I'm concerned about what's going on with those kids."

Before Jennette could speak, Anita stood and walked to Neil Edward's desk.

"Don't worry about the fleet, Sheriff. They're all in. All except the *Steilacoom Witch* and the *Hattie Belle*. Those two haven't come back yet. Still out there."

"Anita, how do you know all this stuff? Phone number for the gas company, best tree trimmers in town, the whereabouts of the fleet?" Neil Edward stared at the wiry woman.

Anita crossed her arms and huffed.

"I am a concerned citizen, Sheriff Longcarver. It's my *duty* to pay attention."

The phone rang again. Jennette answered, listened, and looked up at Neil Edward.

"You better take this one," she said. "It's the headmaster at Hudson. He wants to know what you're doing about the *situation*." She made air quotes around the word.

"Tell him we're on our way out there. Tell him we have an organized team. Tell him we have this under control, and the best thing he can do is reassure all those parents that we're handling it."

Anita returned to the seat beside Jennette and listened as the deputy relayed the message. Neil Edward waited until the call was done. He had planned to invite his "concerned citizen" to hustle back into her rusting death trap and go on home—more diplomatically, of course. But Jennette didn't give him time.

"So, we're taking a team out! This is the police work I live for! Give me two minutes to grab my gear, and I'm ready."

"No, wait. You're not going anywhere, Jennette. Get Leone on the phone and tell him to fire up his skiff. Also, we're out of radio range, but see if one of the other boats in the fleet can reach the two vessels still out there. And try to reach their cell phones. Get coordinates and any information you can. And Anita, it's best if you head on home now."

The silence that followed muted a close clap of thunder. Neither woman said a word. Neither woman moved. They simply stared at him. The phone rang. Jennette lifted the receiver—an inch—and set it back down.

Neil Edward winced. He knew he was the boss—the guy in charge. He knew he made the decisions—his call. And, he knew, he was outnumbered.

"Look." He held one hand up, palm toward Jennette. "We need someone to operate these phones. You said it yourself—it's crazy. Leone and I can handle things."

The women stood tomb still—silent. Each focused on Neil Edward.

Neil Edward swallowed. A flash of lightning scratched the sky—another slap of thunder rumbled overhead. The lights in the office flickered. He swallowed again. He knew it wouldn't work, but he tried. "What about the phones? What about the guy in the back? What if he needs something? What if he needs water or—"

Anita straightened her spine.

"I can answer phones, Sheriff. I have the skills and all of the necessary information."

Jennette placed her hands flat on her desk and leaned forward.

"And you know, that I know, how much you love boats. Don't you, Sheriff?"

Outnumbered. Definitely outnumbered.

"Okay, okay. Jennette, get your gear. I've got to talk to that guy in the cell—something I need him to do before we leave."

He closed his eyes for a second, opened them and looked at Anita. "And," he took a deep breath—exhaled in a sigh.

"I'll have to deputize you."

47

Jennette insisted on helping Neil Edward with the swearing-in of Volunteer Deputy Anita Anderson.

"Look, Boss, as one of the only two paid members on the force, I feel it's my duty to welcome—and support—the volunteer officers."

"It's a temporary appointment, Jennette."

"Yes. But. Remember that time I missed Leone's swearing-in ceremony? Wasted a full day driving to Seattle to try out one of those new-fangled prosthetic legs. But after all that driving, plus two ferry rides, we both agreed—my wooden leg is better than anything modern medicine has to offer."

"Jennette, I don't see what this has—"

"Well, I've never felt good about missing that important police ritual. Had to split a bottle of Jack Daniels with Leone to express my regrets."

Neil Edward glanced at the clock.

"Okay, okay. Let's do this."

Minutes later, Jennette flanked Anita and balanced a tattered, spiral-bound volume on her open palm. Anita stood straight with her left hand pressed on the county's *Guide to Best Practices*, her right hand raised.

"I don't think the *Guide* is appropriate," Jennette said. "Maybe it's not even legal. We really should use a Bible."

"We don't have a Bible in the office, and we don't have time to run around town looking for one. The guidebook will do." Neil Edward cleared his throat and did his best to look serious and official.

"Anita Anderson, do you solemnly swear to perform the duties of Volunteer Deputy, to obey directives from the full-time deputy—"

"That's me."

"I know that, Jennette," Anita said.

Neil Edward cleared his throat. "And to keep all police business strictly confidential?"

"Absolutely."

"And no making Executive Decisions—you run everything past Jennette or me. Got it?"

"Yes, sir."

"And no gossiping—except with me—when it's, you know, official," Jennette added.

"No unofficial gossiping," Anita said. "Except with you."

"Then, as the Duly Elected Sheriff of Otter's Run, I hereby pronounce you Temporary Volunteer Deputy."

Anita squealed. Jennette dropped the *Guide* on her desk, and the two women hugged. Although they were fresh out of Volunteer Deputy Badges, Jennette fixed a small Washington State flag lapel pin on Anita's sweatshirt. Neil Edward grimaced but made a show of shaking Anita's hand before grabbing the cell phone they'd taken from Travis's car. He dropped the phone into his pocket. With a quick, two-fingered salute to the women, he slipped into the back room.

Travis paced the cell.

"Jesus H. Christ. Where the hell you been? I want my lawyer and something t' eat. And I don't wanna see that old bitch anymore."

"Do you have a lawyer, Mr. Drumthor?" Neil Edward selected a key from a ring on his belt and opened the cell door.

"No, but I could. Right? You gotta get one for me. Right? Public defender. This ain't my first lap around the track." Travis glared at Neil Edward.

Neil Edward sighed.

"I believe you. But the thing is, you don't need a lawyer. You're not under arrest. You're simply enjoying a short stay with us while we clear up the issue of your car and a few other details. Besides, it's pouring out there—a real mess. Think of this as shelter from the storm. Let's talk, okay? A friendly-like chat." He sat at one end of the bunk.

Travis sat on the other end of the narrow bed.

"Okay. But I didn't do nothin', so whadda ya want?"

Neil Edward pulled the phone from his pocket, tapped in the password Hailey1234, and gave it to Travis.

"Flip through the photos, okay? Tell me about those kids, and why you think they aren't in school today, and why you think they had your car."

Travis took the phone and thumbed through the photos. "I dunno why they skipped school. Probably bored. But I know why they took the car. My brother told me him and his crew needed it for a job. Said he'd fill it up when they were done. Said he'd give me a split of the take." He paused, squinted at an image, then flipped past the photo.

"What kind of job?"

"Hell if I know. Didn't care. Don't care. Just as long as they got the car back to me in time for me to get to work. But the little bastard didn't bring it back. He left it in that parking lot. I had to hitch out here to pick up my car, but the shit didn't leave the key where we said." He stopped scrolling. "There, that's him. That's Eugene." He handed the phone to the sheriff.

In the photo, the kid in the black leather jacket scowled at Neil Edward. He passed the phone back to Travis.

"So, where was he supposed to leave the key?"

"Top of the driver's tire. Like always. But it wasn't there."

"How'd you know he was going to leave the car at the marina?"

"He called. Left a message. Said plans changed. Said they were taking some boat to Canada, but he'd leave the key where we do."

Travis stopped at another photo—held the phone out. "The pansy-ass surfer-lookin guy? That's Tyler."

"Who's the other guy—the big kid?"

"That hippo? I dunno. Some dufus they hang around with sometimes. I think he lives in the trailer park south of town."

Travis continued to scroll through the photos. He stopped once to scratch his belly, and then he held the phone up to show a shot of Hailey smiling—clear skin, bright blue eyes.

"Now there's a hottie—looks like some kinda goody-goody. Needs some life lessons. Yeah, I could learn her a thing or two."

Neil Edward suppressed a scowl—he wanted to slap Travis with a verbal warning—*have a little respect for Judge Lynden's daughter.* But he'd already faked ignorance about the kids in the photos. He kept his mouth shut, glanced at his watch, hoped this wasn't wasted time.

"So, why were they going to Canada? Any ideas?"

"Nope. But he's gonna get the crap beat outta him when he comes back."

Neil Edward stood up.

"Alright, then. Tell you what. You get that phone call now. Why don't you call your brother—ask him why he stiffed you. You can use that phone but put it on speaker."

"What? I don't gotta let you listen to my private calls."

Sheriff Neil Edward Longcarver shrugged.

"Take it or leave it."

48

Kevin lumbered up the steps, and without another word to Jake, he wandered across the cabin toward Tamara. Jake followed him, but he paused at the top step to watch Emily and the other children as they giggled and whispered to each other. They sat in a semi-circle under the port windows and played a game that involved whispering messages from one to the other.

When a strong gust slapped the side of the *Hattie Belle* and rocked her with brutal force, Lexie toppled over and collided with Karlie. The two girls crashed to the floor.

"Ow!" Lexie said.

"My arm! I hit my arm!" Karlie wailed.

Conrad dropped his cell phone—it slid across the floor, struck the base of the bench with a pop, and spun in circles.

"My camera! My camera is broken." His lips quivered.

Jake guessed tears were on the way.

Emily scrambled from her place. She grabbed the spinning chunk of plastic and gave it a quick once over.

"No, it's not, Conrad. See? The case is cracked, but it still works. Look."

Conrad examined his phone, nodded once, and pointed it at Emily.

"And now for some on-the-scene comments from one girl who was there. Can you tell our viewers what happened?" he asked.

"Only a little wave action. Nothing Miss O's third grade class from the Ruth Hudson Elementary School can't handle!" Emily vamped for the video.

Jake lifted his chin and smiled. But his shoulders slumped forward. Emily was finding her way in the world. And he was not part of that. *Don't dwell on it—not now.*

At the helm, Denny faced forward with his hands resting light on the wheel. He moved it side to side in small motions and kept the bow pointed into oncoming waves. Jake glanced at the narrow mirror over the window. Denny stared straight ahead—his face expressionless. *Biding his time?*

Spike stood to the right of the wheel, wedged between the dashboard and the sliding door. He stared at the chart on the dashboard. Though dots of sweat pooled in the pockmarks lining his cheeks, he shivered in the wet, salt-crusted jacket. Skin sallow—face drawn.

Odds were, Spike had stashed the weapon in his jacket pocket, but Jake couldn't tell for sure, and that made for bad odds. Still, he had to try something. He reached for a handrail and started toward the helm.

"Where the hell you think you're goin'?" Spike said.

"I was coming to see if you guys need any help."

"We don't."

"Well, mind if I come up there? Watch the storm?"

"Yeah. I mind. Get your ass back there." Spike nodded toward the children.

"But I—"

Spike straightened and slid his hand into his jacket pocket.

"Okay, okay." Jake shrugged and turned around. *Not now.*

He passed the aft deck, where Tyler leaned over the rail. The wind whipped the kid's hair and spray drenched his clothes. His body twitched in a jerking motion—puking overboard. *Poor guy.* Jake realized that he hadn't felt any queasiness except for the few moments when he'd first come out of the water. His stomach knotted with a sharp pain—probably from swallowing so much salt water—but no signs of seasickness.

"How are you feeling?" Tamara asked.

"Good. Physically anyway." Jake lowered to the floor.

Tamara scooched closer to him—dropped her voice.

"Spike has a gun."

Jake nodded.

"Didn't know if you knew. You were pretty much out of it."

Jake nodded again. He listened to her but watched the two at the helm.

"Before I knew about the gun, I got a call from Mrs. Johanson—the principal at the high school. Turns out my assistants, my real assistants, had a flat on the way to the marina. These guys simply lucked out. Found a chance to run—from whatever they're running from, and they took it."

"I have to ask—" he said.

"Yeah, I know. I know. I should have said something right at the start. I should have told Mrs. Johanson about them—about the imposters. But I kept thinking how they'd never let the children go on another field trip. I thought that maybe, if we could get through the day, and no one at my school knew about the boys, well, maybe—no excuses. It was totally stupid of me."

"Don't be so hard on yourself," Jake said. "They can't blame this on you. It was a case of mistaken identity—right from the start."

"Yes, but I should have called the high school the minute I saw those boys. Kevin, in his ridiculous shorts and Spike's jacket. I should have known they weren't college-bound seniors."

"You couldn't have known. Kids wear all kinds of weird things to school these days. At least none of them have purple hair or nose rings."

"Maybe you're right, but still, I shouldn't have covered for them. For sure, I'll be polishing my resume when this is over." She folded her hands in her lap.

Jake looked at her and covered her hands with one of his.

"Like I said, don't be so hard on yourself. You're obviously a great teacher. The kids love you, and you're doing everything you can to protect them. You should get a promotion when this is over. And if your school can't see that, well, another one will be thrilled to get someone like you."

"What are we going to do?" She dropped her gaze to his hand—the one that covered hers. She didn't move.

"I'm not sure," he said. He returned to watching Spike at the helm.

Tamara shifted to face him.

"So, Mr. Mechanic, Jake, the Pretend Mechanic, tell me, who are you—really? The truth this time."

Jake gave her hands a quick squeeze and pulled his away. He pushed a lock of hair from his forehead—switched his attention to her.

"Fair enough. I'm sorry I lied. But you can understand why. Right?"

Tamara waited.

Jake cleared his throat. "Not much to tell. Middle-class kid—played football, delivered pizzas. After high school, my best buddy, Richard, and I joined the Navy."

Tamara looked at his tattoo.

"I had a cousin who joined the Navy," she said. "He said it changed him both for the better and for the worst."

"Best thing that ever happened to me. Before her, of course." He glanced at Emily.

"Go on."

"I ran the physical training courses onboard, and when we got leave, Richard and I traveled. Good times until—"

"Until what?"

"The container ship."

Jake closed his eyes—his breathing slowed. He no longer heard rain slashing the windows. He didn't see the children playing. Instead, he heard the deep rumble of the destroyer's engines, and he saw stacks of containers piled high. Brown, yellow, and gray aluminum rectangles packed with consumer goods—shoes, car parts, plastic toys—all bound for Europe.

"A British ship in trouble," he said. He kept his eyes closed.

"Pirates?"

"Thugs."

The sights, sounds, even the smells still haunted him.

"It wasn't a standard operation, but the captain thought we could use the practice. U.S. Navy against a group of goons—no contest."

He opened his eyes and tried to focus on a loose thread on his coveralls, but he heard the blast, felt the weight of the body—Richard's body.

"You don't have to—"

"No, it's okay. I want to."

He picked at the thread.

"We were boarding. They set off charges. Containers fell off the ship. Wrong time. Wrong place. Busted my shoulder, but they slammed Richard. Bad. I tried to swim back, to carry him.

They gave me the Medal of Honor. I sent it to Richard's mother. I was a mess until I met Marilyn."

Tamara gave him a gentle nudge.

"You said you're divorced. Is *that* true?"

Jake searched her face.

"Yeah, but we might have made it except for Marilyn's dad. He was always pushing me. Pushing me to expand my business—pushing me to go into politics—push, push, push. Marilyn didn't like it when I pushed back. Between her dad and the accident—"

"What accident?"

Jake took a deep breath and exhaled slow.

"I bought a gym," he said. "Let parents bring their children to workouts as long they signed a release form, and the kids stayed in a roped-off area. Everybody liked it. Kids played, parents trained, and nobody had to pay for daycare or babysitters. But this one time, a new guy—I never blamed him—forgot to clip his weights on the bar. He was overloaded. I was across the gym training another lifter and couldn't let go. I yelled for him to wait for his spotter, but his left arm gave. A fifty-pound plate slid off the bar. Slid off at the same time a little boy was taking an unsupervised walk-about.

"Did he? Did the boy—"

Jake glanced at her.

"Fifty pounds of cast iron versus a four-year-old boy."

"You lost your gym," Tamara said.

"Lost everything. Gym, house, marriage, lost time with my Emily. That's the worst of it. So, when I heard she'd be on this field trip—" He looked away, avoided Tamara's gaze.

"But the accident wasn't your fault. And the parents signed that release form."

"Turns out release forms aren't worth squat. Marilyn and her father's lawyer convinced the judge I wasn't fit to be around children. I think she wanted out of the marriage—maybe before that even happened. Maybe she wanted someone like her father. I was outnumbered from the start."

"Did you fight it? The custody thing?"

"No. I was tired of fighting. Everyone in God's name lawyered up. Parents, equipment manufacturers, the new guy, other gym members, and most of all, Marilyn. She used our money to buy the meanest lawyer she could find. And when that lawyer couldn't get her everything she wanted, her dad found someone who could."

Jake sagged against the wall.

"Maybe," Tamara said, "you should fight for what you love."

B-B-B-B-Bad B-B-B-B-Bad. Bad to the bone.

Spike's ring tone startled him. He dragged the phone from an inside jacket pocket and hit End Call.

"Hey, why you calling me?" He looked at Tyler.

Tyler didn't answer. He leaned against the dashboard and stared at the rain slicking the front windows.

Spike stepped forward and smacked Tyler's shoulder. He held the phone up. The word, Butterfield, lit the display.

Tyler shrugged. "It's not me. I don't have my phone."

"Well, who's calling me, and where the hell is your phone?"

Tyler stood straight, rolled his shoulder, and grabbed the edge of the dash. He wiped his mouth with the back of his hand.

"I forgot it. Left it in Travis's car."

"What?"

"Hey, look, man. We were trying to figure out a plan, and I saw that sign. Remember? We took off to get on the boat. We forgot to go back to the car."

Spike stared at Tyler.

"What did you do with the key?"

Tyler turned away.

"I said, what did you do with the key, asshole?"

Tyler reached into his jeans pocket and pulled out a single key. The tone started again.

B-B-B-B-Bad B-B-B-B-Bad. Bad to the bone.

"Shit. I did not need this, Butterfield."

Neil Edward and Jennette cowered together at the end of the marina's wooden dock and waited while Leone fueled his boat. Waves splashing against the boards drenched them. Jennette's once neon yellow high-tops, now soaked dark with saltwater, offered little grip on the slippery surface. Neil Edward clutched a strap on her life jacket to keep her from toppling over.

"Hurry it up, Leone," he said.

Volunteer Deputy Dwayne Leone stood at the back of his boat—his legs spread wide for balance. He grappled with a plastic jerry jug positioned over a funnel teetering in the hole at the top of his gas tank. Fuel sloshed over the funnel's rim as waves pounded the vessel's aluminum hull. Leone looked up from the jerry jug—his bald head gleamed with rain, his soaked shirt clung to his chest.

"Almost done, Sheriff. I wanna make sure she's topped off—it's a ways out there."

"So, what was the call about?" Jennette struggled with a buckle on the life jacket Leone had insisted she wear. The thing was too small and had the effect of a cheap push-up bra—a bright orange push-up bra.

"Lots of swearing to start." Neil Edward stood behind Jennette in an attempt to shield her, to offer some protection from the torrent of rain lashing down on them. Looking at her, he realized his efforts weren't working. The arms of his deputy's lemon-colored sweater were plastered tight to her skin, and her full, usually whirling, poodle skirt hung straight. Limp.

"Besides swearing?" Jennette looked down at her chest and frowned. The rain already puddled between her breasts and spilled over the top of the puffy jacket.

"A bunch of threats—gonna slam you, rip you a new one. That sort of thing. But I got the impression our guest was feeling some pride toward his little brother."

Neil Edward tilted his head—cold water poured off his hat's rim and drained down his collar.

"They were trying to speak in some sort of code—talked about the job going wrong but not to worry—no trace. And, big brother warned little brother not to lose his sock."

"His sock?"

"Yes, his sock. Remember Leone found one gym sock in the wheel well of that car? One sock and four boxes of ammo? My guess is the other sock held a gun. I hope I'm wrong, but I'm guessing little brother Spike has the missing footwear."

"Maybe, but without the ammo—"

Leone waved to them. "Okay, guys. You can come on board now. We're full up and ready to move. Jennette, you come on first. Sheriff, you hold one of her hands, and I'll grab the other. Take it easy, now—we're rockin' and rollin' pretty hard."

Jennette stepped toward the edge of the dock and stopped. She held up her left hand.

"Wait. A text came in—it's a picture."

"We should go, Jennette." Neil Edward tugged at her arm.

"Wait, Sheriff, this is important. Look."

She held her phone out to him.

Neil Edward cupped one hand over the phone and squinted at the screen's grainy black and white image.

"Is this what I think it is?"

"Yeah. CCTV photo from the convenience store. My friend in the Clallam County Sheriff's Office sent it. They just got the footage."

"Hold on a minute, Leone." Neil Edward motioned to his deputy, pulled Tyler's phone from his pocket, and entered the password. He scrolled through the photos and then held the phone next to Jennette's.

"Look at this."

"It's the same guy, isn't it, Sheriff?"

"Yeah. Not real clear. But clear enough. Let's go." He pushed Tyler's phone back into his pocket and turned toward the boat.

"No, wait. She's sending another text." Jennette read the message, and dropped her phone into the small duffel she'd packed for the trip.

"Well?"

"Not good, Sheriff."

"Tell me.

"That clerk at the store? He didn't make it. And they found the shell casings."

"Lemme guess. Nine millimeter hollow points."

Jennette looked up at Neil Edward—tilted her head to one side.

"Maybe I should call for backup?"

Sheriff Neil Edward Longcarver pursed his lips into a tight, thin line and inhaled a long breath. When he spoke, his voice was low and flat.

"Roger that," he said.

51

Despite two massive outboard engines—one hundred and fifty horse-power each—*Leone's Lady* bounced like a toy in the rough fetch sloshing near the dock. Neil Edward tensed as the twenty-six-foot aluminum skiff tugged and jerked at the line holding her in place. She fought the tether with her bow thrust high and her stern weighed low from two hundred gallons of fuel. The motion churned his stomach. Neil Edward turned away and looked to the land.

Leone's boat reminded him of a horse, a spirited bronco— one not yet ready to bear the weight of a man—or even the weight of a saddle. While most of his peers had been perfecting their skills at fishing or paddling, Neil Edward had spent his teenage years making weekly trips east to the town of Sequim to learn about the animals of the land. His choice had confused his parents, but they loved him and let him follow his path. Neil Edward thought about the horses he'd worked with and how he'd learned that with patience and a fine-honed skill, he could calm them, train them. Turning back to the raging water and bounding boat still tethered to the dock, he shuddered. He knew that no amount of patience could calm this vessel. He hoped Leone had the skill.

Hoisting Jennette on board the lurching skiff was not as difficult as either man might have expected. With her weight pressed on Neil Edward's shoulder for support, Jennette pivoted fast on her left leg and swung her fleshy limb over the side of the boat while at the same time grabbing tight to Leone's hand. Leone gave a quick, firm pull, and Jennette flew into the boat, twisted, and landed on one of the two vinyl chairs welded to the deck under the boat's narrow canvas canopy.

"Yeeee haaa!" Jennette raised both arms straight in victory.

"Holy moly, girl." Leone snapped a salute. "I've been on the water most of my life, but I've never seen anyone board a boat like that!" He turned to Neil Edward.

"Think you can top that, Sheriff?"

Neil Edward stared past Leone to Jennette, who was now busy digging through the contents of her duffel bag.

"She never fails to blow my mind," he said. "No way can I even come close to that. Give me your hand and help this old guy climb on board."

Although he had tried to joke—to make light of the mo-ment—Neil Edward knew, deep down, his old-guy comment wasn't rhetorical. What had started as a simple sore back in need of a massage had morphed into full-blown pain. Maybe it was the nasty weather with its relentless rain and whipping winds, or maybe the stress of knowing something was wrong out there—in that boat filled with school children, or maybe it was simply old age coming to plague him. Whatever the cause of his physical pain, Neil Edward longed for this day to be over. He longed for the clean sheets of the massage table and the sugary scent of va-nilla frosting.

Deputy Leone leaned over the transom and offered his hand. Gritting his teeth, Neil Edward grabbed on and attempted to hop up and over the cockpit's edge, but instead of a respectful board-ing, he slipped and flopped across the hull to land belly down on the boat's deck with a loud grunt.

Jennette paused her search and assessed her boss.

"You okay, Sheriff? Need me to help you get up?"

Neil Edward saw her grin.

"Buzz off," he groaned. "Someday, you'll be old and feeble too." He pushed to his knees, and with Leone's help, he managed to stand between the two vinyl seats.

"Once we head out, you got to hold tight to the canopy, Sheriff. It's gonna be a real rough ride. And you've got to wear this. It's the law." Leone handed a PFD to his boss, then fished around for another from a cabinet under his seat.

Unlike Jennette's unwieldy life jacket, the personal flotation device Leone handed his boss was slim and comfortable—designed for maximum maneuverability when fishing or working with lines.

Neil Edward caught Jennette eyeing the device. He turned away, braced against the helm, and fastened a buckle. Leone needed the driver's seat to operate the boat, which left only one free chair. Neil Edward was okay yielding that secure place to Jennette—a no-brainer. But he drew the line at giving up his comfortable safety gear in exchange for her puffy, outdated life jacket. Being the boss had to have at least some small perks.

"Okay, everybody ready?" Leone said.

Jennette held up one finger.

"Gimme a minute. I've gotta get a hold of Anita—tell her to call for backup."

"Working with the Coast Guard—yeah!" Leone's face lit up, and he pumped one arm.

"Relax, Cowboy." Jennette punched in numbers. "If we get anyone, it will be the Clallam County Sherriff's Office. Hopefully, their marine unit. Less bureaucracy and a whole lot less paperwork than calling in the Guard." She pressed the phone to her ear.

"Anita. Listen." She scrunched down behind the windshield to talk while motioning to Leone to get on with things.

"Okay, Sheriff," Leone said, "I'm going to untie the bowline. Soon as I get back in the cockpit, you release the stern. Make sure to pull the line in fast."

Neil Edward ground his teeth. He bent low, kept his head down, and edged hand-over-hand the short distance from the helm to the stern. The task of releasing lines was part of an annual Blessing of the Fleet ceremony and Neil Edward's civic duty. So, while he did know a few things about boats, the experience in his grandfather's canoe—so long ago—had permanently put him off water voyages.

When he reached the aft cleat, Neil Edward turned to give Leone a thumbs up, but the deputy had already crawled forward on his stomach to the bow. He'd untied the line, pulled it onboard, secured it, and slithered back to the cockpit on his stomach.

With one final look to shore—to the siren call of dry clothes, warmth, and solid ground—Neil Edward released the line, pulled it into the boat, and turned toward the helm. Leone jammed the throttle forward. The vessel's sudden acceleration thrust Neil Edward backward. He fell hard onto his rump. He gave a quick glance to the front of the boat.

Jennette bent forward, one finger in her left ear, the cell pressed against her right. The phone call spared Neil Edward from a second round of embarrassment.

According to a Chamber of Commerce brochure, the distance from Otter's Run to Vancouver Island was about twenty-six nautical miles—a ninety-minute ride by slow boat on a calm day. Building in time for wildlife sightings and photoshoots, most small whale-watching vessels budgeted over two hours to cruise the scenic route around the Strait of Juan de Fuca. Because international laws required strict clearance procedures, the boats didn't stop on the island or even venture into Canadian waters. Still, they cruised close enough for tourists to admire stunning views of British Columbia. The return trip was generally a straight-line route back to port because, by that time, most passengers were ready to switch modes from nature watching to eating and drinking at the pub in town.

This wasn't a calm day, but on the other hand, Leone's boat wasn't slow. Neil Edward guessed his deputy would take the straight-line route.

"So, we should meet up with the *Hattie Belle* in an hour? Maybe a little less?" Neil Edward yelled over the roar of the huge twin engines. His fingers locked around the canopy rail as the boat fought waves. His body warped one way, then the other, and his arm muscles twisted in pain.

Leone leaned forward, gripped the wheel tight, and peered through the heavy rain pelting the dashboard windows.

"Yeah, about that, I guess." A wide grin split his face—his eyes gleamed. He echoed Jennette's earlier enthusiasm.

"Isn't this the best time ever? Fighting crime on the high seas. Yeeee haaaa!"

"Got that right!" Jennette dropped the phone into the duffel at her feet. Despite the cover offered by the boat's dash and flimsy canopy, the wind dried and filled the light fabric of her skirt, and a multi-colored parachute billowed around her. She clutched a rail with one hand and struggled to hold her skirt down with the other.

"Law enforcement at its finest!" Her grin matched Leone's.

Neil Edward kept his legs wide and his knees slightly bent. He'd stashed his hat under Jennette's chair—wind and salt spray stung his eyes. How could anyone think this cold, wet ride was anything other than body-slamming, mind-numbing, misery?

52

Jake leaned against a pole for support. He rubbed his bare arms as he made a visual sweep of the cabin.

Boxes and trash bags from lunch now littered the floor under the aft bench where Tyler stretched on his back, one arm over his eyes—probably feeling nauseous again—probably trying to hold off another round.

Kevin continued to entertain the children with silly antics. Except for Amanda, the kids seemed to enjoy his clowning—the motion of the boat and the frightening events of the past hour perhaps forgotten, at least for the moment. Tamara kneeled in front of Lexie and helped the little girl pull her sweatshirt hood out from under her life jacket.

Jake focused on the child who sat by herself with her back to the wall, her feet out straight, her eyes closed. Amanda's breathing came both labored and shallow, and though her skin was pale, she lacked the tinge of someone suffering from sea-sickness. Even violent bouts of *mal de mer* were rarely fatal. Severe asthma attacks are. The timetable had changed.

Tamara stepped close to Jake. She kept her voice low, her eyes were wide, her skin flushed.

"Conrad's missing. He was here a second ago—he was filming Kevin and the other children. Now I can't find him."

Jake shot a look toward the companionway. The heavy sliding doors were closed, and the aft deck stood empty. He eased forward, keeping his back against the hull until adjacent to the helm—tried to get closer without Spike's notice. Tamara stayed by his side.

"Not many places to hide. Maybe he went to the bathroom. I'll check," he whispered.

"No. Wait. There he is." Tamara gestured toward a small space under the dashboard. Conrad squatted low—almost hidden from view. He aimed his cell phone upward.

"*Hattie Belle. Hattie Belle. Hattie Belle.* This is the *Steilacoom Witch.* Come in. Over."

The radio's crackling static drew Jake's attention to the helm station and to Spike, who sat hunched forward in the captain's chair. Spike's eyes swung from Denny to the instruments on the dash, to the rain-streaked windows, and back to Denny at the wheel. A spiral of smoke drifted from his cigarette.

Jake followed Spike's gaze to the glowing instruments on the dashboard. On the destroyer, he'd learned to read some of the tangles of lines, dashes, and arrows on digital charts. Now, those symbols spelled out Denny's unspoken plan. Somehow Denny must have tricked Spike into thinking the *Hattie Belle* was heading toward Vancouver Island. But while there was no text, or even a landmass showing on the chart, the digital compass glowed with a steady red S, which could only mean south. South to the marina, south to safety.

"*Hattie Belle, Hattie Belle.* This is the *Steilacoom Witch.* Come in." Again, the scratchy static-broken voice. This time more urgent.

Denny leaned forward to grab the mic.

"Leave it," Spike said.

"We should answer them."

"No." Spike slid off the chair, dropped his cigarette on the floor, and stepped on it. The butt landed a foot from Conrad. "We ain't talking to nobody."

Jake watched as Denny glimpsed down at the dirty smudge of tobacco on the otherwise spotless, gray floor. The captain's eyes narrowed, and he pressed his lips in a thin line.

"*Hattie Bell.* This is the *Steilacoom Witch.* Are you experiencing difficulties? Repeat. You guys got problems over there?"

"We should answer them," Denny repeated. His voice tight—strained. "Everybody sticks together out here. If they think something's wrong, they'll come over."

"Fuck 'em." Spike squinted at the dashboard. "Where are we?"

"We're right here," Denny said. He pointed to an open area on the chart.

"Means squat to me," Spike said.

"Where is Canada on that thing?"

A wave rolled under the bow lifting the boat and setting it down with a tremor. The starboard door slid open as the radio crackled again. Jake felt a blast of cold air rush over him.

"Denny, this is Clint. Pick up, man. Over."

"I'm serious," Denny looked toward the open door. A couple of hundred yards away, a smaller boat rode the churning waves on a course parallel to the *Hattie Belle.*

"That's one of the boats in our fleet. They expect an answer."

Spike let go of the dash, swayed once, and straightened.

"Are you listening to me? What part of fuck 'em don't you get?"

"Hey, Denny. Come in. Repeat. You there, Den?"

Conrad scooted from his hiding place, stood, and panned the room. He pointed to something floating on the water, and aimed his cell phone at the object.

"Hey, look—I think he's hurt."

Spike walked to the window. He peered where Conrad pointed. A mat of mottled gray and white feathers slicked the bird's limp body. One wing stretched open—if the sea had been the sky, the gull would have soared. But it dropped under salty foam and then rose with the swell of a wave. Its slender neck, broken.

"Dead bird. It don't matter. We all die. Every fuckin' one of us dies. You're lucky if you go quick."

"Can you say that again? But without the bad word?" Conrad panned away from the window and trained his phone on Spike.

Spike swiveled to stare down at him.

"Hey, no videos. Gimmie that phone."

Conrad jumped back, out of Spike's reach, and whipped the phone behind his back.

"Who the hell are you, anyway?" Spike said.

"I'm Conrad Huffington. The third. I'm a photojournalist."

Spike snorted.

"Yeah, right. Photojournalist. Right." He returned his attention to the screen, craned his neck, and yelled toward the aft bench.

"Tyler! Get your ass up here. Take a look at this map."

Tyler didn't move, but Kevin wove to the helm, stood next to Spike, and stared at the screen. Jake moved closer—striving to be silent, invisible, to avoid looking at Spike's jacket pocket.

"Wait a minute," Spike turned back to Conrad. "Why the hell are you taking all those videos?"

"I'm filming this for the Ruth Hudson Elementary News channel. This is my best report ever." Conrad swiveled the cell phone toward Spike.

Spike pulled a cigarette from the pack in his inside pocket.

"Stop that shit and go sit down."

Conrad didn't budge.

"You can't stop me," he said. "I have a right to report the news."

Spike slipped the cigarette behind his ear.

Jake tensed.

Spike moved away from the helm and towered over Conrad.

Conrad resumed filming, rotating his cell phone to follow Spike's movement.

"What are you? Like seven?"

"I'm eight," Conrad said, "eight and a half next month."

"I don't give a shit if you're eighty next month. I said stop with the video."

"Spike, leave him alone. He's just a little kid." Kevin pushed between the two.

"Fuck off." Spike jabbed Kevin's chest with two fingers.

Kevin stayed in place.

"Spike, you're a butt. A butt and a big bully. Leave the little guy alone."

Conrad slipped from behind Kevin.

"You can't stop the free press," he said. "People are watching this—important people. Like the librarian. You can't stop freedom of the press." He continued filming as he talked.

Spike glared down at Conrad.

"What are you saying? People are watching this?"

"I already told you. My videos are broadcast live to the school's channel. When this story breaks, I'll be famous. Like my dad!"

"Gimmie that, you little shit." Spike grabbed the phone from Conrad's hand and pitched it through the open door. The phone soared from the boat, splashed down, and sank.

Conrad wailed.

Spike turned toward the boy.

Kevin wedged between them and held his arms wide.

"Spike, you jerk! Leave him alone."

"Move it."

Tamara dashed around the men, swooped Conrad in her arms, and spun away.

Jake moved fast—pushed Kevin aside. He faced Spike. There was no fear in Spike's eyes. No uncertainty, no desperation. Only a hollow-eyed stare. A stare like the one Jake had seen first in the gym, and later in the police photo. The photo of the tweaker who'd pummeled his girlfriend's newborn, stuffed the tiny dead body into a KFC bucket, and pitched it into a dumpster.

Jake drew back for a punch.

Spike jammed his hand into his jacket pocket.

Jake held his hands up, palms open. He took one step toward Spike.

"Look, Spike. What happened in that store was an accident. It's not fair for you to take the blame."

"Back off motherfucker." Spike pointed the gun at Jake's chest.

Jake locked eyes with him.

"I can help you."

"Against the wall. Now." Spike said.

Jake kept his hands up and backed away until his shoulders pressed against the port hull.

Kevin stepped forward.

"Spike," he said.

"What do you want?"

"I want you to get rid of that gun."

"You got no say in this, asshole."

"Spike, we hafta go back. Those kids are wet and cold, and that one little girl, I think she's having a asthma attack."

"We're not going back."

"But Spike, she needs a doctor. She needs one of those breather things."

"I don't give a flyin' fuck about those kids, and I don't give a shit about you." Spike turned from Kevin and waved the gun at Denny.

"You. Crank this thing up. We're takin' way too long. And where the hell are we?"

"We're um—" Denny said.

"No, Spike. You're gonna kill somebody. By accident 'cause you don't know what you're doing. You're a faker."

Spike leaned toward the dash and squinted at the blinking lights.

"I asked you, where the hell are we?"

Denny cleared his throat, glanced at the chart.

"We're about thirty minutes—"

A bubble of spit trembled on Kevin's lip. Sweat streaked his t-shirt.

"I said you're a faker, Spike. Everything you do is fake. Even your name is fake."

Spike stepped to the helm and pressed the gun's barrel against Denny's back.

"Last time, old man, where the fuck are we?"

Denny turned enough to look at Spike.

"We're a half-hour from Vancouver Island. Like I said before, there are rocks and sandbars along the shore, so there's no place to land, but I can get you close. Take the dinghy in."

Spike stepped back and lowered the gun. He slipped it into his pocket and reached for his cigarettes.

"Show me on the map."

Jake pushed from the wall. *Gun out of play.*

Spike spun to face him. A cold stare.

Jake retreated.

Denny started to point to the chart, but Kevin stepped between the helm and the dash.

"Get outta the way," Spike said.

"A loser and a faker, like Travis and your dad. Losers and fakers."

"I said move it."

"No. Spike. I mean, Eugene. Eugene Francis Drumthor."

Spike's punch landed hard. Blood spurted from Kevin's nose. Kevin dropped to his knees.

"Kevin!" Emily broke from the circle of children and stumbled across the cabin. She squatted beside Kevin.

"Emily, get back with your teacher!" Jake shouted.

"No, daddy, he's hurt. He's my friend, and he's hurt."

"*Hattie Belle, Hattie Belle, Hattie Belle.* This is the *Steilacoom Witch.* We're call—"

"Shut the fuck up!" Spike shrieked at the radio. He grabbed the mic from the holder and yanked it from the dash. Whirling around, he threw the mic across the cabin—it smashed against the edge of a bench and splintered into shards of plastic and copper bits.

"Repeat. We are calling to request assistance for you. *Steilacoom Witch,* standing by." The crackling sound persisted through the radio's speaker.

"Fuck you!" Spike's eyes, black beads—his skin, ash. He ripped the gun from his pocket.

Jake dove over Emily and Kevin—covered them with his body.

Denny ducked behind the helm.

Spike pulled the trigger.

Sparks blazed, children screamed, smoke billowed from the dash. Once blinking lights and screens—black.

The stench of gun powder.

54

Neil Edward leaned as close to his deputy as possible without losing his grip on the canopy rail. He strained to duck low enough to see through the skiff's Plexiglas windshield. "How much further?"

Leone pointed across the water. In the distance—to the northeast of Leone's path, two dark shapes emerged from the foamy haze.

"That's them," he said. "The one with the kids is the *Hattie Belle*. And the other one—the *Steilacoom Witch*—that's Clint Tuckerson's boat. We'll be there in a flash."

Jennette glanced back at Neil Edward.

"You okay?" she said.

Neil Edward flipped a thumbs up—a lie. He was not okay. Not okay at all. Wet to his bones and cold even deeper. His arm muscles screamed—twenty-five minutes hanging from the aluminum rail had almost pulled them from their sockets. His legs wobbled—barely held him upright, and he knew that his knees would be sore for weeks. At times, the skiff cut through waves. At other times, it jumped—air-borne—slammed down to the surface with a smack. Standing in Leone's skiff, this ride was worse than the ride he'd endured when he'd broken the meanest bronco ever born. And that was over forty years ago. No question, it would take a whole lot more than a massage to ease his pain this go around. But at least the rain had slowed, and visibility was better—clear enough to see the outlines of the two boats in the distance.

Leone slowed the skiff—a flush of water swarmed the hull only two inches away from spilling over the sides and swamping the small boat.

"Radio check. Radio check. Radio check. *Steilacoom Witch* over."

With the skiff's engine no longer at a full-out roar, the call's static crinkle became audible.

Deputy Leone grabbed the mic.

"*Steilacoom Witch*. This is the Otter's Run Deputized Marine Vessel. You're loud and clear."

"That you, Leone?"

"Ten-four." Leone slipped the gear shift into low and nudged the skiff through the waves.

Neil Edward looked at Jennette. He mouthed the words.

"Deputized Marine Vessel? Ten-four?"

She glanced at Leone and rolled her eyes.

"Well, listen, Buddy, I've been trying to raise the *Hattie Belle* for the last half hour or so. They aren't answering. I wasn't sure if my unit was working or not, but since it is, I'm worried about him. It's not like Denny to ignore a radio call. Over."

Jennette reached down and grabbed her canvas duffel bag. She slid off the chair and patted the seat. Neil Edward started to refuse, but she wrinkled her nose and stuck out her tongue as she pushed past him. He had no idea what Jennette was up to, but he was too rattled to argue with her. He eased onto the vinyl seat and sighed. A wave of relief washed over him.

On the radio, a green light flashed—Clint was transmitting, but the radio hissed and crackled so much that his words scrambled in the static. While Leone fiddled with the controls, he glanced toward the rear of the skiff.

"What's she doing back there, Boss?"

Neil Edward swiveled the seat to face aft. Jennette had wedged herself between the hull and two fuel cans. She stood on her right leg—her back to the men—her left leg propped on the edge of the transom. She hunched over—her skirt pulled high over one thigh. Neil Edward rotated the chair forward.

"I don't know, Leone. Maybe it's best not to ask," he said.

"You copy that?" The voice came through again.

"No. Had to switch channels. Repeat. Over"

"We were heading back—the whole fleet. We were planning to grab a beer later—Denny's shout—but something changed, and he reversed course. I watched on the radar for a while, and when he turned south again, I figured no big deal. Figured he saw something—a seal or something. Figured he'd give his passengers one last chance to see wildlife. But after about a quarter of an hour, I noticed he wasn't on the radar anymore, and when I couldn't raise him, I decided to turn around—look for him—see if he needed help. Like I said, it's not like Denny to ignore a radio call. Over."

Neil Edward nudged Leone.

"Ask him about his passengers. How do they feel about staying out longer in this weather?"

Leone relayed the message.

"I was worried about that at first, but it's a small group today. College kids. I told 'em we were going to help out another vessel, so we'd have a short delay getting back. My mechanic broke out our secret stash of Coors and a couple bags of pretzels. They're happy campers. Over."

Leone turned toward Neil Edward.

"Boss, I got a bad feeling about this. You sure Jennette called for backup? I mean, it's just you and me and," he lowered his voice, "old peg-leg back there. She's gutsy, for sure, but we might need a little more firepower—if you get what I mean."

Neil Edward shifted slightly for a better view of the two boats.

"Don't worry about Jennette. Besides, if she said she called for backup, she called for backup. But I sure wish I knew what was happening on that boat."

The green light flashed again.

"Hey Leone, I'm gonna drop our dink and go over there—see what's going on. Over."

"Wait." Neil Edward leaned forward and motioned for his deputy to hand him the mic.

"How do I do this? Three calls to the other vessel before talking?"

"It's just us, the *Steilacoom Witch*, and the *Hattie Belle*, now. Nobody else in range, Boss. You can skip the formalities and talk—that's Clint. He's cool. He's the captain of the *Witch*. Great guy. Drinking buddy. Good boat handler too."

Neil Edward clicked the mic switch.

"Clint, this is Sheriff Neil Edward Longcarver on the, um, Otter's Run Deputized Marine Vessel. Can you hear me?"

"Loud and clear, Sheriff. Only this is Bob Fields—I'm the mechanic on the *Steilacoom Witch*. Clint, he's in the back gassing up the dinghy motor. What can I do ya for, Sheriff?"

"Okay, Bob, tell your captain—tell Clint—to hold off. There are children on that boat, and we have reason to believe there are at least three, possibly four men who have boarded illegally. We also have reason to believe that at least one of the men is armed. We don't know the entire situation yet, and I don't want anyone getting hurt. We're almost there, so get Clint to hold off until we reach you."

"Too late, Sheriff. On account of he's already on his way."

Neil Edward swore under his breath. He handed the mic to Leone.

"We've got to—" He stopped mid-sentence when Jennette leaned against the back of his chair. She pressed her hand on his shoulder.

"Look, Boss. I think we've got some real trouble," she said.

Both men looked to where Jennette pointed. They were close enough now to see a small dark speck speeding across the water between the two vessels. And they were close enough now to see that while one boat appeared steady despite the rolling waves, plumes of dark smoke billowed from the other.

55

Travis rattled the bars on the cell door.

"Hey, you old bat. Get me something t' eat. I get meals. Three squares. I know my rights, ya skinny bitch. And hurry up! I die of starvation, and it's on your ugly ass." He waited a beat, spit on the floor, and rattled the bars again.

Anita pressed the phone receiver tight against her ear to muffle Travis's rant. She'd left the door to the cell area open to keep an eye on the prisoner, but now she regretted the move.

"We want to be sure those children are alright. And who's in charge? Does the sheriff have this under control?" the caller said.

Anita went for calm, professional.

"Yes, absolutely. The sheriff is in charge, and we—he has this completely under control. You can rest assured, Sheriff Long-carver is a veteran law enforcement officer, and he's doing everything by the book."

The caller fussed another minute. Anita listened for a few seconds before interrupting. "Thank you so much for your concern. We'll call you if we need any more input. Thank you. Good-bye." She hung up and exhaled.

That had to be the tenth call about the boat with a load of school kids. The rumors were spreading fast. So far, her favorites were that the Russians had kidnapped American children to hold Washington, D.C., hostage. And that the second graders were being taken to Canada aboard the whale-watching boat to be sold as sex slaves to tourists in Vancouver. Finally, the captain got lost in the San Juan Islands in the storm and was waiting for the U.S. Coast Guard to rescue them. The last rumor might have made sense if Anita didn't know about Captain Denny and his superior boating skills—no way would that man get lost at sea.

"Hey! Bitch, I am talkin' to you! Get me food, or my lawyer will sue your ass."

Anita pressed her lips together and took a deep breath. She glanced toward the cell. That foul-mouthed cretin needed to be taught a lesson, but how to do it was the question. The sheriff had been clear—no executive decisions. She was only to answer the phones and take messages. Period. But she had to shut the criminal up—his caterwauling was giving her a headache, and besides, what if a member of the public dropped by and witnessed his disgusting behavior? It might reflect poorly on her new place of employment. Well . . . volunteer employment.

Anita considered her options. Close the door and ignore him? Address the food issue? March in there and give him a piece of her mind? She straightened her shoulders and walked across the office to confront the prisoner.

"'Bout time. You got a hearing problem? I been yellin' at ya forever. I'm starving in here."

"Well, sir, it's Mr. Drumthor, I believe, right? Much as I'd like to accommodate you—maybe order you a pizza or a nice big juicy burger and fries, or something more fitting for an important man like yourself—" She sighed and held her palms up. "Truth is, my hands are tied. I'm only here to answer the phones while the sheriff and his deputy are on a call. I don't have the authority to make executive decisions, which means I can't help you."

"Fuck. Feedin' a guy don't require no executive decision, lady." Travis scratched his belly and spat on the floor again.

"So now I'm a lady, eh?" Anita said.

"Well, yeah. I'm sorry about calling you a bitch. Ain't your fault—probably—that this shit hole town's got old maids running the police station. They probably don't even have enough bucks to feed the saps they arrest—probably have to send for supplies from Port Angeles, or shit, maybe from the rez." He scratched his belly again.

"Damn, I'm hungry."

"Hmm, let me see if there is anything I can do for you." Anita scrunched her face as if in deep thought. She snapped her fingers. "I've got an idea. Wait right there," she said.

Anita dumped the contents of her bag on Jennette's desk—her phone, a collection of free bumper stickers, a box of hair coloring, three catnip mice from the Dollar Store for Mr. Snivels, a pair of sneakers, and two books from the give-one-take-one lending library. She found it at the bottom of the bag—lunch for Mr. Travis Drumthor. At least while she was in charge, Travis's only meal would consist of one wounded banana and three-fourths of a granola bar. She'd planned on freezing the banana for muffins down the line. The granola bar had been too stale to finish. Maybe not what the sheriff would have fed the prisoner, but on this one small matter, Anita made an executive decision.

"What the fuck is this?" Travis squeezed the banana between his thumb and finger. Brown goo oozed from a slit in the peel.

"Fruit," Anita said. "It will build up your strength for when you and your lawyer present your case."

Travis grunted.

"The power bar has protein and fiber. In case you need, you know, fiber."

Travis squeezed the banana in one fist and the granola bar in the other. He turned and shuffled to the bunk.

The office phone rang again. Anita held up one finger. "I have to get that, Mr. Drumthor. I'll be right back."

Though Travis seemed focused on peeling the banana and was not looking at her, she gave him a quick nod then hustled out of the cell area. She closed the door behind her.

"Otter's Run Sheriff's Office. Deputy Anderson here."

"Deputy Anderson, I'm Leslie Brody at the Ruth Hudson Elementary, and on behalf of—"

As Anita listened to the caller, she reached for a message pad and pen, but she stopped short of making any notes. After a few minutes, she glanced at the clock. For sure, the Clallam County Sheriff's Office would have organized their team by now. For sure, help was speeding toward the sheriff at that very moment.

" . . . so, we hope to have a law enforcement representative come and reassure the parents and the staff. Is that possible?"

For the second time in less than an hour on the job, Anita Anderson made an executive decision.

"Yes, of course," she said. "We're always happy to meet with those we serve and protect. I'll be there in," she glanced at her watch, "about ten, maybe fifteen minutes. See you soon."

Before locking up, Anita looked in at the prisoner. She hadn't heard a peep from him for a while. Travis lay on his back, eyes shut, snoring. One hand clutched the rotten banana peel, and the other wedged down his pants. Anita rolled her eyes, stepped back, and closed the door.

A tall woman met her at the Ruth Hudson Elementary School door and shook Anita's hand.

"Leslie Brody. Thanks for coming so quickly."

"No worries. We, at the Otter's Run Sheriff's Office, want to do everything we can to assure our citizens are safe." Anita had switched out her rhinestone-studded hat for a dark blue baseball cap with the embroidered initials O.R.S.O. with the hope that the Washington State lapel pin, plus the official cap, would give her more authority—more control.

Leslie led Anita to a crowded conference room humming with anxious voices. Anita counted fourteen men and women wearing "GUEST" badges and four women who stood off to one side—teachers, Anita guessed. At the head of a long oak table, a squat man in a rumpled suit whispered in the ear of a well-coiffed man who wrung his hands as he listened. A woman with a microphone and a man wielding a large video camera jockeyed for position among the others. When the cameraman turned to pan the room, Anita saw Five Alive's familiar logo. She squeezed her shoulders back and stood straighter.

"Excuse me, excuse me. May we have your attention, please?" Leslie cleared her throat and waited for the group to hush.

"Thank you all for coming. And now, we will hear from our headmaster." She turned to the hand-wringing man in the expensive suit. He cleared his throat and stood.

"Parents, I know you are concerned—the video posted this morning was confusing, but rest assured, the faculty and staff at Ruth Hudson Elementary hold the safety and welfare of your children as our top priority. To that end, we've alerted the local law enforcement about our concerns, and we've invited a representative of the Sheriff's Office to speak with us regarding the situation. Ms. Brody will introduce our guest."

Leslie Brody introduced Anita—Deputy Anita Anderson—and requested that everyone hold their questions until the end of the briefing.

Anita attempted to spin a "we have everything under control" speech, but before she could finish what she'd practiced during the drive over, the questions and comments started. They were shouted fast and loud and filled with anger and fear. Some of the questions were directed to Anita, others to the headmaster.

"What are you people doing about this?"

"She's a first-year teacher—why didn't you send a more senior person along?"

"Why are there strangers on that boat?"

"Did you call the Coast Guard?"

"What about the F.B.I.?"

"You're going to hear from my lawyers."

The headmaster didn't answer any of them. He simply turned to Anita for her input.

Anita did her best. She'd organized—and participated in—dozens of community meetings and public hearings, and she knew a thing or two about angry citizens. The more questions they flung at her, the more confident she became. While she didn't lie, she exaggerated the Sheriff's Office's efforts—made it sound like there was a well-oiled team handling every aspect of the current situation. The truth was, according to what she'd heard from Jennette, nobody had a clue what was going on.

Anita only knew two things for sure—first, she'd made the call to the Clallam County Sheriff's Office and had requested back-up. Second, Sheriff Longcarver, one full-time deputy, and one part-time volunteer deputy were heading across the Strait, in rough weather, in a small, aluminum skiff.

It wasn't much, but it was enough for Anita to spin the news.

Forty minutes later, on the drive back to the sheriff's office, Anita reviewed her performance. From her perspective, she'd calmed an angry mob, soothed anxious families, and appeased an antagonistic attorney. Maybe she was wasting her talents in her role as a concerned citizen. The deputy—Volunteer Deputy—job could very well be the steppingstone to something much bigger, much more important. She pulled into Neil Edward's parking spot. For a few moments, before returning to the job of answering phones, Anita Anderson sat in her Camry, closed her eyes, and dreamed of great things.

56

For a moment, Jake stayed still—so still that even with the boat's rolling, he could feel Emily's breathing, and even with the stink of the smoking rubber and hot wires, he could smell Kevin's fear. He turned his head enough to see Spike standing in front of the helm wearing a cocky half-grin.

Jake pushed up and brushed bits of plastic and metal from his shoulders. He reached for Emily's hand and helped her sit. A streak of blood smeared her face. Jake wiped her cheek with his thumb—her skin wasn't cut—the blood wasn't hers. Emily looked up at him with a brave smile. Jake gave her a quick hug, and glanced down at Kevin.

The teenager remained immobile, curled to almost fetal. He held his eyes shut tight and breathed through his mouth. A thin line of blood trickled from his nose.

Jake twisted around in time to see Denny grab the edge of the helm and pull himself to standing.

"You ignorant piece of dirt," Denny said. His voice came out in a growl. "You messed with my girl. I've had enough of you." He moved toward Spike with both fists raised.

Spike spun and slammed the gun against Denny's temple. Denny went down, his right leg twisted, buckled. He landed on his knee and shrieked.

Jake pushed Emily down and leaped to standing—he lunged at Spike.

Spike made a pivot and pointed the gun at Jake.

"Stop it right there, asshole. Take one more step, and I'll do you like I did that fucking radio."

Jake halted. Spike had pointed the gun at him before, but this time, something was different. Despite the sweat slicking Spike's face, he showed a different sort of calm. A different kind of confidence.

"Spike! What the fuck?" Tyler pushed himself from the floor. He rushed to the helm.

Denny lay curled on his side. Groaning, he held both hands wrapped around his knee, a dark lump already forming on his temple.

Spike took two steps back. He gripped the gun with both hands and scanned the cabin.

"Now listen to me—all of you. I'm in charge here. Anybody got a problem with that?" He slowly panned the room, pointing the gun at each adult for a moment before moving on. No one spoke.

"That's what I thought. So, here's what's gonna happen—" He waved the gun at Tamara. "You're gonna get all your brats together and stay over there, against the wall. And I don't want to hear any talkin' or cryin' or anything. Got that?"

Tamara stood still and stared at Spike.

"And gimmie your phone. You ain't gettin' any more calls."

Tamara walked to the helm. She maintained eye contact with Spike as she slid her cell from her back pocket and handed it to him. With a quick look at Jake, she retreated.

As he'd done with Conrad's, Spike sent Tamara's phone flying through the open door.

He turned to Kevin.

"Fat Ass, you go with her. I'm done with you."

Kevin stood and took Emily's hand. He wiped his bloody nose with his other hand and then wiped it on his shirt. He and Emily stumbled across the cabin.

Spike pointed the gun at Denny.

"Okay, Gramps. You program that GPS to take us to Canada. And don't give me any shit about sandbars or crab pots. Got that?"

Denny had managed to sit up, but he continued to hold his knee between both hands.

"I can't do that because you shot the instruments. Nothing will work now."

"Shit!" Spike stomped his foot and spun around. "God damn it. Fuck." His face blanched white, his eyes narrowed. He paced and mumbled.

Jake caught Tamara's eye. She'd clustered the children tight together against the port wall under the window. She and Kevin sat close together in front of them. They'd formed a two-bodied human shield.

Jake ground his teeth but forced himself to slow his breathing. He needed to calm Spike, or it would be impossible to get the gun away.

Spike stopped pacing. He stood over Denny and spoke to Tyler.

"Tyler. You take this loser to the back and tie him to the bench. Take his phone and toss it. If he gives you any shit, knock his ass overboard too."

Tyler started to speak, but Spike cut him off. For the third time, he pointed the gun at Jake.

"You. You're gonna drive this boat to Canada—and you're gonna step on it, and you're not gonna try anything funny. 'Cause if you do, I'm gonna shoot a kid. Maybe I'll shoot your kid. And don't for one fucking minute think I won't. Got that?"

Jake forced himself to remain perfectly calm—perfectly controlled. He stepped to the wheel. He'd watched Denny enough to have a general idea of what to do. He found the gear shift and moved it from neutral to forward. The engine growled with the shift. Jake pushed the throttle. The *Hattie Belle* rocked from side to side and then moved forward. He added more fuel, the boat steadied and picked up speed. He turned the wheel with the small, wedge-like movements he'd seen Denny use. As if in a dance, the

Hattie Belle twirled in a semi-circle until Jake held the wheel firm. The compass now pointed north.

"Okay." Spike backed off a few more steps and leaned against the starboard window. "You keep heading to Canada, and don't forget what I said about those kids—about your kid."

57

When the bullet struck the electronics, the windshield wipers halted mid-swipe dividing the windows with two diagonal stripes. A serious problem if the heavy rain had continued, but now only a drizzle tapped the glass. Jake squinted through the salt-crusted panes. Dark clouds drifted away leaving a patch of pale blue in their wake, and while the water still churned and salty froth capped confused waves, the sea was calming—the storm was clearing.

Jake checked the compass. They continued to head north despite his less than steady steering. He could hear Tamara shushing the children, and though he couldn't understand her words, he felt their soothing reassurance. Not everything, though, was settling down. Tyler was tying Denny to the aft bench, and Denny had to be in severe pain. Jake twisted to look aft.

"Eyes forward, asshole. You got one job, nothin' else." Spike stuck the gun under his armpit and pulled the cigarettes from his pocket. He lit one and peered at Jake.

Jake pursed his lips and faced the bow. He looked straight ahead at the waves slapping the *Hattie Belle*'s hull, but he kept Spike in his peripheral vision.

"So, Moose. Tyler says you ain't a mechanic. At least not a very good one." Spike made a snorting sound.

Though he'd only turned for a few seconds, Jake had seen a rubber dinghy bounding over the waves. *Fisherman? Guy checking crab traps? Someone taking their dog to shore for a pee break?* It didn't matter who was in that rubber boat or why they were there. It was only important that someone else was out on the water—someone who might be able to help them. Keep Spike talking—keep him distracted. Figure out how to hail the person in the dink with-out Spike knowing.

"Guess I'm in the wrong place at the wrong time. It's my life, if you catch my drift." Jake shrugged.

"Welcome to my world."

"So, why Canada? I'm guessing you didn't sign up to save the whales." Jake looked at Spike—tried to make eye contact—another distraction.

"Fuck the whales." Spike took a long drag, tilted his head back, and blew a perfect smoke ring. It floated above his head for a moment before ghosting away.

Keep him talking.

"So, what's so great about Canada?"

"Retard been talkin' to you?"

"He might have, but I don't usually listen to guys like that. Know what I mean?"

"He's an idiot," Spike said. "He probably don't even know what's happening. Bottom line, we were—" Spike stopped. He squinted at Jake. "It don't matter to you what we're doin'. You get this boat to Canada, then me and Tyler, we're outta here."

"You got family in Canada?" *Keep him distracted.* Keep him from looking toward the back, toward the rubber boat powering here.

"Fuck family." He took another drag, pitched the half-smoked cigarette out the door, and pulled the gun from under his arm. He pushed away from the window and stretched. He twisted at the waist and started to look aft.

Jake faked a slight fall from balance and jerked the wheel hard to port. The *Hattie Belle* paused her forward motion, then jolted left.

Spike grabbed for the helm chair and steadied himself.

"What the fuck are you doing?"

"Sorry. There was a crab pot. I was trying to go around it."

"Tell me next time you're gonna do something stupid. And fuck the crab pots—run 'em over." Spike pulled the pack from his jacket.

Jake risked a peek at the mirror above the windows. The rubber skiff was closer now, close enough for Jake to see the driver. Young guy, standing upright, legs wide. He held onto a long pole attached to the dinghy's throttle. Even from this distance, even from a reflection in the narrow strip of mirror, Jake could see the lines of concern etched on the man's face. *Did he suspect something was wrong? Was he on his way to the Hattie Belle?*

Spike scanned the cabin—his eyes narrow. Jake pointed to a stretch of land in the distance."

"Check it out," he said. "That must be Vancouver Island."

Spike followed Jake's gaze.

"About fucking time."

They stared at the land without speaking until something rammed the boarding platform.

"Spike! There's a guy in an inflatable behind us—he's trying to board." Tyler yelled from the companionway.

"Tell him to get lost," Spike said. He turned to Jake and held the gun even with Jake's face.

"This some kind of a trick?"

"How could it be a trick? I've been here, in front of you, the whole time. You've been pointing that gun at me forever. Right?"

"Spike, he wants to talk to the captain," Tyler said.

Spike turned to look toward the back—only for a few seconds but long enough for Jake to slide the gear shift into neutral. The *Hattie Belle* continued to glide forward.

"Get rid of the fucker. I gotta watch this guy. You handle it." Spike turned back to Jake, gripped the gun with both hands, and leveled it at Jake's chest. He stood braced against the side door and stared toward the aft deck.

Jake glanced at the mirror the moment Tyler swung an aluminum boat pole in a wide arc. The pole caught the dinghy driver on the side of his head. The man shrieked as he fell from the mirror's view. Jake heard a heavy thump—he swiveled aft—saw Tyler raise the boat pole with two hands and slam it down. Again, the man cried out.

Spike turned and glared at Jake.

"Drive."

Jake pushed the throttle forward. The old diesel roared—a good sound effect, but only inertia moved the *Hattie Belle*.

58

Neil Edward pointed across the water.

"There. At the stern."

Jennette fiddled with the binoculars—adjusted an eye piece. "Clint's in trouble. That kid smacked him in the head with some kind of pole. He fell—but I can't tell if he landed in the dingy or went overboard." She handed the binoculars to Neil Edward.

"What's happening now?" Leone asked.

Neil Edward squinted into the binoculars.

"The kid with the pole is in the dink. He's messing with the engine. No—wait. He just climbed out—he untied the line and pushed it off. I still can't tell if Clint's onboard." He pointed at the dingy now roaring away from the *Hattie Belle*.

"Leone, catch that—"

Before Neil Edward could finish his sentence, Leone slammed his vessel into forward and opened the throttle. The forward thrust knocked Neil Edward against the seat. He spun to grab Jennette, but her arms were already wrapped tight around the chair's back. She wasn't going anywhere.

The small rubber boat careened and smashed into the breakers while racing in wide circles. Neil Edward strained to find Clint, but staring through the binoculars while bounding over whitecaps at top speed brought that bite of scone back in a rush.

"Here." He tossed the binoculars to Jennette, leaned over the side, and heaved.

Leone turned downwind long enough for Neil Edward to go dry. Back on course, the deputy gave Jennette a quick grin. "Never spit, or piss, or puke, into the wind, right?"

Jennette grabbed Neil Edward's collar and pulled him back to the chair.

Leone resumed the chase. His skiff, bigger, faster, and under expert steering, overtook the smaller boat.

"Look!" Jennette clung to the canopy railing with one hand and pointed down at the dinghy. Clint lay sprawled on the aluminum floor. He appeared unconscious. His right arm wedged between the throttle and the gas can, steered the small vessel in circles.

"I'm gonna T-bone it, Boss. You gotta jump in and stop it," Leone yelled. He spun the skiff's wheel to starboard.

Neil Edward closed his eyes for a second, opened them, and took a deep breath. He slid across the chair and grabbed the edge of the skiff with both hands.

Leone eased back on the throttle as he steered around the small rubber vessel in ever-smaller circles.

Swinging his right leg over the skiff's side, Neil Edward reached for a rail and held on tight.

Jennette moved into the empty seat and grabbed his belt. She yelled into his ear.

"I gotcha. You tell me when you're ready to jump."

"Thanks." Keeping his rear lowered into the boat for ballast, he pulled his left leg over the edge. He glanced at the swirling water below. Big mistake. The taste of vomit rose. Neil Edward spit foam. He avoided looking down again but followed the dinghy as Leone circled closer and closer. Only a moment to jump into that moving target. Missing it meant he'd be fodder for two sets of knife-sharp spinning propeller blades—blades that would slice him to deli-meat in seconds.

Leone made a pass around the dinghy, slowed, and threw the skiff into reverse. It jerked and paused. The dinghy plowed into the skiff's side, lingered only a blink, bounced backward, rotated, and took off in another dizzy circle.

He'd missed it. Missed the moment to drop down and stop it. He stared at the retreating vessel and swore.

Leone shifted into forward. He goosed the gas and took off after the dinghy again.

Jennette continued to grip Neil Edward's belt. She pressed her chest against his back and spoke low in his ear.

"No whales here. It's just you, and me, and Leone, and a guy who needs your help."

Neil Edward turned his head enough to see her smile.

Leone made another pass around the dinghy.

"We're close, Boss. Ready?"

"Yeah, ready."

Several yards before they reached the dinghy, Leone threw his boat into reverse again. *Leone's Lady* slowed. As before, the rubber boat thumped against the side of the skiff and lingered for a second. Neil Edward shoved away from the skiff and dropped. He landed in the dinghy and flopped over the prone man. Raising to his knees, he pulled Clint's arm out from between the tiller and the gas can. He twisted the grip on the throttle, and the motor went from a roar to a purr.

"Cut it," Leone yelled.

Neil Edward pressed a button at the end of the throttle and cut the engine. With no forward motion, the dinghy rocked up and down, and for the third time, he fought rising nausea.

"Here, grab this," Jennette dangled a line over the edge of the skiff.

"Leone—you got him! Right on, man!" The radio hissed with Bob Field's voice. Behind him, cheers from the passengers aboard the *Steilacoom Witch* crackled over the airwaves.

"Sheriff Longcarver gets it done," Leone answered the radio call. He glanced at Jennette. She flashed him a smile.

"Is Clint alright? Over." Again, the *Steilacoom Witch*.

"Looks like a nasty gash, but he's breathing. We're gonna tow the dink over to you guys—get him onboard the platform. Over."

"Roger that. We're ready. Over."

After securing the dinghy to the skiff and after checking Clint's pulse, Neil Edward gave a thumbs up and sat cross-legged on the floor between the dink's bench and the motor. Lower center of gravity—less movement. The weight of the two men helped to steady the boat—kept it from bouncing. He slid a cushion under Clint's head as *Leone's Lady* towed the dinghy over the water. Twelve feet of rope separated the two vessels.

The ride to the *Steilacoom Witch* didn't take long. But long enough for Neil Edward to suck in deep breaths of cool, clean air and allow himself to calm—allow his muscles to relax.

The rain had stopped, and the dark clouds had drifted away. A hint of sunlight peeked through soft, white puffs against pale blue. He looked across the waves toward the shore. A small cove offered refuge for a sailboat resting at anchor. In the distance, someone ran a chainsaw. Closer, a dog barked.

They were almost to Vancouver Island—maybe they'd already crossed into Canadian waters. It occurred to him that even if backup from Port Angeles didn't arrive, the Canadian Coasties might be nearby. That meant paperwork, the hassles of international law, and the issue of jurisdiction, but he let that go. The Canadians were friendly, skilled, and efficient—he'd welcome their help, paperwork or not.

For the first time in six decades, Neil Edward felt at peace on the water. In that peace, he broke his promise to himself. He remembered the whale.

The creature swam straight for his grandfather's canoe—its sleek fin a gleaming black sail. A few feet from the vessel, the fin stopped. Neil Edward held his breath and stared as slowly—deliberately—the fin lowered flat to the water's surface, and the great black and white creature rolled to its side. One large, unblinking eye stared at Neil Edward. Neil Edward wet his pants.

The whale sank, almost soundless, below the surface. Nothing remained but a low swirl on the face of the sea.

When his heart finally stopped racing, Neil Edward knelt on the bottom of the canoe and copied his grandfather's motions. His paddling was not as graceful or as quiet, but with his best efforts, the canoe moved toward the beach.

His arms ached, and his knees hurt, but he kept swinging the heavy paddle from side to side—kept gliding the canoe forward. He heard someone call his name. Shadowed figures lined the shore. They would be his parents, his cousins, and maybe others too. Fear and exhaustion turned to shame. He knew he would have to tell them about the whale, but he could not let them see how afraid he'd been.

He looked over the edge of the canoe. In the pale moonlight, he thought he saw the shimmer of sand through shallow water. He grabbed the line tied to the bow and tumbled out of the vessel. Neil Edward had expected to land on his feet—to walk to shore pulling the canoe—to look brave and strong.

But the sea was deep, and when he dropped, the shock of the cold water slammed the air from his lungs. He gulped saltwater. Still gripping the line, he bobbed to the surface, kicking, and spitting, and coughing. His eyes stung, but he'd managed to hang tight to the line—to dangle in the frigid water until his father scooped him up.

The adults prepared a feast in honor of his bravery, and the elders told him over and over again how the whale was now his Spirit animal and how the whale would guide him and keep him strong and brave. But Neil Edward didn't feel brave—he felt shame. So, when he was old enough, he switched from canoes to horses and, later, to his black and white police cruiser.

A sharp whistle cut the sound of wind and sea. Jennette leaned over the stern of *Leone's Lady* and waved at him. Her face lit with a grin—her puffy skirt billowed around her legs. Clearly, she was enjoying every moment. Neil Edward waved back.

Jennette was the only one who knew his story. And he knew she would never tell.

59

Spike wiped the sweat from his brow and reached into his pocket. He dug through the crumpled pack—worked to extract a cigarette.

"Tyler, what the hell is going on? Get your ass up here."

"Man, we are so screwed." Tyler arrived at the helm, still holding the boat pole. His chest heaved—he panted for breath. A thin line of blood dripped down one side of the pole.

"Damn it," Spike said, "smokes got wet." He squinted at Jake. "You got any?"

Jake shook his head.

"Forget your stupid cigarettes, Spike. I'm not kidding—we're fucked."

Spike scowled at Jake and lit the damp cigarette. He eyed Tyler through a stream of smoke.

"What are you talking about? You got rid of the guy, right? He's not a problem. Besides, we're almost to Canada." Spike took a drag, blew smoke, and looked toward the open door.

"Yes, he is a problem, you asshole," Tyler said. "You don't get it. Another boat picked him up. A guy jumped into the dink, and he was wearing a uniform."

"What kind of uniform?"

"I dunno—he had a life-vest on, but what difference does it make? Coast Guard? Cops? Whatever. We're screwed."

"You're an asshole and a loser, Butterfield. You wanna rob a store—get cash to impress some bitch—but you don't wanna use guns. Hell, you didn't even wanna use masks. I should go by myself—leave you and that fat retard to go home and cry to your mamas." Spike spit on the floor.

"Fuck you and your bullshit, Spike. You don't know what you're doing—you don't even know how to use that gun. You probably killed that guy in the store, and if you keep waving that thing around, you're gonna kill someone on this boat. If you kill a little kid, we'll rot in prison just like your dad."

"Shut up."

"Your dad and Travis—they're both gonna die in prison. But you think they're such hot shit. You're the asshole looser, Drumthor."

The two stood face-to-face—two feet apart. Spike held his cigarette in one hand, the gun in the other. Tyler clenched his left fist—he gripped the boat pole in his right. Blood seeped between his fingers.

60

The dinghy bumped into the *Steilcoom Witch*. Three college-aged kids—two boys and a girl—and a guy in canvas coveralls helped Neil Edward secure the dinghy to the back of the larger vessel and then lift the unconscious man onto the boarding platform. They moved him into the boat's main cabin and stretched him out on a bench.

Leone pulled his skiff alongside the *Steilacoom Witch* and tossed a line to the ship's mechanic. Once the skiff was secure, he climbed over the bow onto the larger vessel. Jennette stayed onboard *Leone's Lady* and punched numbers on her cell phone.

"Your captain needs medical attention," Neil Edward said.

The mechanic pointed forward. "Take him to his cabin. I'll be down there in a minute to check him out."

"I took first-aid last term," the girl volunteered. "I can check stuff."

The mechanic eyed her for a moment.

"Okay. Go." He turned and extended his hand to Neil Edward. "Sheriff Longcarver. Bob Fields, mechanic for the *Steilacoom Witch*. Good to meet you in person."

"Wish the circumstances were different," Neil Edward said. He stepped onto the deck. Bob followed.

"So, Sheriff. What now?"

Neil Edward shielded his eyes against the bright sunlight.

"Now you get Clint to a doctor. I don't want to alarm your passengers, but he needs help—fast."

"What about you guys?"

"We've gotta get on that boat." Neil Edward turned toward the *Hattie Belle*. "Find out what's happening with those kids. Thing is, I don't know enough to make a solid call. Also, we need backup."

Bob scratched his head. "Well, we called the Clallam County Sheriff's Office for help. We figured their marine unit would come out right away."

"And?"

"And they said they got a call from someone in your office, but that was during the storm, and the line went dead part-way through the call. They've been calling your office for more information, but they haven't been able to reach anyone."

Neil Edward ran his hand through his wet hair and cleared his throat.

"Strange. We left a deputy in charge of the phones. Gotta hope she's not in trouble. He wavered a moment, then went on. "Time to get those passengers out of this area. We don't need any more civilians in harm's way. Stay in touch with Leone on the radio or his cell—I wanna know when your captain comes around, and when he does, what he can tell us. Got that?"

"Yes, sir. On it."

"And one more thing, Bob."

"Sir?"

"Call me Neil Edward, or Sheriff if you want. I need to borrow your dinghy for a while. That okay with you?"

"Yes, of course, sir—I mean Sheriff. I'll fill the tank and pull it around behind the skiff. Give me a few minutes—won't take long." Bob saluted, blushed, and thrust his hand behind his back.

"Much appreciated." Neil Edward entered the *Steilacoom Witch* and made his way to the starboard side where Leone had tied the skiff. With the help of one of the passengers, he dropped into *Leone's Lady*.

"Leone, come on. We're out of here."

"On my way, Boss."

Jennette touched his arm.

"Sheriff, while you were over there, I got through to my friend in the Clallam County Sheriff's Office. She said there was a delay—something about not getting through to our office. So, I don't know what that's about. But she said the video—the one with the wet kid and the big guy with his daughter, well, it's all over the news. At least the local news." Jennette caught her breath.

Neil Edward eyed his deputy.

"There's more, isn't there?"

"Yep. Also, on the broadcasts is our own, newly deputized Anita Anderson. Sounds like she's giving news briefs to the media and to the public."

Neil Edward groaned. He sat on Leone's helm chair.

"Well, at least she's okay. What else?"

"Well, this is good news. Clallam County is sending out their marine unit."

"Coast Guard?"

"My friend wasn't sure, but she thinks they're going to coordinate with the Canadians in case the boat is in international waters. Which, in my humble opinion, it is," Jennette said.

Leone leaned over the side of the *Steilacoom Witch*.

"Hey, Boss. Clint's awake now, and he's talking. He says he got a quick look inside the *Hattie Belle* before that kid hit him with the pole."

Neil Edward swiveled around in the helm chair and looked up.

"Well? Could he see what was happening? Could he tell if anyone was hurt?"

"He says he only got a glimpse, but they've got Denny tied to the aft bench—he says Denny didn't look so hot."

"Anything else?"

"Nope. Only he's pretty sure that the kid who hit him was taking orders from someone else—someone inside the *Hattie Belle*."

"Okay, if that's all we've got, it will have to do. Tell those guys, thanks. And, come back on board—we're going over there." Neil Edward looked across the water and then back at his deputy. "One more thing, Leone. Ask him if the kid who hit him was wearing a black leather jacket."

"One second, Boss." Leone ducked back into the wheelhouse. A moment later, he reappeared, climbed over the edge of the *Steilacoom Witch*, and dropped into the skiff.

"He says nope. The kid was wearing a t-shirt and jeans. Looked like he was covered in soot or something. But no jacket."

"Right. Well, it's something. Let's get going."

"Sheriff?" Again, Jennette laid her hand on his arm.

"Jennette?"

"We don't have much information, right?"

"Not enough."

"I've been thinking. You've got that kid's phone—the one our guest back at the station used for his one call, true?"

"Yeah."

"Well, why not call those boys? Figure out what they want. Maybe, and I'm not sayin' this is according to the book or anything, but maybe tell a little white lie?"

61

B-B-B-B-Bad B-B-B-B-Bad. Bad to the bone.

The ring tone broke the tension. Spike shifted the gun to his left hand and pulled the phone from his inside pocket.

"That's gotta be Travis. He musta found your phone. I'm gonna put him on speaker." He punched a button and held the phone toward Tyler.

"I don't wanna listen to your lame-ass brother." Tyler leaned the boat pole against the dashboard. He slid onto the helm chair, slumped back, and closed his eyes.

Jake exhaled—this was a bonus. Maybe Tyler wouldn't notice that the boat wasn't making headway—that it was slowly drifting closer to shore, riding the tide—but making no real progress. Good—keep it that way as long as possible.

"Travis. Hey, man. You ain't gonna believe the firepower in your piece. I mean, I blew the fuck outta this old tub. Big hole— over-the-top man."

Spike continued to hold the phone toward Tyler and waited— no answer on the other end.

"So, we're workin' a job here, and we're gonna need you to get us some cash and a ride." Again, he waited. Again, no answer.

"Travis? That you?"

A man at the other end of the line cleared his throat.

"Spike? Spike Drumthor?"

"Who the hell are you? Put Travis on."

"Spike, this is Sheriff Neil Edward Longcarver from the Ot- ter's Run Sheriff's Office. Your brother loaned us the phone."

"What the fuck? Where is Travis?"

Tyler jolted upright—stared at Spike.

"He's taking a little break—hanging out with us while we help him locate some missing items."

Jake continued to move the wheel as if he were steering—feigned indifference—hoped Spike would leave the phone on speaker.

"What do ya mean, missing items?"

Again, the caller cleared his throat.

"Oh, nothing much. But it does seem he's missing the keys to his car, and his driver's license, his wallet, and—" the man waited a beat, "one white sock."

"Fuck." Spike swore under his breath.

"Why are you calling me? I ain't got his keys, and I sure as hell don't got his sweaty old gym socks."

Jake looked out the starboard window—an aluminum skiff—some sort of recreational vessel with a small rubber dinghy tied behind, made lazy circles around the *Hattie Belle*. Could that be law enforcement? Or a fishing vessel? He knew he would face the consequences of boarding the *Hattie Belle*. Worse, he would face Marilyn's wrath. But the hope that trained officers might be close offered reassurance—increased the odds in his favor—increased his confidence. The children would be okay. Emily would be okay. At least, *he had to believe* that would be the case.

"Spike." The man's voice even—neutral. "I'm guessing you want something. Maybe you need something. So, maybe we can talk. Maybe we can work something out. Do what's fair all the way around. How does that sound?"

Tyler nodded and mouthed, yes.

Spike clicked the phone off speaker and pressed it to his ear. "Sounds like bullshit to me. Sounds like something a cop would say right before he busts your ass. Fuck off."

Spike hung up and crammed the phone back into his pocket. He looked at Jake.

"You. We almost there?"

Jake made a show of checking the compass and then looking out at the shoreline.

"Close," he said. "I'll have to start looking for places where we can pull in."

Spike wiped sweat from his upper lip.

"Yeah. You do that. And you do that in a hurry."

62

B-B-B-B-Bad B-B-B-B-Bad. Bad to the bone.

"What the fuck do you want now?" Spike yelled into the phone.

"Two things, Spike. I want to know if you have any injured people on board, and I want to know what you want—what you need. How can I help you?" Neil Edward said.

"No. We don't got no injuries." Spike glanced toward the back where Denny slumped against the ropes tying him to the bench. The captain's face was drawn and pale. His eyes were closed.

"Well, nobody died if that's what you wanna know. What we want—me and my partner—is to get the fuck off this boat. In Canada. If you can't help us with that, we're done talkin'." Spike hung up again. He paced the four feet between the door and the dashboard until he noticed Tamara whispering in Kevin's ear.

"Hey, what's going on back there?" Spike looked toward Tamara and the children.

Tamara held onto Kevin's shoulders with both hands. When she pulled back—Kevin shook his head, no. Tamara leaned in again, and whispered again.

"I said what the fuck's going on?"

Kevin shambled across the cabin and stood in front of the helm—in front of Jake. If Jake *had* been steering, Kevin would have blocked his view.

"Ah, Spike?"

"What the hell are you up to?"

"We've got a problem." Kevin spit tiny bubbles as he spoke. His face blushed the color of bruised raspberries and gleamed slick with sweat. His nose had swollen to twice its size. A crust of dried blood clung to one nostril—a dark bruise formed under one eye.

"You're the problem, asshole," Spike said.

Kevin licked his lips. He shoved his hands into his pockets, pulled them out again and clasped them first behind his back, then in front of his belly.

"Spike, you have to hear this."

Spike glanced at Jake—watched him continue to turn the wheel in small motions—then glared at Kevin.

"You got two minutes before I punch your face again. This time, it will hurt."

Kevin swallowed, glanced toward the back of the boat, and took a ragged breath.

"There's a girl back there who's real, real sick, Spike. She's got asthma—bad. She can't breathe."

"Not my problem."

"Spike. She's a little girl, and she might die if she doesn't get a breather thing. It is your problem."

Tyler slid from the chair.

"Spike, Kev is right. If that kid dies, there is no place on earth we can hide—not Canada, not even Russia. We're totally fucked."

"What do you want me to do about it?" Spike took up pacing again.

B-B-B-B-Bad B-B-B-B-Bad. Bad to the bone.

"God damn it," Spike said, "it's that fucking cop again."

B-B-B-B-Bad B-B-B-B-Bad. Bad to the bone.

"Answer it, Spike—maybe we can get him to take the girl or something." Tyler nodded to the phone.

B-B-B-B-Bad B-B-B-B-Bad. Bad to the bone.

Spike answered.

"What?"

"Spike, look, I know you want to go to Canada. I get it. Smart call. You have a plan. And you can do that, but you have to cross an international border, and you're going to need some help getting in. I can help you. But first, I need to know about the injured people on board. I know you've got at least one person hurt. Any others?"

Spike hit mute.

"How the fuck does he know about that guy?" He looked toward the back—toward Denny.

"Maybe that guy who was trying to climb on the boat saw him. If he did, that means I didn't kill him." Tyler wiped a slick of sweat from his forehead.

"It doesn't matter," Kevin said. "Tell him about the little girl who can't breathe. Tell him about Amanda."

Spike took a deep breath and hit Unmute. "Look, we got a guy with a few bruises—nothin' big. And some kid who's havin' a asthma attack. She lost her inhaler. But that's all. Now, what are you gonna do for me?"

"Thanks, Spike," Neil Edward said. "I'm gonna see what I can do for you. Give me five minutes, okay?"

Spike turned to Kevin. He raised the gun.

"You got three."

63

Neil Edward tapped Tyler's phone off. His brow knit into tight lines.

"What?" Jennette leaned toward him. "What did he say?"

"It's not good," Neil Edward looked across the water to the *Hattie Belle*. "They've got a kid on board, a little girl, who's having an asthma attack. He says she's having trouble breathing." He stopped and took in a deep breath.

"Jennette, how long until the marine unit gets here?"

"She said about fifteen, maybe twenty minutes. They didn't have the coordinates until a while ago. Leone sent a text."

Neil Edward shot a look at Leone.

Leone shrugged. "We're out of radio range. Sometimes texts get through when calls don't. I don't know how this stuff works. I just try everything."

"Twenty minutes could be a long time for someone having an attack. I don't—"

"I've got an inhaler, Boss," Leone interrupted. "Don't use it much. Mostly during hay fever season—mostly on land. But I keep it onboard, you know, in case. Maybe she could use that?"

Neil Edward frowned.

"Is that like a prescription? Would it be safe for her to use your inhaler?"

"I dunno. Like I said, I don't use the thing much. Don't have much of a problem. So maybe it's a light dose. I don't know."

Neil Edward turned toward Jennette.

"What do you think?"

"I'm taking IT, Sheriff, not nursing."

Sheriff Neil Edward Longcarver held onto the canopy railing to steady himself as *Leone's Lady* rose and fell on the waves in the calming but still confused sea. He studied Jennette for a minute before he turned to Leone.

"Do you have a first-aid kit on board?"

64

Spike leveled the gun at Jake and glanced toward the shoreline.

"Listen to me, asshole. We're close. You can pull up there and let us off."

Jake looked out the port window. They had drifted close enough to the land to see a ribbon of road bordering an open stretch of rocky beach. Though he couldn't read the words, he could discern a bright red maple leaf on a large green and white sign at one end of the beach—the area was probably some sort of provincial park—maybe a campground.

Two thoughts flickered—neither of them good. First, a campground meant people—more innocent people in the dangerous range of Spike's anger—in the range of Spike's gun. Second, a low, rocky beach could indicate a long sandbar extending away from the shore—or worse, hidden rocks. Boats, and shoals, and rocks—him at the wheel, Spike calling the shots, and a boatload of second graders.

"We can't land there. There's no place for you to get out. I think we need to find a better spot."

"I don't give a fuck what you think. You can drive this piece of shit right up on the beach for all I care."

"Wait, Spike," Tyler said. "Maybe he's right. Maybe we need another plan."

Spike looked at Jake, at Tyler, and finally, at Kevin.

"What the hell are you staring at, Fat Ass?"

Kevin swallowed, sucked in a shallow breath. He pointed to the dinghy hanging off the stern.

"That captain guy said we could take the little boat to shore. Maybe we could get close to land with the big boat and take the little boat the rest of the way. We could get away, and these guys can turn around and go home. Or whatever they have to do. It's just a thought."

Spike spat on the floor.

"I don't need any more of your thoughts. And there ain't no *we* to this—it's me and Ty—you are outta this. We already decided that. Get your fat ass back with those brats—I'm sick a lookin' at you."

As Kevin shuffled past, Jake gave him a quick, conspiratorial wink. Kevin paused for a moment, gave his head a slight tilt, and continued on his way. Jake had meant to give the kid some confidence, some hope, but he couldn't tell if Kevin had registered, or had even seen, his gesture.

"Well?" Spike looked at Tyler.

"He's got a point. We get close, drop the dinghy, and motor to shore. Gets us away from this boat faster."

"You know how to drive that thing, Butterfield?" Spike glanced toward the stern.

"I can drive anything."

"Right." Spike snorted. He ran his hand through his hair and took a step closer to Jake.

"You heard him. We're goin' closer. Do it."

Jake reached toward the throttle and paused.

"But what about that sheriff who called you? Don't you wanna wait and see what he has to offer you?"

"Fuck him! I don't give a rat's ass about what he has to offer. And that don't have nothin' to do with you. You drive this fucking boat to the beach. Now." Spike took one more step closer to the helm—now only a foot from Jake.

Jake exhaled, pushed the throttle forward an inch, and revved the engine. He waited for a beat and pushed the throttle forward the rest of the way. The engine raced.

Tyler stepped next to the wheel—next to Jake.

"That didn't sound right. Something's wrong—move over," he said.

Jake clamped his lips together. He edged past Spike.

Tyler clutched the wheel with his left hand and grabbed for the throttle. He looked at Jake and then at Spike.

"We're in neutral," he said. "I think we've been in neutral this whole time. He's been givin' it gas, but we aren't going anywhere."

"You fucker!" Spike raised the gun, but Jake was ready.

He slammed his fist into Spike's stomach.

Spike grunted and folded forward.

Jake chopped his knuckles against Spike's neck.

Spike dropped to the floor—face down.

Jake lunged for the gun but missed as the aluminum boat pole cracked across his jaw. He spun around and smashed against the wheel.

Tyler raised the pole for another strike.

Jake caught the tip of the pole and pulled it toward him.

Tyler stumbled.

Spike scrabbled across the floor and grabbed Jake's bare leg. Before Jake could jerk away, Spike buried his teeth in Jake's foot. Broken skin. Blood.

Jake screeched—loosened his grip on the pole.

Tyler wrenched the pole away and stabbed Jake's shoulder.

Spike let go.

Jake careened around the wheel.

Tyler slashed the pole against Jake's neck.

Jake stumbled back two feet—a foot from the edge of the open engine room hatch.

Tyler rammed the pole into Jake's gut.

Jake collapsed and fell backward into the gaping hole. He crashed to the steel floor, twisting his left knee under his body. He fell back against the hot engine—his arm landed on the exposed pipe. He shrieked. Lurched forward. A strip of burned flesh tore from his arm.

65

Neil Edward and Dwayne Leone stood in the back of the skiff and watched Jennette work. She'd dumped her personal items onto the helm seat and now loaded first-aid gear from a white plastic box into her duffel bag—band-aides, rolls of gauze and tape, a spray can of antiseptic, Leone's inhaler. The last thing destined for the duffel was her cell phone on an open call to Neil Edward's cell. Neil Edward set his phone to mute.

"I don't know, Boss. It might work, but I'm still worried about what could happen if they go through the bag and find the phone. They'll know we tricked them, and they'll be pissed, for sure."

Leone lifted his ball cap, wiped his brow with his sleeve, and replaced the cap.

"You're right about that. I agree it's a risk. But we need to know what's going on over there, and I can't think of any other way."

"Well," Leone mumbled the rest of his comment. "She could stash the phone in her garter. I don't think they'd check that."

"No!" Jennette jerked up straight.

Her response was so quick—so sharp—that Leone jumped, and Neil Edward held his hands in a defensive posture.

"Whoa. Hold on there. We didn't mean anything."

Jennette scowled at the two men and returned to organizing the duffel bag.

The three stayed quiet until Jennette reached for her phone. She stared at it a moment, and looked up.

"There is another way," she said.

"Well?"

"I could stuff it in my bra. Of course, the sound might be muffled, but I don't think anyone will pat me down. Especially if I leave the vest on the whole time."

The two men stared at her. Neil Edward spoke.

"Let's do a test run."

His two deputies leaned in close as Neil Edward tapped the keys on Tyler's cell. He'd put the phone on speaker mode so all three of them could hear the conversation.

"Yeah. What?" Spike's disdain came through loud and clear.

"Okay, Spike," Neil Edward said. "We got a hold of the RCMP, and they are going to work with us to give you safe passage into Canada. Sound good?"

"What's the RC—whatever?"

"Jesus, Spike. It's the Royal Canadian Mounted Police, you idiot." The voice of another young male.

"Shut up. I knew that."

Jennette covered her mouth—suppressed a snicker.

Neil Edward cleared his throat.

"So, I need to know your conditions. What do you want?"

"I'll tell you what I want." Spike's voice was steady. "We're gonna take a dinghy to that park over there. See it?"

"Yes, I do."

"We're going over there, and we don't want nobody trying to stop us. And when we get there, you're gonna have a car parked up on that road. And no cops. Anywhere. Got it?"

"I understand," Neil Edward said.

"Car. No cops . . . and we want money—in the car. Five hundred bucks," Spike hesitated—then added, "No, make that a grand."

Neil Edward looked at Leone. Leone shrugged his shoulders.

"Okay. I understand. You want a car and a thousand dollars and no cops. Anything else?"

"Hold on." The phone went mute. Seconds later, Spike came back on.

"And we want food. I don't care what—sandwiches, whatever. And cigarettes. A carton. And a bottle of whiskey. The good stuff they have in Canada."

"Okay. I'm going to go over it again—you know, to make sure I've got it right. You want a car, and I'm guessing you want it full of gas. And you want a thousand dollars and a bottle of Canada's finest whiskey. Right?"

"Yeah. That's right. And food. And smokes. No cops."

"Cigarettes. Food. And no cops. Got it."

"Good. You get it. But to be sure, we're gonna be takin' some insurance policies with us. So, like I said, no cops and no tricks."

Neil Edward stiffened. He mouthed the word "children."

Jennette's solemn expression spoke volumes.

"Okay, no cops. No tricks. I'm going to pass all of this on to the RCMP, and they'll get you set up with what you want. But it's going to take a little time. And during that time, you need to give us something."

"We don't gotta give you nothing."

"Well, we're making a deal here—a fair agreement. So, you want a car, smokes, food, cash, and booze—well, you've got to give us something in return. That's how fair agreements work."

Spike waited a few beats before he answered.

"What do you want?"

"We know you have an injured person over there. You told us that. And you said you have a little kid who's having an asthma attack. We're worried about that child. We have a midwife on board. We want to send her over so she can take care of that little girl and whoever else needs medical attention. Fair?"

"No way. We don't want any cops over here. No deal. Fuck off." Spike hung up.

Neil Edward redialed.

Spike picked up on the first ring.

"I said, no cops."

"She's not a cop, Spike. She's a midwife. She delivers babies, and besides, she's an old lady with a wooden leg. She's no threat to you at all."

Jennette leaned over and smacked Neil Edward's arm. She mouthed the words "old lady" and gave her boss a one-finger salute.

"What do you say, Spike? Fair?"

"Nobody's havin' a kid over here, so you keep her. Besides, how come you just happen to have a nurse with you?"

"Like I said, she's not a nurse. She's a midwife. A woman on one of the islands is about to deliver, and there aren't any doctors around. We do this all the time. Most women on these islands don't want to go into the city to have their babies, so we bring a midwife out to help them with the delivery. But the thing is, she does have some nursing skills and some supplies."

"Gimme a minute," Spike said. The phone went flat.

Leone looked at Neil Edward.

Neil Edward mouthed the word, mute.

Spike came back on.

"She can come over," he said. "But only her. I don't want nobody else."

"I've got to send my deputy over to drive the dinghy for her."

"No. She can deliver kids? She can drive an outboard. Only her, or the deal's off. Take it or leave it."

"Okay," Neil Edward said.

"Just her. But remember, she's an old woman. A senior citizen with a wooden leg. She's going to need help getting out of the dinghy and onto your boat."

"That's not a problem. We got this fat ass who can help her. But I wanna know how long 'til we get the car, and the cash, and stuff."

"I'm going to call the Canadians and get that rolling as soon as we hang up."

"Good," Spike said. He hung up.

Jennette leaned across the helm chair and smacked Neil Edward's arm again. This time, harder.

66

Jennette smiled at Kevin.

"Better tie it tight, son," she said, "you don't want this dink getting away from you."

Kevin leaned down and tried to grab the line. He missed it twice. On the third try, he caught the line from Jennette and wound it around the boarding platform's cleat.

"That's a nasty shiner," Jennette said. "Looks like you ran into a big fist—maybe a couple of big fists. When we get on the boat, I'll clean you up."

"I'm okay," Kevin said. "I fell. You know, when the boat was rocking. During that storm. But you should fix Amanda—she's really sick. She can't breathe." He offered his hand.

Jennette gripped his arm and reached for the rail. Despite the bouncing of the rubber dinghy, she managed to get her right foot secure on the platform, spring upward, and pull herself to standing.

"Wow, that was cool," Kevin said. "Spike said that sheriff guy said you're an old lady and that you couldn't get on the boat by yourself. But that was awesome—you didn't even need my help."

"Never underestimate the power of an old lady." Jennette winked. "Now, let's go see who needs what."

Tamara sprinted across the cabin and grabbed Jennette's arm.

"Thank God! Did you bring an inhaler?"

"I did. Where is she?"

"Over here, in the corner." Tamara pulled Jennette to the huddle of children.

"Wait a damn minute." Spike stopped the two women. He pointed the gun at Jennette. "I don't trust that cop, and I don't trust you. I wanna see what's in the bag."

"I only brought medical supplies," Jennette said.

"Shut up and hand it over."

Jennette held the duffel out to Spike, but he stepped aside.

"Tyler—dump everything on the floor. I wanna make sure this isn't a trick."

Tyler took the duffel and unzipped it. Instead of pouring the contents out, he shuffled through them.

"There isn't anything in here except band-aides and stuff, Spike."

"No gun? No phone?"

"Nothing like that. Mostly stuff like first-aid cream and shit."

Spike glared at Jennette.

"Fix the kid." He walked toward the helm, then turned back to Tyler.

"Watch 'em."

Tamara sat on the starboard bench and cradled Amanda in her arms. The child's pale skin shimmered with a thin sheen of sweat. Each shallow breath carried a low wheeze.

Jennette fished the inhaler from the duffel. Tamara grabbed it from her. She gave the device a quick shake, placed it between the girl's lips, and pressed the tube.

Amanda gasped and gulped a breath.

"It will take a while, but not long. Maybe ten minutes. She'll be okay." Tamara watched Amanda and let out a long sigh.

"Nice work. You've done this before," Jennette said.

Tamara looked up at Jennette, her cheeks flushed.

"I shouldn't have grabbed that. I should have let you do this. I'm so sorry. I was just so panicked."

"No, no. That's okay. Whatever works." Jennette looked around the room. "So, looks like you've got, what, eight children on board?"

"Yes," Tamara whispered the word. She bit her lip, wiped Amanda's brow, and gently embraced the little girl.

"Looks like there's one little guy wrapped in a sweater, but other than being maybe scared and cold, everyone seems unharmed. And there are three guys—boys. And you and the captain back there?"

"Well, actually, there's one more—"

"Quiet. Stop talking. You do what you came here to do." Tyler glared at the two women.

Jennette looked up at him.

"There's no reason for you to be rude, young man. We were just chatting." She reached out and touched Amanda's face. In the short time since she'd received the medication, the girl's color had warmed to soft pink, and the wheezing had almost stopped. Jennette stood. She lifted the duffel bag and glared at Tyler.

"I should take a look at that man back there. He looks like he's in pain."

Tyler stepped aside and let Jennette pass but stayed close to her.

Jennette sat on the bench next to Denny and touched his swollen knee. Denny winced.

"What happened to you?" Before he could answer, she snapped at Tyler.

"Why is this man tied to this bench? He's hurt—broken kneecap is my first guess. He should be able to elevate this and have ice—he should be seen by a doctor—immediately."

"Not my call," Tyler said. "Just do whatever."

"Is there any ice onboard?" Jennette struggled to help Denny into a more comfortable position.

Denny spoke through clenched teeth.

"Captain Dennis Thompson. I'm—"

"No talking, damn it!" Tyler's brow furrowed with deep lines—a bead of sweat ran down his face from his forehead.

"You. Nurse. Fix this guy if you can. Then, if you're smart, you'll get back in that dinghy and get the hell out of here."

Jennette stood and walked to Tyler. She stopped six inches from him.

"Young man, my guess is that you are in way over your handsome little head. You're taking orders from your buddy in the jacket—probably because he's got a gun. Where did he get a gun anyway? Never mind, that doesn't matter. What matters is that you still have a chance to get out of this mess. If you cooperate with that sheriff, he'll help you. I've known him for years—he's a good guy. Get your friend to give it up—you still have time to make things right." Jennette paused for a moment. She studied Tyler's expression.

His sallow tone and drawn skin gave him the look of an exhausted old man. He picked at the flesh on his thumb. When his gaze swung from the cluster of frightened children to the bow, Jennette's attention shifted as well.

Spike stood at the helm, one hand resting on the wheel. He shielded his eyes with the other and faced toward shore.

They were close enough to the land to see a stretch of dark sand and a rocky beach ringed by thick stands of evergreen trees. A narrow road curled like a strand of beige ribbon around the base of the tree line.

"Tyler! Get your ass up here—there's a tent on that beach. And those campers have a car. Fuck the Canadians and fuck that cop—we got us a ride!"

"You don't belong with him," Jennette said. She kept her voice hushed. "Take my advice. Do the right thing. Save yourself."

Tyler hesitated—he looked toward Spike and back to Jennette.

"Forget it," he said. "It's too late." He pointed to Kevin.

"Put some cream or something on that guy's nose and get off this boat. You take my advice—get as far away from this mess as you can." He left her and stomped across the cabin to the open door by the helm.

Jennette sighed and turned toward the companionway. With her back to Spike and Tyler, and her voice low, she gave her report.

"One shooter. One accomplice. Nervous. Frightened. No sign of the big man. Blood on the floor around the wheel. Lots of blood."

"Who are you talking to?" Kevin stepped next to her.

Jennette cooed soft as she reached over and touched the bruise on his face.

"Nobody. I was mumbling to myself. It happens to everyone when they get old. Come on," she said, "let's sit on the bench and get that nose of yours cleaned up. Okay?"

67

Tyler gripped the door jamb, one foot inside the cabin, the other outside, on the deck.

"Spike, maybe we should rethink this. I mean, maybe if we call it now, we can do some sort of plea bargain—like, get points for cooperating with that sheriff."

Spike stared straight ahead and pushed the throttle forward enough to race the engine.

"Stop talking, Butterfield."

"I'm serious," Tyler said. "The store thing was an accident. And even if that guy dies, it was still an accident. A lawyer could probably get us off. And the boat? All we did was not pay for a ticket. But now—" He gestured toward the dash. "We trashed this place, and that nurse back there says the captain has a broken kneecap."

"I didn't do that," Spike said. "He tripped and fell. That's not my fault."

"Spike, you hit him in the head with the gun."

"Doesn't count. He fell."

Tyler exhaled. "What about that guy in the engine room? Maybe we killed him."

"You killed him. Maybe you killed him."

"Spike, he was going for the gun. He could have shot you. Or me. Or both of us. What was I supposed to do?"

"Hey, chill. I'm just pointin' out that you're in this deep. We give up now, and we'll do fifty thousand years. You might never see that hottie you're so hard for."

"For sure I'll never get to see her again. I didn't have much of a chance with her as a mechanic—but as a kidnapper? Ha." Tyler bit at his thumb—the skin now thin, raw, close to splitting.

"What do you mean, kidnapper?"

"You know what I mean."

"We're not kidnappers. We're just using a couple brats for insurance. They get hurt? That's on the cops."

Tyler gaped at his friend.

"Spike, I'm not spending the next twenty years in prison 'cause of you."

"Shut up, Butterfield. I told you before—you wanna run home to your mama? Go. I don't need you."

Tyler turned and faced the land for a moment and looked up. He squinted and pointed toward the sky.

"Jesus, Spike. It's a helicopter."

Spike let go of the wheel and dashed to the door.

"That fucker! I said no cops!" He spun around and pulled the phone from his pocket.

"Tyler—grab the wheel. I'm calling that cop, and then I'm gonna start shooting."

68

Neil Edward shielded his eyes and scanned the sky. The blue and white helicopter buzzed over the Strait on a direct beeline toward the *Hattie Belle.*

"Not good," he said. He tapped the incoming line on Tyler's phone.

"You fucker! What part of no cops didn't you get?"

"Spike. Slow down. That's not ours. That's not law enforcement."

"You liar! I thought we had a deal. I let your old lady come over here. No cops. That was the gig."

"Spike. Listen to me. It's a news helicopter. Look up. It's from Channel Five News. I've got nothing to do with them."

The phone went mute.

Neil Edward turned to Leone.

"Can you see them?"

Leone balanced against the helm chair and trained his binoculars on the *Hattie Belle.*

"Yeah. Two guys on the port side. Nope, one went back inside."

"You still there?" Spike growled into the phone.

"Yes. I wasn't lying, right? Did you see the Five Alive logo on that chopper?"

"If I find out this is a trick, I'm gonna start puttin' bullets in those brats."

"Spike, I'm not lying to you. It's not a trick. That robbery you pulled in Port Angeles—it's all over the news. And those little kids? Their parents are freaking out. This is a big news story."

"What makes you think that I—that we—had anything to do a robbery in Port Angeles?"

"There's footage of you. The security camera has clear footage of you and your friend. It shows you firing your weapon and the clerk going down."

"You sure it's me?"

"The footage is crystal clear. No doubt." Neil Edward lied.

"Well, what about the guy? That guy in the store? Did he—?" Neil Edward lied again.

"We don't know for sure, Spike. He's in intensive care—lost a lot of blood. He might make it, but it's too early to tell." He waited a beat and added, "If he doesn't make it, you'll hear about it—even in Canada. Like I said, this is a huge news story, and I can't control the press."

"You better control the goddamn press. I want that chopper out of here. Now. Or that news story is gonna get a lot bigger." Spike hung up.

Neil Edward looked at his deputy. "Leone?"

"Already done, Boss. I managed to get a hold of Anita. She's calling the news station now—everything should be—oh shit."

Leone pointed to the *Hattie Belle*.

69

Conrad bolted from his place with the other children and dashed for the companionway.

"Dad! Dad!"

"Conrad! Come back. Now!" Tamara called to him.

"I wanna see! I wanna see!" Jenny chased after Conrad—her red braids flying, her bare feet slapping the steel floor. She managed to slip past Tamara and join Conrad on deck. The two of them jumped up and down, and with faces turned skyward, they waved to the helicopter now circling above the boat.

"Me too!" Ryan raced to the door.

Tristan followed him.

"I wanna see it too!"

Kevin grabbed Emily's hand, and they ran to join the others on deck. Tamara sprinted after them.

Conrad clutched Ryan's arm and pointed to the helicopter.

"That's my dad! That's my dad!"

A man in khaki slacks, white shirt, and a maroon bowtie strained against thick straps as he leaned from the chopper's open door. He wore earphones and held a video camera. He pointed the camera toward the *Hattie Belle* and waved to the children.

The boys jumped, flapped their arms, and yelled to him.

"Mr. Huffington! Look down here!"

"Daaaaddy!"

"Children, come inside. Now! Karlie, get down!" Tamara shouted against the rotor's roar as she grabbed at the girl who'd climbed to the top of the boarding platform's rail—the same rail

Ryan had fallen from earlier. Tamara wrapped her arms around Karlie and pulled her down.

Kevin, Jennette, and the children gawked at the helicopter, which twirled above them like a great, shining dragonfly. They waved, clapped, laughed, and called out to Conrad's father.

Tamara did a headcount—*something's not right.* Seven children. She squeezed Karlie, told her to stay off the rail, and then poked her head through the companionway. Only one small girl had remained inside the cabin. She lay curled and sleeping on a bench in a patch of sunlight. Tamara started toward the bench, but Spike pushed her aside.

"Move it, bitch." He grabbed the little girl's arm, jolted her from sleep, and dragged her from the bench.

"Leave her alone!" Tamara tried to pull the girl from him, but Spike punched her in her stomach. Tamara staggered backward.

Spike pulled on the child's arm.

"Owww," she squealed. She started to wail.

"Shut up, kid. You cry, and you're dead." He pulled her behind him and marched through the companionway.

"Shut up! Everybody shut up, or I'll shoot her."

The children, and the adults, stopped what they were doing and stared at Spike. He gripped the girl's arm tight and jerked her close to him. He pointed the gun at her.

The girl's lower lip trembled. She looked at Tamara—her eyes wide with fear.

Holding her stomach, Tamara took a step toward Spike.

"Let her go."

"You say one more word, and I swear to you, I will blow her head off. Do you understand me?" Spike's eyes narrowed to slits, and his lips pressed flat—small gobs of spit pooled at the corners.

Tamara stopped. Blinked. She took one step back, and while still looking at Spike, she knelt and embraced the girl she'd pulled from the railing.

Spike yelled above the roar of the blades.

"Okay, now, everybody listen to me. We're all going back inside, and I'm gonna tell you what to do. Got it?"

Nobody moved—all eyes on Spike.

"Kid. What's your name?" He tugged at the child's arm.

She whispered something—impossible to hear.

Spike jerked on her arm.

"I said, what's your name?"

"Lexie," the girl answered. This time she looked up at Spike—no tears—and though her body quaked, her gaze held steady.

"My name is Lexie."

"Okay, everybody. You do what I tell you, and Lexie here doesn't get hurt. Any questions?"

Again, no one moved—now they stared at Lexie.

Spike glanced up at the helicopter in time to see the heavy machine make two rotations in place, lift, and fly off toward the shore.

"Good," he said. "Now, inside. No talking."

Jerking Lexie's arm, he backed through the companionway and crossed the room. He waved the gun between the group of children and the wide-eyed little girl at his side.

Neil Edward shielded his eyes and watched the chopper leave the area.

"Anita must have made contact with them—passed along the message," he said.

"I've got her on my phone," Leone answered. "The guys in the helicopter radioed the station, and they're talking with her now. She's got me on her private cell."

"Could they see anything?"

Leone held up one finger as he pressed his phone to his ear. "Right," he said. "Okay. Keep us in the loop." He hung up and turned to Neil Edward.

"The guy in the chopper says the kid in black has a child at gunpoint—a little girl—seems to be holding her as a threat to the others. Looks like the other children are okay. At least he couldn't see any injuries. They took off as soon as they got the word from the station."

"He seem okay? The guy in the chopper?"

"Why?"

"His son is on that boat."

Jake dragged himself to one of the plastic crates. Blood from the wound on his head had pooled at his eye and sealed it shut. His burned arm raw—the nerves on fire. The searing sting of scorched skin competed with the stabbing pain in his knee. None of that mattered. He could live through pain—he couldn't live through losing Emily.

The hatch cover stood open—he was only a few steps from reaching the cabin—from Spike. But his leg had swollen as far as Dickerson's canvas bibs would allow. His knee was misshapen and dislocated. He'd popped a lot of shoulders into place over his years at the gym, and he knew what to do. He also knew his current pain would be nothing compared to what he'd feel when he pushed the knee back into its socket. At least that suffering would be quick. Didn't matter. He had to climb the stairs. He clasped the swollen joint in both hands, took a deep breath, exhaled with a whoosh, and pushed the bone into place. He'd been right about the pain.

The phones were silent. Anita took a deep breath and stretched. She gazed around her place of employment—voluntary employment—voluntary, at least for the time being. She reassessed her performance. So far, she'd been a valuable asset to the team—definitely ready for a promotion. But there was one pesky exception. Those executive decisions. Clearly, her decision-making skills were stellar. Even so, she might have crossed a line. The sheriff had been specific about her responsibilities—answer the phones—nothing else.

Anita paced the room, opened drawers and cupboards, and read files. She pulled a cardboard box from under Jennette's desk. Neat black lettering on the top spelled out "Travis Drumthor—Personal Effects." Anita peered inside.

The box contained filthy clothing, a small plastic bag containing a hand-rolled cigarette, something that looked like a small rabbit's foot, and four boxes of ammunition. Jennette's handwritten notes included mention of an expired registration, missing driver's license, and one short line—a question. *Stolen gun?*

Anita closed her eyes and pinched the bridge of her nose. Something nagged at her. Something she'd read on one of the many community pages she followed. What was it?

"Hey! Woman! I want another call. Where the hell is my brother? Get him on the phone—tell him to get me outta here, or I'll drag his sorry ass back to Sequim and beat the shit outta him." Travis rattled the bars on the cell door.

Anita snapped her fingers. Sequim! That was it. Robbery. A pawn shop robbery in Sequim—what? Two months ago? Guns and ammunition. Wouldn't take anything at all to look up the details—do some police-type investigating. If she could tie Travis to that robbery, any concerns the sheriff might have about her decision-making would be history. Anita closed the box and pushed it back under Jennette's desk.

"Listen, bitch, I'm warning you. You're gonna hear from my lawyer. You listenin' to me?" Travis's squalling had gone up a decibel—so loud now that Anita couldn't think straight.

She marched into the holding area.

"Mr. Drumthor, you have to settle down. The sheriff and his team are doing everything they can to help your brother. There isn't anything I can do for you right now, but as soon as the sheriff has the crime scene secured, he'll give me further instructions. But I won't be able to hear him if you don't stop yelling. So, pipe down, okay?"

"What do you mean, help my brother? What crime scene? What's happening?"

Anita eyed Travis, contemplating what she should say and how much information she should share. Executive decisions were becoming easier.

"Your brother shot and, we think, killed a man. He kidnapped a boatload of children and is holding several adults hostage across international lines. Law enforcement from both sides of the border are chasing him—it's an international incident. Sheriff Longcarver is doing whatever he can to keep your brother alive. That's all I know. Now, can you be quiet so I can hear when new information comes in?"

She stood in the doorway glaring at him as a wide grin spread across Travis Drumthor's face.

He sat on the cot's edge and flopped onto his back, hands behind his head.

"Well, I'll be damned," he muttered. "My baby brother is all growed up—turned into a real man. Maybe the kid was payin' attention to me all along. Who woulda thought? Wait till the old man hears this."

He might have said more, but Anita didn't wait to hear. She closed the door and, with a disgusted huff, walked across the room to answer the incoming radio call.

"Otter's Run's Sheriff's Office. Over." She tapped one finger on the edge of the radio as she listened to the crackling message.

"*Clallam County Sheriff's Marine Unit.* We've got the target on radar—we should have a visual soon. ETA five to seven minutes. Over."

"Copy that." Anita thanked the caller for the update, wished him success, and signed off. She punched Leone's number into her cell phone. When Leone answered, Anita relayed the message from the marine unit, asked him to tell the sheriff she'd solved the issue of the stolen ammo, told him to be careful out there, and hung up.

Now, only one more thing to check, and she'd have all the pieces in place. Anita settled at Neil Edward's desk and dialed the number she'd Googled.

"Mrs. Drumthor? Mrs. Clive Drumthor?" No reply. Anita waited a few seconds, then spoke again.

"This is Deputy Anita Anderson with the Otter's Run Sherriff's Office. Mrs. Drumthor? You there?" Long silence.

"Yes." A single word.

"Mrs. Drumthor, this is a courtesy call. Do you know where your son is?" Again, a long silence.

Joyce Drumthor hesitated. "Eugene?"

"Does he go by Spike?"

"Yes."

"Mrs. Drumthor, we need to know some information about your son. About Eugene—um, Spike."

"I—I can't help you." Her voice wavered.

"But Mrs. Drumthor. We think your son may be in trouble."

"You don't understand. He'll—"

"We're only trying to help your son."

"I can't. I just . . . I just can't."

The line went dead.

Jennette leaned against the companionway door out of the way but close enough—maybe Neil Edward and Leone could hear.

"Okay, all you brats line up against the wall. I don't wanna hear one peep outta any of you. The first one who cries or says a word gets shot." Spike gripped Lexie's arm and dragged her along as he paced the room's width, waving the gun at the other children.

The little girl trotted to keep up with him. She squeezed her eyes shut, but she didn't call out. Jennette waited.

Tamara kept one finger pressed to her lips and hustled her students into place. One by one, the children sat down, their backs against teak, their hands in their laps. Six terrified children lined against the wall. No cries, no whimpers, no words. Pale yellow liquid soaked through Karlie's shorts and wet the floor beneath her.

Kevin took Emily's hand and moved to join the others, but Spike stopped him.

"No, that one stays with Tyler," Spike said. "Tyler. Get your ass over here and get hold of this kid."

"Spike, I don't want to—"

"Shut up, Butterfield. She's insurance. Hold onto her."

Tyler took Emily's hand.

Kevin glared at Spike.

"You. Sit down." Spike flicked a look at Kevin, then turned toward Tamara.

Kevin balled his hands into fists.

Spike spun around to face him.

"I said, sit down. Now."

Kevin lowered his head and slouched toward the children.

Spike refocused on Tamara.

"And you—teacher—you sit down too. I don't wanna have to mess with you."

Tamara straightened, lifted her chin, and walked to him. She stared into his eyes.

"They're just little kids, and they'll be a lot of work for you. Take me instead."

"Nice try, bitch. But nobody cares about you. Those brats are worth a lot more to me."

"Spike, if you take those girls off this boat, you'll be kidnapping, and you'll go to prison. They'll never let you out."

Spike dropped his hold on Lexie and took one step forward. He backhanded Tamara across her face. Hard.

She stumbled sideways—reached to her cheek.

Tyler gasped.

"Hey," Jennette shouted.

Spike ignored her—he scowled at Tamara.

"Now go sit down, you fucking bitch. You got no say in this. These kids are coming with us until we don't need 'em anymore. I'm in the mood to shoot somebody, and you're right at the top of the list."

Face red from the slap, Tamara turned and walked to the children. When she sat down, Tristan and Amanda wrapped their arms around her.

Jennette sucked in a deep breath—still waiting.

"Stupid cow," Spike said.

"Spike, you don't need to do shit like that. You don't need to hit a woman. I don't like this—any of this," Tyler said.

"Your problem, Butterfield? You got no balls."

"Jesus, Spike, I hurt that guy in the boat—maybe bad. And what about that other guy? He might be dead." Tyler gestured toward the engine room. He bit at a hangnail, watched, silent, as blood pooled on his thumb.

Spike glanced at the blood, then looked toward the shore.

"Listen to me, Butterfield, I have a plan."

Jennette coughed—caught Spike's attention.

"Sorry," she said. She looked down—didn't engage but took a couple of steps closer to the two. She leaned against the support beam. Closer now. *Neil Edward needs to hear this.*

Spike scowled at her but spoke to Tyler.

"See that park over there? And see that tent? There's a car and food and probably booze. I bet those campers have cash—credit cards for sure. So, we're gonna pay those guys a visit. And after that, we're gonna take a little road trip—make a couple of detours to lose the cops. After a while, we drop the brats somewhere in the woods. The cops will go ape shit lookin' for 'em. We slip away, and by Happy Hour, we'll be drinkin' beer and eatin' burgers in some Canadian dive. It's a perfect plan. So, you want in? You grow a pair."

Spike grabbed Lexie's arm again without waiting for Tyler to respond. He took a deep breath and glared at Tamara and the other children.

"Now I'm gonna tell all of you what's going down, and you're all gonna listen. If anybody tries anything cute, well, you can say goodbye to your little buddy." He yanked on Lexie's arm.

She winced but still didn't cry out.

"Me and my partner, we're taking the nurse's boat over to Canada. Lexie and Blondie—they're coming with us."

He paused and scanned the group. No one moved.

"You are all gonna stay exactly where you are. No movin'. No talkin'. No doin' nothing for one full hour. And then, you can do whatever the fuck you want."

Jennette raised her hand.

Spike blinked. "What do you want, Gimp?"

The group had gone so quiet that when Jennette walked across the room, her wooden foot, strapped in its fitted tennis shoe, made a soft clunking on the cabin's floor. Her skirt swished against her thighs. She stopped six feet from Spike, out of immediate striking range.

"I get why you want to go to Canada. You want to get away from American cops. But if you steal from those Canadians—or if you hurt any of them—you'll have to run from the Mounties." She tilted her head and paused.

Spike started to say something, but Jennette continued. She raised her voice. "The teacher was right. If you take those little girls off this boat, it will be kidnapping. That's a federal crime. Why don't you wait until the sheriff gives you what you want? The sheriff should be here soon." She almost shouted the last sentence.

"What's your problem, you old bat? Why are you yelling?" Spike narrowed his eyes and stared at Jennette. He said, "Take the vest off."

She shook her head.

"I need to keep it on because I can't swim. I can't swim with the wooden leg, so I need to wear a life vest."

"I said, take it off." Spike gestured with the gun.

Jennette swallowed and fumbled with the vest's buckles.

"Hurry up."

Jennette slid one arm out and turned, a half turn, toward the back of the boat. She slipped her other arm out of the vest, dropped it to the floor, and stood facing Spike with her shoulders hunched forward.

"Okay, happy now?"

Spike stared at her for a moment.

"Tyler. Go feel her up. I think the old bitch is wired."

Tyler dropped Emily's hand.

"Spike, you're out of your mind. I'm not gonna feel up anybody."

Spike glared at him. He said, "Suit yourself, Butterfield. We'll deal with this another way."

He focused again on Jennette—made direct eye contact. "Okay, bitch, lose the clothes. All of them."

"For Christ's sake, Spike." Tyler's face gleamed with sweat.

"Not talkin' to you, Butterfield. I wanna see if she's wired." Spike stared at Jennette.

"There are children—" she said.

Spike pointed the gun at her heart. "I don't give a shit. Strip."

Jennette raised her head and took in a long breath.

"No," she said.

Spike didn't say another word. He cocked the gun.

Neil Edward focused the binoculars on the object skating the edge of the horizon. He'd seen the vessel before. The refurbished U.S. Coast Guard cutter—now painted deep blue with an ever-green stripe—flew massive U.S. and Washington State flags. Large white lettering along the hull spelled out Clallam County Sheriff's Marine Unit. The impressive, intimidating ship approached fast—with purpose. Neil Edward knew the vessel would slice the sea in two sparkling curls as it powered toward them. He knew that the three large-bore guns, mounted on the foredeck, would point directly at the *Hattie Belle* and that a line of highly trained men and women—all wearing helmets and full combat gear—would stand at the bow aiming their weapons at the little whale-watching boat.

Leone hit a button on his phone.

"Breathe, Boss. Anita says they'll be here in five minutes. And she said something about solving the stolen gun and ammo crime. Think she's talking about that stuff we found in the car this morning?"

Neil Edward didn't answer. He registered but ignored the information about stolen ammo—he would address that and Anita later. Now, he focused on the muffled voices on the muted phone. He heard Jennette say one word, and then he heard something else. He slipped the phone into his pocket.

"Move it, Leone. We're going in."

"But, Boss, we'll have backup in five minutes."

"Jennette doesn't have five minutes."

Jake heard Spike's demand and Jennette's one-word reply. He heard the round click in the chamber.

He eyed the stairs from the engine room to the cabin. Stairs on the left side—injured left knee. He made one jump up two steps—rammed through the pain. Palms flat on the cabin floor, he pushed to the top step.

Spike dropped Lexie's arm and spun toward Jake. Both hands on the grip—he fired.

A hot explosion of pain—a blast of blood from Jake's shoulder.

The *Hattie Belle* slammed the seabed—her hull shuddered, lifted, rolled to starboard, and plunged down again. Her wooden beams groaned. They ground against rocks, sand, and broken shells. Throttle in forward, she plowed into the sandbar until her prop mired in thick silt.

Jennette teetered and fell against a bench.

Tyler slipped in the blood by the helm.

Spike stumbled forward—discharged the gun again—smashed the port window. Glass shattered, showering the children huddled beneath.

Emily grabbed Lexie's hand and dragged her behind a support beam.

Jake's knee buckled. He dropped back, crashed down the steps, hit the floor. Dickerson's toolbox skidded across the engine room and struck the hull. One metal drawer screeched open. Jake grabbed a tool, took a deep breath, and vaulted back up the steps.

"Fuck!" Spike staggered, steadied, and then stood.

Jake swung the wrench—the forged steel pipe wrench. He swung with the full power of his pain, the full force of his rage, the unleashed fury of grief. Jake slammed forged steel into Spike's kidney.

Spike yowled and dropped to his knees.

Jake smashed the wrench between Spike's shoulders.

Spike fell forward. His head cracked against steel. The gun flew from his hand—clattered across the floor.

Tyler dove for it.

A neon yellow tennis shoe fitted over a carved wood foot stomped Tyler's outstretched fingers.

He yelped.

Jennette pressed one foot hard on Tyler's hand and planted the other firm on the floor. She aimed her service revolver at his head.

"Are you sure?" she said.

77

Sheriff Neil Edward Longcarver didn't wait for Leone to tie his skiff to the side of the *Hattie Belle*. When they were close enough, he let go of *Leone's Lady* and leaped the distance between the two boats. He grabbed the old trawler's wooden handrail, pulled himself onto the deck, and slipped on the wet wood. Adrenaline caught him. Neil Edward yanked his gun from its holster, burst through the side door. And stopped.

Except for a couple of sniffling children, soft words of encouragement from a young woman, and a sharp scraping sound as the boat ground deeper into sediment, the sun-dappled cabin of the *Hattie Belle* was quiet.

The space smelled of burned rubber, diesel smoke, gun powder, vomit, and maybe—he wasn't sure—urine.

A hulking man, dirty, bloody, dressed in work bibs two sizes too small, gripped a pipe wrench. He stood over the guy Neil Edward had seen in the photos—the kid in the black leather jacket—the kid who called himself Spike. The kid lay face-down. He didn't move.

Two little girls stood next to the bloody man with the wrench. The girls held hands. One of them, a thin child with a torn, bloodsplattered dress and wispy blond hair, smiled up at the man. And then, she turned and smiled at Neil Edward.

Children clustered close together under a blown-out window—a window Neil Edward guessed had been destroyed by the shot he and Leone heard as their skiff sped across the water. Some of the children hugged each other, a few whimpered, and a couple of them helped brush shards of safety glass from small shoulders.

The teacher he'd seen in the video cooed soft reassurance to her students and to a heavy-set teenager who appeared dazed and confused.

Neil Edward recognized the man tied to a metal bench in the back of the cabin. One of the captains of the whale-watching fleet. The man nodded once to Neil Edward.

And, in the middle of it all, standing in a patch of sunlight, with her wooden foot in its bright yellow high-top pressed firm on the hand of a prone boy—the boy with the crush on Judge Lynden's daughter—was Jennette. Her skirt hiked up around a leather holster buckled below a yellow silk garter. She pointed a Smith & Wesson .38 Special at the motionless teenager. Jennette glanced at Neil Edward, cocked her head, and raised one eyebrow.

78

At the sheriff's bidding, Jennette took charge.

Once he'd tied the skiff to the side of the *Hattie Belle*, Leone jumped on board and followed her lead, followed her instructions. When the Clallam County Sheriff's Marine Unit officers boarded the *Hattie Belle*, they started straight for Neil Edward, but he directed them to Jennette. For her, that was worth more than any raise.

She pointed around the cabin.

"We've got some wounded folks," she said. "The kid on the floor hit his head. And he might have some internal injuries. The guy in the back? My guess—is a broken kneecap. Worst though, that big guy. Gunshot and bad burn to start. And more."

The medic gave her a quick nod and headed to Jake.

"What should I do?" Leone asked.

She gestured toward Tyler and Kevin.

"Cuff those two. I'm sure there's a brig on the cutter. Our boy, Spike, might have a spinal injury. He's going out on a stretcher for sure, but keep an eye on things in case he makes a rapid recovery."

"What about the big guy?"

Across the cabin, the medic worked on Jake's burned arm. Emily leaned against her father, his good arm wrapped around her.

"Give me a minute on that one," Jennette said.

"Right, Boss." Leone straightened his shoulders, squared his jaw, and strode toward Kevin with cuffs in hand.

Jennette turned to Tyler and made eye contact with the boy. He looked at her for a moment, then hung his head.

Leone pulled Kevin's arms behind his back and fussed with the handcuffs. The chubby teenager looked more confused than frightened. Jennette guessed he'd have an easier go of things than his buddies because it would be her sworn duty to testify—to tell the truth.

Tamara wove her way through the now much happier group of second graders. She stopped next to Jennette. Earlier, she and members from the marine unit had wrapped blankets around the children. Now, the crew handed out juice boxes and offered navy blue baseball caps sporting the emblem of a Coast Guard cutter.

"I can't say how grateful I am for what you did back there, the inhaler and everything," she said.

"No problem," Jennette said. "Happy to help. But you're going to have some explaining to do. That sound about right?"

Tamara reached up and brushed a curling strand from her forehead.

"I'll probably lose my job. Worse, maybe the chance to work with children for a long time—maybe forever."

Jennette draped her arm around the younger woman's shoulders and gave her a quick squeeze. Not police policy, but Jennette didn't always follow policy.

"You're going to be fine. I watched you with those children— I saw what you would have sacrificed for their safety. The judge? The administrators? They're going to ask me. And I'm going to tell them."

Tamara gave Jennette a weak smile.

"But there is one thing I want to ask you before you go back to the kids. Something I want to get your thoughts on," Jennette said. She glanced across the cabin toward Jake.

After a few minutes of discussion, the women shook hands, and then they hugged. A real hug this time. Again, not police policy. Again, Jennette didn't care. But she did need official sanction on one issue.

"So, you can get where I'm coming from on this, right?" She and Neil Edward stood off to one side. They spoke in low, hushed tones.

"I do, Jennette. But the fact of the matter is—"

"The fact of the matter is, love can make a person do stupid things. Doesn't matter whether it's love for another adult, or a dog, or love for your kid. Probably especially love for your kid."

Neil Edward lifted his hat and ran his hand through his hair.

"Jennette, I don't know."

"Come on. You'll be there the whole time. And we'll all be on the cutter together, except him, of course." She nodded toward the helm.

Denny sat in the captain's chair with an ice pack strapped to his knee. He and a crew member from the cutter were poring over a digital chart on an electronic tablet.

"What are his plans?" Neil Edward said.

"He'll be in charge, but a couple of the Clallam guys will drive his boat back—dock it at the yard in Port Angeles. First, though, they have to wait for a tug to push it off the sandbar. The Canadians are sending one out."

"Hope he has good insurance."

"So, about the other thing—" She put her hands on her hips and looked up at him.

Neil Edward shook his head and sighed. "You win, Jennette."

79

Jake cradled Emily in his right arm—his left, salved and band-aged, rested in a gauze sling. A black patch covered one eye. Both wrists cuff-free. He leaned against the Clallam County Sheriff's Department's steel hull and squinted at the diamonds glinting on the strait.

Sheriff Neil Edward Longcarver stood at the railing facing the land and the colorful patch that was Otter's Run. Since their brief exchange on the *Hattie Belle*, the two men had not spoken. They'd remained so quiet that Emily, wrapped in a wool blanket, held snug against her father, had fallen asleep. Neil Edward pushed back from the railing and sat on a bench. He spoke first.

"They'll take you to the hospital, of course, but I do have to arrest you once we land."

"I get it."

"I don't think Captain Thompson will press charges, but I don't know enough about marine law to know how all that works."

"I'm not worried about any of that—the real problem is dealing with my ex."

"Yeah. I met your ex. No offense, but she's something else."

Behind them, a window slid open, and children's high-pitched laughter wafted from the cabin. Emily stirred in her sleep. Wisps of her hair danced in the breeze. She didn't wake when Jake kissed the top of her head but she nestled closer against his shoulder.

He gazed across the water to the shoreline, to the gray boulders tossed against the land, to the emerald trees guarding long stretches of rocky beach.

"The thing is, Marilyn has something on me, and she says if I'm not careful, she'll use it to make sure this temporary restraining order turns permanent."

"What's that?"

"You know about the accident in my gym?"

Neil Edward nodded.

Jake shifted his weight from one foot to the other and exhaled a sigh.

"The accident happened in the early afternoon. I'd closed on a new building that morning—a newer, bigger building. I'd ordered all the equipment for another gym—even hired two new trainers." He waited.

When the sheriff didn't respond, Jake went on.

"A few of my buddies took me out to lunch to celebrate. We all ordered beer. I made the mistake of telling Marilyn, and she's hung that over my head ever since. Calls it her secret weapon."

"How much did you drink?"

"Not enough to matter. But she blew it up. Made a big deal of it. She and her old man hired the meanest lawyer they could find. I didn't fight it."

"Geez, I'm ancient." Neil Edward groaned as he stood.

Jake studied the older man. He could almost feel the sheriff's aching muscles—his exhaustion.

"Hey, I didn't say it, but thanks. Thanks for—" he looked at Emily.

"No problem," Neil Edward said. "So, what you are gonna do now? Since—you know."

Jake peered skyward. The Five Alive chopper hovered over the vessel, circled twice, lifted, and flew in the town's direction. Jake glanced at Neil Edward, then looked toward the land.

"I'm gonna get a meaner lawyer."

Neil Edward touched the brim of his hat and nodded toward the shore.

"Well, you enjoy the peace now because it's bound to be a zoo over there. I'm gonna use the head while there's still time." He pulled on the heavy steel door to the ship's cabin and stepped inside.

They were close enough for Jake to see the flashing lights of ambulances and patrol cars. Close enough to see the crowd gathering in the marina parking lot. Jake smiled at his sleeping daughter, then looked across the sparkling water. He let his gaze move beyond Otter's Run to the curving coastline, to the soft gray smoke curling from the chimneys of summer cabins, to the gulls gliding on the winds above. He took in a long, deep breath.

Everything smelled of the sea.

ACKNOWLEDGEMENTS

I sincerely appreciate the following people who helped make this journey a delight.

Lisa Dailey of Sidekick Press, and Andrea Gabriel of Paint Creek Press. Talented, witty, and supportive women—working with the two of you is pure joy.

Deborah Rein, Karen England, Curt Joyner, and Ray Leone. Best beta readers ever.

Sam Devlin, for taking the time to answer a zillion boat-related questions. You're a generous man and the finest boat designer on the planet.

Lieutenant Michael Munden of the Blaine Police Department. Thanks for helping with "bad guy" speak. And to Darin Rasmussen, retired Whatcom County Law Enforcement, for help with guns and ammunition.

Spencer Kope, Crime Analyst for the Whatcom County Sheriff's Office and thriller author. Over cups of coffee, you taught me about bodies and blood splatter, and your mysteries have given me many hours of tension and thrills.

Just Fridays Critique group for the support and silliness shared by friends.

Village Books and Paper Dreams—for everything.

Cami Ostman, Laura Kilpakian, Nancy Adair, and all the incredible wordsmiths in the Red Wheelbarrow Writers of Bellingham, Washington. In a word, community.

Great thanks to J.D. Barker—an extraordinary author and stellar mentor who promised to tell the truth and kept his promise.

Most profound appreciation to Jack Remick, a true writer's writer and master of the poetics of prose. A challenging but cherished teacher to whom this book is dedicated.

And, to that guy in the waterfront bar decades ago, who told me a story.

PREVIOUSLY PUBLISHED WORKS

Under: Jessica H. Stone
Blood on a Blue Moon—A Sheaffer Blue Mystery
The Last Outrageous Woman—A Novel
Doggy on Deck—Life at Sea with a Salty Dog (Nonfiction)
How to Retire on a Boat (Nonfiction)

Under: Dr. Jessica Hart
The Fool Stories—Book One: The Adventure Begins (Children's)
The Fool Stories—Book Two: Dreaming of Dreams (Children's)

ABOUT THE AUTHOR

Photo by Melanie Cool

Jes Hart Stone is a blue water sailor and author of the popular guide to traveling with pets, *Doggy on Deck—Life at Sea with a Salty Dog*. Her novels include *Blood on a Blue Moon—A Sheaffer Blue Mystery* and *The Last Outrageous Woman*. Jes collects fountain pens and lives by the sea. https://jeshartstone.com

Printed in the USA
CPSIA information can be obtained
at www.ICGtesting.com
LVHW041625311024
795367LV00005B/34

9 781958 808047